THE CHRYSALIS PHASE

A Novel of Emergence

CAROL BOUVILLE

To Jannah – I hope
you enjoy the book.
Carol Bouville

JALA PUBLISHING PARTNERS
Bethesda, MD

THE CHRYSALIS PHASE

A Novel of Emergence

by Carol Bouville

Published in the United States of America in 2022

by Jala Publishing Partners, Bethesda, MD

Library of Congress cataloging-in-publication data available upon request.

Cover Art by Carol Bouville
Project Management: Della R. Mancuso
Design: Donna Murphy
Copyediting: Ellen Henrie
Printed in the United States of America

Soft cover: 978-1-7354964-4-3
E-book: 978-1-7354964-5-0

The Guest House

This being human is a guest house.
Every morning a new arrival.
A joy, a depression, a meanness,
Some momentary awareness comes
As an unexpected visitor.
Welcome and entertain them all!
Even if they're a crowd of sorrows,
Who violently sweep your house
Empty of its furniture,
Still treat each guest honorably.
He may be clearing you out
For some new delight.
The dark thought, the shame, the malice,
Meet them at the door laughing,
And invite them in.
Be grateful for whoever comes,
Because each has been sent
As a guide from beyond.
Rumi

TABLE OF CONTENTS

ACKNOWLEDGEMENTS

I have been working on this novel since 2017 when my daughter became ill, and my husband and I relocated to Los Angeles to care for her. With so many emotions charging through me, I somehow found an outlet in writing. The original manuscript flowed directly from my heart and mind onto my iPad as this exercise took on a life of its own. Along the way, my daughter slowly but surely got well and encouraged me to continue writing, to re-evaluate and then rewrite, but always to believe in this project. Thank you, Fabienne. In addition, I'm grateful to my son and my husband, who were willing to read and reread the manuscript multiple times, especially my husband who corrected my many typos as well as some errors in French. I also wish to thank my friend and editor Alice Heiserman, President of Write Books Right, who went way beyond our contractual agreement with ideas for character and plot development as she gave me her constant encouragement.

On the technical side, I am very lucky to have worked previously with Della Mancuso as my publishing consultant on another project and now again with her to prepare this manuscript for publication. Thank you, Donna Murphy, for doing a wonderful job designing the book and turning my butterfly collage into a beautiful book cover. Thanks also to Ellen Henrie who, as copy editor, corrected and fine-tuned the manuscript. Finally, I wish to thank my other family members and many friends who encouraged me along the way. I am truly grateful for all their support.

DEDICATION

To my family, without whom I could not have written this book.

1

THE STORM

Mid-May, 2015—Gaithersburg, Maryland

Today's going to mark a turning point in my life, Sarah Aubert assures herself as she unexpectedly awakens at sunrise. She curls her 5'10" frame into a fetal position as a rush of turbulence churns in her gut, then rises into her throat. But will I be able to go through with my decision? After a moment's hesitation, an irresistible surge of excitement seeps back into her body. Yes, I will, she vows. Jumping off the bed, she quickly puts on a pair of shorts and a T-shirt and heads downstairs. Her twin sister, Margot, is already in the kitchen eating breakfast.

"My God, Sarah!" Margot exclaims. "What are *you* doing up this early?"

"I decided to go for a run before it gets too hot," Sarah replies nonchalantly as if this were always part of her daily routine. "Want to come with me?"

Margot shakes her head, then focuses her carob-brown eyes on her sister. The girls, born twenty minutes apart, are opposites, except for their imposing height and slender build. Margot resembles her father's side of the family from southern

France with olive skin and straight, sable-brown hair, square jawline, and aquiline nose. She was named after her paternal grandmother, Marguerite. Their mother, Abigail, chose 'Sarah' to honor her deceased grandmother in keeping with Jewish tradition. With her lighter skin, lapis eyes, and abundant auburn curls, Sarah's features echo her mother's as a descendant of eastern Europeans.

Since the girls left for college in Washington, DC, last fall—Margot for Georgetown, Sarah for George Washington—they haven't seen much of each other. Even though the campuses are just a few miles apart, Sarah joined a sorority and, with a basketball scholarship, had a rigorous practice schedule. In contrast, Margot spent her free time at art openings and the many small theaters in the Washington cultural scene.

When Sarah is playing basketball, she thrives on pushing her athletic body to be the best rebounder and scorer on the court—as if her entire self-worth depended on how well she performed. On the other hand, Margot loves being a spectator, especially of theater, becoming engrossed in the finite world that the actors construct. Margot believes that acting is about projecting emotions, whereas basketball is about projecting force.

For a moment, Sarah holds Margot's intense gaze, then abruptly turns and strides out the back door. "See ya later," Sarah calls back as the screen door bangs shut.

The morning stretches toward noon, and the heat and humidity intensify, unusually so for the middle of May. By mid-afternoon, the sky begins to darken, and wind gusts whoosh through the trees as the rumblings of distant thunder increase in intensity.

Margot vaguely wonders where Sarah might be. She hasn't

seen her since much earlier when Sarah left for a run. Margot looks around on the main floor then calls her sister's name. When there is no answer, Margot is drawn toward the picture window in the den overlooking the driveway. Despite the rain that now blurs the glass, she sees someone moving along the blacktop. To her surprise, but then, not really, she recognizes Sarah, dancing in rhythm with the worsening storm, her russet ringlets circling her head, sending water flying away like a dog shaking off after a bath.

Margot pounds the window with the palm of her hand. After a moment, Sarah hears something or senses Margot's distress as she looks up and waves, beckoning her sister to join her.

Margot shakes her head emphatically, yet, at the same time, she wants to be there with Sarah, to prove to her that she, too, is capable of impulsive folly. She goes to the hall closet to retrieve a hooded jacket, wishing she didn't care so much what Sarah thinks of her. Finally, she runs into the garage and presses the door opener. "What on earth are you trying to prove?" Margot shouts.

"Fuck you!" Sarah yells back, but she smiles, holding her hands out to her sister. "Don't you want to have some fun before we start our internships next week?"

Margot isn't sure about 'fun' as she ventures into the open driveway. Almost immediately, the wind forces the hood off her head. Within seconds, rain hammers her cheeks, and streams of water slide down her neck as her bobbed hair is plastered to her scalp. She turns toward the garage, but Sarah grabs her hands so she can't go back, her eyes ablaze with feigned malice as she laughs at her sister's distress. Sarah disregards danger as if nothing harmful could touch her. Margot is the one who obsesses over all the worst outcomes, hoping she can somehow thwart anything she can name.

Suddenly, a loud crack follows a burst of lightning. The sound distracts Sarah enough to loosen her grip on Margot's hands as she wrestles herself free.

"Baby!" Sarah hurls at her sister as Margot retreats into the garage, closing the heavy metal door behind her.

The next time Margot looks out of the window, the driveway is empty.

Sarah doesn't show up the rest of the afternoon or evening. Only much later, as her parents head into the den to watch TV, does Michel, her father, ask Margot if she knows where Sarah might have gone.

"I have no idea," she answers with a shrug of disinterest.

• • •

When Margot arises the next morning, Sarah's door is closed. She assumes that Sarah is catching up on much-needed sleep.

Margot enters the empty kitchen, starts a pot of coffee, then opens a cabinet to retrieve several mugs as her father walks in. Michel Aubert is no longer the trim young man projecting a hesitant semi-smile from his wedding picture. His nut-brown eyes still radiate the same vibrant energy as they did twenty years ago. However, he has gained weight, mostly around his belly, as it protrudes over his pajama bottom. At this early hour, he's still blurry-eyed and scruffy around the chin. Looking at the wedding photo, Margot can see why her mother interrupted her education to accompany him to France.

Abigail, her mother, has told the story about their courtship many times. "I was at a party when I met this cute Frenchman with enormous, dark-brown eyes and a sexy accent. We hardly had a language in common, but we started going out together. Then your father had to cut short his stay in the US to fulfill his mandatory military service back in France. He asked me to go with him, and by then, I was in love with him, so how could I have possibly said no?

"We stayed in France for almost three years so he could complete his doctorate, while I did my best to assimilate. I learned the language and the customs enough to stop feeling like a perpetual foreigner. Then, the two of you came along!

"Papa didn't earn much money during those years, so we lived with his parents in a village outside of Toulouse. Luckily, just when things became too difficult for three generations to function together under one roof, he received a job offer as a research physicist back in the States."

• • •

"What are you doing up so early, *Pitchoune*?" Michel asks, interrupting her reverie. Margot looks at him adoringly, her eyes as shiny as tempered chocolate. She loves it when he calls her that. In Occitan, a dialect from the south of France, it means 'little one'.

"I wonder whether Sarah ever came home last night. Did you hear her at all?"

"Nope," her father replies. "I guess she came in very late and was careful to be quiet."

"Do ya think?" Margot asks with exaggerated skepticism. She picks up her coffee mug, places a kiss on her father's scratchy cheek, and goes out to the back porch. She sits in one of the Adirondack rockers and looks through the screen into the yard. After yesterday's storm, a carpet of blush-pink petals has accumulated under the flowering cherry trees. Haze rises off the lawn as puddles from the rain start to evaporate. Margot missed this house while away at school, with its mishmash of furniture styles and travel souvenirs.

Margot is aware that her time to live under the protective umbrella of her parents' care is fast coming to an end. In October, she and Sarah will turn twenty. Margot recognizes that part of the process of becoming an independent adult is to figure out how to emerge from one's adolescence intact, like a butterfly unfolding its wings as it frees itself from its cocoon.

• • •

Sarah is not up by the end of the morning. When 1:00 rolls around, Margot decides to find out if her sister came home at all last night. As she approaches Sarah's bedroom, even before she opens the door, Margot senses with a stab of dread that Sarah isn't there and that she won't see her twin sister again for a long time.

The door isn't locked, so she slowly pushes it open. The curtains are closed, and the room is in shadow. The bed is lumpy, and, for a moment, Margot assumes that Sarah is under the heap of entangled sheets and gaudy throw pillows, sound asleep. But then, she intuitively knows that this isn't true. Sarah is gone! Her closet door is ajar, and when Margot pulls it fully open, she can see that some of Sarah's clothes are gone, too. "What's happened?" she cries out into the musty room.

Immediately, Margot worries that Sarah could be in trouble. She is about to bolt out of the room when she spots a piece of paper on the dresser, set neatly to one side, away from the chaos of junk jewelry and hair do-dads; a pen rests on top of the paper so it wouldn't blow away when the door opens.

The note, which looks hastily scrawled across the page,

reads: *Dear Family, I've been invited to spend some time in Ghana with my good friend from school, Daren Owusu. I'm sorry I didn't tell you about this before, but I was afraid you would forbid me from going. I know I'm letting you down with the internship and all, and I'll call to explain it better when I get to Daren's. Love, Sarah.*

Margot is flabbergasted. "Daren? Who the hell is Daren?" She shouts into the deathly silent room. "How could you leave the country for Africa, for God's sake, with someone I've never heard of? And what about Mom and Papa? You had to know they'll be devastated!"

Rage mounts and engulfs Margot like the storm from yesterday. She wants to sweep all her sister's trinkets off the dresser and watch them scatter around the room. Instead, she starts to shake, and the tears she has been holding back now stream down her face. She flops on her sister's bed and sobs—her face buried into Sarah's pillow, trying to find comfort in the lingering scents from Sarah's sweat and shampoo.

After a few moments, however, Margot's rage returns. She realizes that she will be the one who will have to tell their parents unless one of them finds the note first. Neither is home now, and she can't decide if she should call one of them. As she is mulling over what to do, she hears a car pull into the driveway, and the garage door starts to lift. She recognizes her father's heavy footsteps as he trudges up the stairs, down the hall away from the twins' rooms, and into his bedroom. Then she hears the sound of running water. Margot grabs her purse, tiptoes downstairs, and leaves the house by the back door. She can't face having to tell her parents that her zany, impulsive, pain-in-the-ass of a sister has run away from home!

2

THE GUEST

Mid-May—Kumasi, Ghana

I can't believe I'm in Ghana!" Sarah exclaims to Daren as they climb out of the chauffeur-driven 4x4. "Until we became friends, I'd never met anyone from Africa, much less from a city as exotic-sounding as Kumasi."

She stares in awe at the imposing white house as the mahogany double front doors suddenly fly open. A statuesque woman with a radiant smile rushes out, throws her arms around Daren's shoulders, and kisses him several times on both cheeks. A stocky man as dark as charcoal, presumably his father, follows close behind. When they turn toward Sarah, the woman's expression changes from pure joy to polite formality.

"Welcome to Ghana," she says as she extends her hand.

"Thank you so much for having me," Sarah replies. She has the urge to embrace Daren's mother; instead, she grasps her hand as long as she dares.

Sarah follows Daren and his parents as they walk across the threshold into a high-ceilinged foyer. The marble tiles echo as they walk through the palatial space and into an expansive living room. Sarah is agape as she surveys the velvety couches and acajou tables interspaced with enormous pots of tropical plants. Exotic, carved masks and intricately patterned tapestries adorn the walls.

By now, Daren's two younger sisters have raced down the stairs and rushed toward their brother. His mother tries to speak above the noise in a local dialect to a maid. At the same time, his father peppers Daren with questions as he talks over the din. Sarah feels as though she's been projected into an alternative reality. She can't understand what anyone is saying, and no one seems to realize she is even there. Finally, Daren disengages, then takes Sarah's hand to introduce her properly to his family.

"Quiet down, everyone! This is my special friend, Sarah Aubert. From the day I met her at school, she welcomed me—not as a clueless foreigner—but as a regular person worthy of her friendship. She included me in her circle of friends and helped me over a serious hump of feeling out of step with everyone else."

Suddenly, Daren's family goes silent, then turns toward Sarah with wide, welcoming smiles. A moment later, everyone starts talking again as Daren takes her aside.

"I know this must seem like a bit of a circus," he says. "Let's go upstairs so you can unpack and rest for a while. Some other relatives are coming over for dinner this evening, so I hope you can get some sleep first."

"Thanks; I would love to take a shower and then a nap. What language was your mother speaking to the maid? It sounds so different from anything I've ever heard."

It's Ashanti Twi, a dialect derived from a local language, Akan. The Ashanti people have inhabited this part of Ghana since the 1600s. We even have a king. You're going to get to see him in a week or so at the traditional ceremony that occurs every couple of months.

"Thanks so much for inviting me here. You saved me from what was shaping up to be a very difficult summer."

As they climb the stairs, Daren glances sideways at her with his almond-shaped, velvety black eyes fringed with mile-long eyelashes. Sarah flashes him a gleaming smile as if she were discovering for the first time how attractive he is.

From the day he met her, Daren was drawn to Sarah—her inquisitive blue eyes, her infectious smile, and the rusty freckles that pepper the bridge of her slender nose. He was deeply touched that this attractive, popular, American girl befriended him as if his social awkwardness and thick accent didn't matter. He could have invited any of his other friends to come to Ghana this summer, but he chose Sarah as a way of expressing his gratitude.

Daren leads her down a wide hallway, then shows her into a cozy bedroom with a private bath. He cranks up the AC unit on the wall, places her suitcase onto the bed, and then turns to leave. "Just let me know if you need anything."

Sarah pushes her suitcase aside, removes her sweaty T-shirt and flops on the bed. She finds it impossible to relax, however, knowing that her parents have undoubtedly discovered her note and are likely quite distraught that she left the way she did. Now that it's too late to take any of it back, the reality of what she has done is beginning to seep into her consciousness: how reckless she was to sneak off with Daren, jump on a plane with him, and fly almost halfway around the world to Ghana.

Her stomach knots up in a tight ball as she admits what

a despicable situation she has created—prioritizing her exasperation at what was in store for her over the summer above her parents' expectations. She backed out of her internship and probably jeopardized her basketball scholarship. Right now, though, she is too tired to think straight. Instead, overcome with the need to sleep, she suddenly feels kissed by Hypnos.

• • •

A knock at the door arouses her from what seems like a very short nap, as a woman's voice echoes from the hall, "Dinner will be served shortly."

"Oh, shit!" Sarah says aloud. She jumps into a cool shower then brushes her teeth. Afterward, Sarah wonders if she should have used the bottled water in her room, so she re-rinses with it. She twists and then piles her thick curls on top of her head, securing them in place with the one clip she brought, puts on some shorts and a halter top, and rushes downstairs.

As she enters the dining room, Sarah notices right away that all the women are wearing brightly patterned dresses or long skirts and ruffled blouses. Even Daren's younger sisters have on dresses, their hair neatly braided into cornrows and secured with rings of tiny beads. Oh, Jeez, she surmises in a panic, but I had no idea! She seeks out Daren's mother, afraid to look at any of the other guests who silently sit and stare at her. "Please excuse me," she chokes out, feeling her cheeks growing hot. "I'll just go up and change." She wonders if she even threw in a sundress; she packed so quickly. Daren's mother can barely hide her disapproval as she replies to Sarah that it isn't necessary—this time.

When they finally settle down to eat, fourteen people are seated around an enormous table, cut directly from a large, hardwood tree. Sarah marvels at the elaborate table settings: the shimmering royal blue and white china plates atop woven bamboo chargers, bookended on one side by brass napkin rings in the form of crocodiles and three glasses in different sizes on the other side, that gleam like crystal statues.

In addition to his parents and his two younger sisters, Daren's older sister, her husband and a toddler are among the guests. George is also an older brother who is away in graduate school in England. And all the rest are aunts, uncles, cousins—first, second, and first once-removed.

Sarah's head begins to ache; she does not recognize anything on her plate as the type of food she has ever eaten before, and she is a little afraid of it. She keeps glancing over at Daren, trying to take cues from him about how to act. She is embarrassingly aware that she has landed in an upper-class Ghanaian family with its own codes of established traditions and social behaviors that she cannot access. Daren's mother is a pediatrician. His father collaborates with several Chinese firms to build roads and housing complexes. He also manages properties he rents to ex-pats from Europe and the United States, mostly in Accra, the capital of Ghana, causing him to be absent much of the week.

As the meal wears on, everything starts to blur together for Sarah into an exotic soup of chitchat, laughter, glasses clinking, and utensils going from plate to mouth. She is too tired to pretend she is enjoying herself, so Sarah whispers to Daren that she would like to be excused. Everyone stares at her as Daren escorts her from the room.

"Please tell your mother that I'm so sorry to have disrupted the meal," she tells Daren as she looks at him for a sign of approval.

"It's understandable, so please don't worry. I hope you sleep well," Daren answers as he gives her a peck on the cheek. Then he turns around and heads back into the dining room. From the hall, even before she starts up the stairs, Sarah hears the energy level rise again, and she realizes that, other than Daren, nobody cares that she has left.

• • •

Sarah sleeps fitfully. When she awakens, daylight is poking through the slats of the heavy mahogany shutters that shroud the windows. Sarah looks for her phone to see what time it is, but the battery died sometime during the night. She brought the charger, but the plug doesn't fit into the weird socket next to the bed. Sarah knows that her parents and sister have texted and left voice messages multiple times. She wants to feel some regret that she is unable to reach her family right now, but in reality, she is relieved that she has a valid reason not to call.

She throws on her one sundress and ventures downstairs, following her nose until she finds the kitchen. The cook is scrambling eggs and toasting up fresh bread. She nods to Sarah, then turns her head toward a doorway.

Sarah exits the kitchen onto a wide veranda where Daren's mother sits at a table facing a large swimming pool. The table is set with coffee cups and juice glasses for breakfast. "Do sit down," Mrs. Owusu says, indicating the chair across from her. "Did you sleep well?" she asks, her dark, deliberate eyes scrutinizing Sarah's demeanor.

"Yes, thank you," Sarah mutters. "I'm sorry about last night. I couldn't keep my eyes open."

"Please, don't worry about it." A slight smile animates her face, and her eyes soften as she changes the subject. "You are very lucky to be here at this time. A week from Sunday is *Adae,* a traditional ceremony for the king. We will all be there. In the meantime, I hope you will enjoy some sightseeing."

The cook brings the eggs, toast, and coffee for Dr. Owusu. She eats hurriedly, then says, almost as an afterthought, "Feel free to use the pool this morning. Daren plans to take you to Kejetia later, and it will be hot."

As Daren's mother heads toward the house, Sarah realizes that she has forgotten to mention anything about an adapter for her phone. When the cook arrives with her breakfast, she tries to ask her about it, but the woman just shrugs her shoulders and mutters, "*Ne comprends pas.*"

Sarah assumes she is from one of the French-speaking countries that dominate this part of West Africa. Sarah smiles at the cook as she tries to explain in her limited French the difference in the electrical outlets. The woman shrugs again and walks back into the house.

When Sarah finishes her breakfast, she returns to the house, wondering if she dares to explore some of the rooms herself. Most of the doors along the hallway are closed, but at one end, she peeks inside a room with an open door that appears to be an office. She sits down at a massive wooden desk, opens one of the drawers and rifles through the various contents inside, searching for an adapter.

"Whatcha lookin' for in der?" asks a small voice behind her. It was one of Daren's younger sisters.

"Oh, I'm sorry, but my phone is dead. I'm trying to find an adapter for the outlet."

"It's not in the desk. I'll find it for ya."

She crosses the room, opens a closet door, and retrieves

what Sarah needs. Then she skips off toward the kitchen before Sarah can thank her.

Sarah returns upstairs to charge her phone, change into a bikini, and then go back to the pool. The cool water buoys up her mood as she swims a few laps. Just as Sarah decides to get out, Daren appears in shorts, his torso bare. Sarah is surprised that she is attracted to him as his dark skin glistens in the sun. "I just did a few laps, but I'm game to go back into the pool if you are as well."

"I'm going to have some breakfast first. How did you sleep?"

"Okay, thanks, but my phone gave out during the night. Your sister found an adapter for me. I really should call my family to tell them how I am. I just left a note, but I didn't say anything about coming here ahead of time." Her whole upper body sags forward, her hair dripping water down her face.

"You mean, they didn't know you were coming to Ghana with me?" He sounds truly astonished.

"It's a long story," she replies, raising her eyes to meet his. "I doubt they would have been okay with it, even though you bought the ticket. I'm supposed to start a summer internship on Monday."

"Jesus, Sarah! I had no idea! Yeah, you'd better get in touch with them soon. I plan to take you to the Kejetia Market later. It's the largest outdoor market in West Africa. You can buy anything there, and it's fun to bargain."

It's obvious to Sarah that Daren does not want to become involved with her family problems. She wishes, though, that she could confide in him about the turmoil roiling through her right now. Instead, she asks, "Haven't you ever felt like you are in the wrong place, going for the wrong things, and other people's expectations trap you?"

"All the time...," he answers quietly.

"Really? Your parents seem so easy on you. Mine expect so much of me at school because of the basketball scholarship—like this is my only chance to be in college. Plus, I was supposed to work over the summer, so I can at least pay for some of my expenses next year."

"Well," he responds, "isn't that expected of all of us?"

She is taken aback by this response and quickly determines that he couldn't possibly know what it's like to have to earn money when it's obvious that his family is as rich as God. But then it occurs to her that his parents are professionals and undoubtedly expect him to excel in school to have a lucrative career eventually.

Sarah tries to hold his gaze, but the cook brings out his breakfast. Now that she can observe him in his environment, she discovers a more self-aware side of him that he hadn't shown her before. She wonders if there could be an opening to connect with him at a deeper level than they have so far.

Sarah excuses herself to check on her phone, and, since it is almost charged, she is out of excuses not to call. Still, she cringes at the thought of hearing the disappointment in her parent's voices, or worse, an ultimatum that she return home immediately. Instead, she sends off a text to explain in a few sentences why she left as she did:

After pushing myself all year to stay on top of my classes and basketball, I couldn't face an entire summer of going through it all again—in my internship, at practice, in everything. You three are smart and accomplished, and therefore multitasking is just so much easier for you than for me. I know what I did was extreme, but I couldn't bring myself to have this conversation with you beforehand. When Daren invited me to come with him to Ghana, it felt like a way to avoid a lot of pain. I'm really sorry I've caused you all so much anguish.

When she rereads what she wrote, it sounds lame and full of self-pity, but she hits *Send* before changing her mind. A sinking feeling overcomes her as she revisits how irresponsible it was to sneak off to Ghana with only the note on her dresser as an explanation. Emotions she has tried to hold back come spilling out. She lies down on the bed and cries herself into a semi-sleep—her hair and pillow wet with snot and hot, salty tears.

3

DILEMMAS

Mid-May—Gaithersburg, Maryland

No one found Sarah's note from the day before, and it sat unnoticed on her dresser. Her parents, Abby and Michel, figured she was with friends or in touch with Margot about her plans. When her mother finally reads Sarah's text the next morning, she is shocked, hurt, and enraged. Abby has always felt a special closeness to Sarah, but she can't muster any empathy for her wayward daughter in this moment of high emotion. She wants Sarah to absorb all the blame and ensuing guilt for her recklessness. Without allowing the why to emerge, Abby acknowledges that she never actually discussed with Sarah whether she was on board with the commitments that her parents planned for her over the summer.

Instead, Abby focuses on what might happen to Sarah's scholarship if she isn't back in a month or so. The thought of Sarah losing her scholarship, after she and Michel have worked for years to build up a college fund, provokes another surge of anger quashing all other concerns.

Abby throws a light robe over her curvy body, then rushes

downstairs to seek out Michel as if he were somehow complicit in all this.

"Are you aware that Sarah jumped on a plane to Ghana last night with some guy from school?" Abby's gray-green eyes bore into his calm face, her nostrils flaring as her thin lips tighten into a pout.

"Yes, Abbs. I saw her text, too. I'm not happy that she didn't tell us ahead of time, and I'm very surprised she never said anything to Margot."

"How do you know she didn't?" Abby challenges him. "Maybe Margot just didn't want to be the one to tell us."

"Why are you so quick to accuse Margot? She's a good kid. I'm pretty sure she would never have done what Sarah just did. But it's upsetting if Sarah was so unhappy about what we planned for her this summer that she thought leaving was her only option."

"We didn't plan anything she ever objected to. But what if she loses her scholarship? Who's going to pay the difference?"

"She'll have to get a job and take fewer classes. It'll take her longer to graduate, but maybe, if she can overcome all this uncertainty, the experience will eventually help her to settle down."

"Well, I don't think any of that excuses her from doing something this extreme. I expect she'll need a ticket home and money while she's there. If she had consulted us earlier, maybe we could have worked something out. But to up and leave like this...I think it was very immature!"

"You're right, it *is* immature, but she's nineteen. Sarah has never been as predictable as Margot in making decisions and following through. Don't you see a little of yourself in her at that age? You ran away with me to France, and you learned a lot by living in another country. I honestly believe that experience helped you decide, eventually, what you wanted to do with your life."

"Maybe so," Abby struggles to admit, her eyes clouding to gray as they change color with her mood.

Michel gets up from the kitchen counter and wraps his arms around his wife. "Things haven't worked out so badly, have they? C'mon, Abbs; you and Sarah have always been able to connect. Somewhere deep down, you have to know she'll be okay." He finishes his coffee then places a wet kiss on Abby's forehead before leaving the kitchen.

Abigail pushes away some of her chestnut curls that keep falling around her forehead. She sips her coffee and remembers how she had arrived at her decision to leave home. She releases a deep sigh as she reflects for the umpteenth time about why she left for France as abruptly as Sarah did for Ghana. Abby never got along that well with her mother, and she knew that running away to France wasn't just an act of love for Michel. At some level, it was also a statement of anger that she had hoped her mother would take personally. She spent much of her teenage years weaving back and forth between responsible and risky behavior—trying drugs occasionally in college and having unprotected sex with several men she had casually dated.

Now, as an adult, Abby realizes that she had craved her mother's attention, no matter how she got it, and it was because Abby didn't want to disappoint her father that she never entirely crossed over that bright red line. After she left for France with Michel, her life changed completely because of that impulsive act when she wasn't much older than the twins are now.

Michel's parents were *les français de souche*—those whose roots were solidly French, Catholic, mostly working-class—the salt of the earth. Michel was the first person in his family to graduate from high school, much less earn a doctorate. Abigail's upbringing was quite different, being raised in an upper-middle-class, Reform Jewish family who only celebrated Hanukkah, Passover, and the High Holy Days. And although they never brought it up in front of her, Abby always suspected that Michel's parents weren't too pleased that their only child married a Jew.

Michel asked her to marry him because, at one point, she threatened to leave. In the end, she stayed because she loved him and reasoned that the difficult situation with his parents wouldn't go on forever. By then, Abby was pregnant, although neither of them knew it the night he proposed. She realized that she couldn't leave him as long as she craved that frothy excitement of tenderness and passion each time they made love. She smiles as she reminisces about how that same spark managed to survive all these years, sometimes as a flame and sometimes a fragile ember that never completely died out.

4

THE INTERN

Mid-to Late May—Washington, DC

When Margot awakes on Monday morning, the first day of her internship, she is immediately aware of the fluttering in her stomach. As a straight-A student at an Ivy League school, she has faith in her ability to learn what she needs to know to do her job well. Her apprehensions have more to do with her realization that she is entering the working-woman's world—dressed in a suit and heels, commuting into DC on Metro. She fears that in just a few short years, she could be part of this cycle that the French call *métro*, *boulot*, *dodo*, transport, work, sleep—entrapped in a strive-to-survive society. But today, she is at the beginning of this process, and, as she boards the train into DC, her confidence rises, replacing her trepidation with excitement at taking on a new challenge.

She arrives promptly at 9:00 at the law firm of Davidson and Hammer, where her mother had worked just out of law school and arranged for Margot's internship. Margot will be assisting seven attorneys, tracking the growing environmental threats to the Chesapeake Bay, the largest U.S. estuary. More than 150 rivers and streams flow into the Bay's drainage system, covering parts of six states. The entire watershed is under siege, as legal challenges arise from often ignored and unenforced laws and regulations.

When Margot walks through the glass doors and approaches the front desk, the receptionist greets her with a welcoming smile, then escorts her into a conference room and closes the door. Several minutes later, a tall, skinny young man in horn-rimmed glasses, wearing a short-sleeve shirt and Dockers, strides into the room. Margot is relieved to see how casually he is dressed, and it puts her at ease.

"Hi, Marguerite, right? I'm Jason Applegate. Nice to meet you. We're going to be working together over the summer. Let's go up to the fifth floor, where most of the lawyers in my division are housed. You'll have a central space there so we can all interact. First, you'll need to fill out some paperwork and then get settled."

She follows him out of the conference room and into an elevator. "Please call me Margot," she says as they quickly arrive on Five. Jason leads her toward his small office at the end of the hallway. Margot notices that practically all the other offices along the corridor are empty and wonders with a sinking feeling if she will be working up here mostly on her own.

As if he anticipated her concern, Jason says, "Many of the other attorneys and some staff have gone to Annapolis for strategy meetings at the CBLAC. We're in the early stages of collecting evidence for a possible lawsuit against some of the integrators who manage almost all of the chicken farms on the Delmarva Peninsula."

"I don't want to sound ignorant, and my mother has told

me a lot about this firm, but what is the CBLAC, and who are the integrators?"

"All these acronyms can be confusing. Besides the several well-known nonprofits, there are alliances such as the CBLAC, the Chesapeake Bay Legal Action Coalition that group many smaller organizations together as they specialize in different ways to protect the Bay and its watershed. We collaborate with these entities to help their members stay current on existing laws or, as in this case, to prosecute offenders thwarting the laws. When you get up to speed, you'll also be working with the people in Annapolis as they prepare what could be a seminal case against the polluters.

"The integrators are the food companies. They don't own the land, but they manage every other step of bringing a chicken from an embryo to someone's kitchen."

He picks up a clipboard from his desk, then leads her back into the hallway. "As an intern, you'll be managing emails, phone calls, and doing research. We need someone who's a quick learner, organized, and not afraid to take the initiative. This work will be great training for you, no matter what you end up doing in the future. Who knows, maybe you'll decide to become an environmental attorney someday, like your mother. Even with President Obama in the White House and most of the legislators in the affected states wanting to protect the watershed, plenty of people and companies are looking for ways to get around as many regulations as they can. We help the watchdogs be as effective as possible within the laws."

As they continue down the hallway, Jason's phone buzzes; he points to an empty cubicle across the hall and nods, mumbling that he'll be back soon. Then he disappears into his office.

• • •

Jason was right. Margot spends most of her time fielding a load of incoming calls and emails, directing them to the proper people within this department. Some are from professionals wanting access to court documents not available online; others are tips from the general public reporting possible legal infractions. The majority, however, are requests for information about the panoply of environmental issues affecting the Bay. Margot is responsible for researching the answers to many of these inquiries.

As Jason started to explain to Margot on her first day, the CBLAC in Annapolis is working on an important case to determine whether the integrators can be forced to pay more toward the waste disposal from their contract farms. Now he wants to get Margot more involved.

"Several years ago, the federal government's Environmental Protection Agency (EPA) intervened in the three states of the Delmarva Peninsula (Delaware, Maryland, and Virginia), forcing them to live up to their voluntary dumping agreements, called Total Maximum Daily Load (TMDL). To put it crudely," Jason comments, "how much crap are they legally allowed to dump into the waterways? A federal judge will determine whether the large food conglomerates must pay more to provide other ways for their farmers to stay within their TMDLs. We expect a verdict by the end of the year."

"So," Margot surmises, "this case is primarily about money."

"Yep," Jason sighs as if he doesn't expect the final outcome to work in their favor.

"Even though I know my outrage isn't going to change anything," Margot commiserates, "I feel like I have to do more to inform everyone how our waterways are becoming so polluted."

Jason beams a smile at her and replies, "That's why you're here. Would you consider relocating to Annapolis for a month or so to work directly with the CBLAC staff?"

Margot's spirits lift at the prospect of becoming more involved with a cause that inspires her. She's anxious to learn as much as she can about the area's history and people. Native names keep swirling around in her head: Susquehanna, Choptank, Rappahannock, Potomac. Major rivers feed fresh water into an enormous ecosystem from the north, mixing in the Bay with saltwater washed in from the Atlantic tides to the south, creating a balance, enabling the region's life to evolve over millions of years. Margot recalls one article in particular she read online while doing some research about the history of the region. It focused on the negative evolution of the entire Chesapeake watershed over the past several hundred years as ever-more rapacious societies forced out the native peoples who named the rivers and who had lived for millennia in peace with their environment.

On her way home from work that evening, this awareness of injustice, greed, and the ongoing degradation of the Bay roll around in her head as Margot sways back and forth with the lurch of a Red-Line Metro car. Most of the other people are the same commuters she sees every morning and evening. Many have blank expressions as they stare into space, lost inside their thoughts. Some sleep as others read, and some completely isolate themselves with earbuds or headphones. Margot wonders what years of commuting do to a person's ability to engage with others outside of family, friends, and work.

As she reaches her stop and exits the train, Margot thinks of her sister, probably having the time of her life in Ghana. She sighs as she wishes that sometimes she could be more like Sarah. I guess our parents are glad that there's only one Sarah. She's impulsive and goes her way, regardless of the consequences. I'm not like that; I've always been called the 'reasonable' one. And since I was thirteen, I learned to fear any unanticipated, dreadful outcomes. Instead of going for it like Sarah, I tend to pull back. But this time I'm all in with going to work in Annapolis. I can't wait to get started!

5

KEJETIA MARKET

Late May—Kumasi, Ghana

When Sarah awakes from her nap, she returns to the pool to see if Daren is still there.

He's swimming laps, and after watching him for a minute or two, seeing his torso twist and rise rhythmically in and out of the water, Sarah can't resist the temptation to tease him a little in a provocative way. She dives into the deep end and blocks him as he propels himself toward her. He mutters something about her being a pain, then tries to circumvent her, but she grabs onto his arms as he swerves.

"Hey, Sarah, what's the deal?" He is annoyed as he bobs around, treading water beside her. Then, he reaches for the side and climbs out of the water. Sarah follows him and sits down on a lounge chair next to him. She's not sure why he is upset, but she's sorry to have pissed him off.

"Daren, what's up? I was just fooling around." She smiles weakly then looks at him with fervent eyes from under her dark, wet lashes. Daren puts his feet on the cement as if to get up and leave, but instead, he leans over and takes her hand.

"You're a beautiful girl, Sarah, and a good friend, but ever since we got here, I've been getting the message that you would like to take our relationship in a different direction. You know how much I care for you, but not in that way. I'm pretty sure I'm not that kind of guy."

For a split second, Sarah assumes that he does not believe in premarital sex because of his culture and upbringing. But then, as she stares back into the wells of his woeful eyes, it hits her. "Holy shit," she pauses. "Are you telling me that you're gay?"

His silence says everything.

"So, no one in your family knows?"

"You haven't been here long enough to see how religious this country is. People name their shops and taxicabs after quotes from the Bible. We all go to church every Sunday. It's just what people do here. I can't tell anyone, and you can't act any differently toward me, especially around my family!" He tries to smile at her, but his eyes start to crinkle as if he were holding back tears.

"But how can you live like this? Does anyone at school know?"

"Look, I'm trying to deal with it. I'm a mess right now. So, let's not talk about it anymore and just go on being good friends."

"Well, that's not hard because it's the truth as far as I'm concerned!" She gives him a peck on the cheek, then stands up, grabs her towel, and heads toward the house.

Sarah is disappointed as the impact of what just happened sinks in. She was hoping to talk to him more about her own identity crisis if nothing else. But now, she admits that it's probably not an option either.

She showers and dresses to go to Kejetia, but her thoughts keep returning to Daren's revelation. She sits on the bed, head bowed, hands clasped tightly together in her lap. In the end, what the fuck am I doing here? Sarah asks herself. I'm causing so much stress to my family, and now this situation with Daren feels like a kick in the ass. She is on the verge of another crying fit, but instead, she forces herself to go into the bathroom and wash her face in cold water, then heads back to the veranda. On the way, she makes a mental list of all the things she needs to buy: another dress or at least a skirt, a pair of flip-flops, some tampons, and a couple of scrunchies to hold back her unruly curls. She packed so fast and was so worried about being found out that she had forgotten a lot of essentials. She also couldn't bring much money, but Daren told her that shopping at Kejetia is a kind of game and that you never accept the quoted price.

She sits at the breakfast table, waiting for Daren to show up. The day is fast becoming hot, as the sun radiates full force into her face from above a row of bluish-green eucalyptus trees. She adds a wide-brimmed straw hat to her growing list of must-haves as she wonders if they take U.S. dollars in the market.

Daren soon arrives wearing shorts and a T-shirt. Sarah would like to change into shorts, but he urges her not to. "Best not to show too much of yourself in town. You're young, attractive—and White. That's a combination that will invite stares but not advances if you're dressed modestly. My presence helps, but it's pretty tight in the alleys at the market. As it is, you need to be careful of pickpockets. Does your bag zip?"

As he talks, he leads her to the chauffeured 4X4. Once outside the property, they drive down a rutted side road, then turn onto a larger avenue lined with small shops and fruit stands. Dotted in between are barbershops and hair salons, shoe repair stalls, and taxi pick-up areas. Many shops and businesses, including the taxis, display signs that say "Pray for Salvation" and "God is Master."

Sarah can better understand now why Daren was so afraid to reveal his sexual orientation. Her opinions about LBGTQ people were strongly opposed to what she perceives as baseless prejudice. Sarah respects and feels empathy for Daren, a kind, sensitive person forced to play a vicious game with himself and his family. She has the urge to take his hand and squeeze it, but she doesn't. He is lost in his own space as a strained silence fills the car. Sarah tries to change the dejected atmosphere by asking him about finding a dress long enough to cover her tall frame.

Daren turns to her with a wistful expression, but then a half-smile starts tugging at the corners of his mouth. "Wait and see," he says. "I'm pretty sure you will find something in the market that's okay for most places you might go."

"But what about church on Sunday and then the King Thing?"

He chuckles. "The 'King Thing' is called *Adae*, and you're right. Normally we all put on our best clothes and lots of jewelry. But you're a tourist, so even if you wear a sundress, my mother can give you a shawl or something. Look, we're going to be there soon." He takes her hand and looks into her eyes with a soft, almost loving expression. Sarah wonders if things could ever be different between them. Maybe he isn't devotedly gay. Maybe he's just confused. She smiles back at him, her eyes locked into his. I'm confused, too, about what he wants me to think.

They arrive at a parking area across from the market jammed with cars and minivans. Drivers are milling around, smoking, snacking, and texting. Many stray dogs lie willy-nilly under bramble bushes and in the deep purple shadows of parked cars. Mingling among them are children carrying baskets on their heads with mangoes, fried dough, and small bottles of water; their skinny bodies supporting far more weight than kids this young should be carrying under a blistering sun.

As they enter the market's maze that stretches as far as the eye can see, the humidity becomes oppressive. A yellowish haze blurs the edges of the distant buildings, and murky water stagnates in the shallow ditches between stalls. Sarah is acutely aware that they could be breeding grounds for malarial mosquitoes. She instinctively shrinks back, but Daren takes her elbow and propels her along the narrow alleyway and into an area where a variety of clothing hangs along a makeshift fence. The patterns woven into the cloth are striking, with geometric designs and vivid swirls suggesting the tropical flora that grows everywhere. Some skirts and dresses are adorned with appliqués that look like letters from some ancient language.

"All this clothing is made from locally woven Kente cloth," Daren explains. "But I'm not sure you'll want to wear any of it once you are back home."

"Well, I can't live indefinitely in this same dress!" Sarah saunters up to the fence and examines the clothes hanging there. She agrees with Daren that they all look too bright and flouncy. Then she spots a long straight skirt with more subdued blues and greens interwoven with small pink and yellow flowers. "I would certainly wear this at home."

Immediately a woman rushes up to them, plucks the hanger with the skirt from the jumble of other garments, and starts to usher Sarah toward her stall. "Here, Missy, change-place here." She smiles a toothy grin, except that some of her teeth are missing. Still, she has a kind face, and her stall is relatively clean and private. Sarah steps into the skirt as best she can without dragging it across the ground. She pulls her dress up around her waist so she can see in the dingy mirror how well the skirt fits. "Look beeutifool!" the lady gushes. She nods to conclude the sale, and Sarah asks her the price. "Do you take U.S. dollars?"

"No exchange," she answers. "Ask boyfriend to pay. He from here, no?"

Sarah takes off the skirt and carries it out. "How much?" she asks in front of Daren.

"Fifty cedis," the woman answers.

Daren grunts and offers 25 cedis.

"How much is that in dollars?" Sarah inquires, but they were already bargaining and quickly settle on 35 cedis. Daren hands the woman the money, takes the skirt, and pulls Sarah on toward the next grouping of stalls before she can say anything.

"How much is that in dollars?" she practically shouts.

"Thirty-five cedis is less than seven dollars," he answers.

"But, that's nothing! I'm sorry you even bargained with her. She looks like she could have used the full 50 cedis more than you or me."

"She would like to have the extra money, but she would lose some of her dignity if I had accepted the original price. This is not the United States. Money is a necessity to most people but not necessarily a status symbol."

"Well, you wouldn't know that by looking at your family." Sarah spits out before she even thinks how that must sound.

"Okay," Daren responds in a monotone. "Way back, my ancestors were village elders and landowners, and probably even slave traders. Their grandsons and great-grandsons went to England to be educated. We've gone along to get along, as you say, and it's paid off for us. But we've always worked hard and still work hard. That's also why what I do now and what I become later are so important to my family."

Not only has she insulted him, but she can see that she has caused him pain. "Oh, Daren, I'm so sorry. I didn't mean to upset you. I'm just a know-nothing American tourist. Please don't be mad at me."

"I'm not. It's okay. I know most Americans judge people more by the size of their wallet than their brain."

"You can't think that of me! I didn't know anything about your family when you asked me to come here, and I accepted because I consider you a close, trusted friend. It's just that I feel sorry for those kids working out there in the hot sun. Do they even go to school? And what about that lady and her missing teeth? She probably isn't all that old!" Sarah suddenly realizes that she must sound like some overwrought activist.

"Your sense of fairness is very admirable, but this is Africa. Most people are closer to survival mode than worrying about what's fair and what's not. They are also religious and have a strong bond to family and community, supporting each other. They even have a separate economy based on bartering. In some ways, I like it better than in the States, where it often feels like absolutely everything has to do with money." He stops abruptly, aware that now he is the one sermonizing.

"It's okay, Daren," she replies. "I get that you're stuck between a rock and a hard place right now in more ways than one."

"You got that right, Girl!" He grins at her, and the cloud that had settled over him starts to float away. "C'mon. I want to show you some other areas of the market where they sell more stuff than you've ever seen in one place."

They burrow further into the endless ribbon of wooden stalls with tin roofs and narrow, rutted passageways until it feels to Sarah as if they were lost in a labyrinth. The clothing section morphs into another with trinkets, jewelry, African masks, and souvenirs. Then they come to women's articles, including several acres of panties, bras, hair and body-care products, and makeup. Eventually, Sarah can buy tampons, a straw hat, and a pair of flip-flops. They turn into another area that sells tools, everything for kitchens and bathrooms, and hand-crafted furniture. Finally, they move on to a whole separate market the size of several football fields that only sells food.

By now, Sarah's jet lag resurfaces, causing her to feel slightly dizzy and disoriented. Her feet hurt, and she is thirsty but afraid to eat or drink anything, especially the water from the unmarked plastic bottles children keep hawking to them.

Daren understands that she is beyond enjoyment or curiosity. He leads her out of the market and onto a square with a couple of outdoor bars and cafes. Sarah plops down at the first empty table she sees under a huge, sheltering tree.

They have a cocktail with ice from a God-knows-what water source, but she's too tired to resist. Daren orders a dish of fried plantains, *tatale*. Both the food and the drink taste wonderfully exotic, and Sarah can relax as she surrenders to the buzz from the cocktail. She stares out at the darkening shadows as they lengthen, and the fading light from the sunset slowly turns into sparkling streaks of flamingo pink and violet.

Suddenly, she feels a vibration in the air as she looks up to see a black cloud of bats streak across the sky above them. She shudders as if she were propelled into a scene from *The Birds*. As the bats cross over the market and fly eastward, their numbers seem to grow until they obliterate the visible sky.

"Oh my God, they are so fascinating and very creepy!" she says as the audible fluttering from so many wings fills the air.

Daren barely glances up. "This happens every night around dusk. They're fruit bats, and they eat mosquitoes; so, be happy they can survive with all this pollution and other human-made shit!"

Sarah desperately tries to take a couple of photos with her cell phone, but by now, the afterglow from the sunset has disappeared, and the bats fade into the starless night.

6

IN BETWEEN

Early to Mid-June—Annapolis, Gaithersburg, Maryland

When Margot eagerly accepted to relocate to Annapolis, Jillian Sinclair, Margot's immediate boss at the CBLAC, offered her their guest house for the duration of her stay. The property is about eleven miles from downtown and extends from the road to a small beach on the Bay's Western Shore. It was once a working farm that had been in Jillian's family for generations. Twenty years ago, her family converted the massive barn into an upscale version of a Maryland coastal cottage, with white shiplap siding, blue wooden shutters, and a traditional widow's walk atop the shingled roof. A few years later, they tore down the small farmhouse and rebuilt it as a guest house.

Margot's attitude toward her internship has changed since she has relocated to the CBLAC. She works tirelessly for long hours with her dedicated colleagues and shares their commitment to being on a mission rather than simply working at a job. Margot believes that the slow but steady degradation of the Chesapeake Bay is one of the most important environmental issues of the 21st century. She is anxious to contribute in any small way she can.

Jillian would have preferred that Margot continue working with the CBLAC even after her internship. Unfortunately, she doubted she could create a new position for her. Instead, she has been looking for other possibilities to entice Margot to remain in the area and to continue working in the same field.

Among her other clerical duties, Margot is responsible for writing progress reports following weekly meetings with other non-government organizations related to the same legal issues that the CBLAC is pursuing. On some occasions, these meetings are open to the public and state officials. Members of the press are also invited to attend.

At the most recent open meeting, Jillian pulled Margot aside. "It's my opinion that you need something more challenging than your internship can provide. I'd like you to meet Steven Rich, a local reporter employed by *The State Capital Ledger*. If you two can find a mutually productive way of working together, I believe you'll be able to take on more responsibilities than I can offer you—and probably more money. Steve has been scouring the area for over a year, trying to expose the most egregious environmental problems caused by the unchecked growth of chicken farming all over the Delmarva Peninsula. Until now, he's been doing it all on his own. I've convinced him that he needs an assistant, and I also think I could persuade his boss to pay for it. Look, he's right over there. Let me introduce you."

Margot's mouth drops open in delighted surprise as her eyes begin to glow, and her ear-to-ear smile reveals her excitement. As she tries to digest what Jillian has proposed, a large man, tall and somewhat burly, strides over to greet them. "Steve, so glad you're here," Jillian says as he hugs her. "I've just been telling my intern, Margot Aubert, about you."

"All good, I hope. Nice to meet you, Margot. Jason Applegate also spoke to me about a sharp, hard-working intern who is ready to take her job prospects in a new direction—hopefully working with a handsome, hard-nose reporter like myself."

Margot is drawn to Steve's energy and his exuberant smile. Steve has a mop of curly, reddish hair, a prominent nose, not unlike her father's, and a round face. When he looks straight at her with his expressive hazel eyes flecked with gold, Margot is surprised that she finds him attractive in a scruffy way. On this hot summer day, his beige cotton trousers have lost their pleats as they bag around the knees.

Jillian suggests that they break for a coffee so Steve can explain to Margot how they might make a good team. As they exit the building and amble toward the only local coffee shop that is not a Starbucks, Steve jumps right in. "*The State Capital Ledger* is a news outlet that primarily covers the proceedings of the Maryland State Legislature. It's pretty dry stuff, but last year the online publication editors decided to report more vigorously on the human-made threats to the Bay due to over-the-top growth in chicken farming and a surge in housing and infrastructure construction.

"Jillian is right; I could use an assistant to help me dig around for anecdotal evidence about how increased pressure from the integrators to raise more chickens affects the farmers in general and the Chesapeake Bay in particular.

"One of my goals is to keep these issues before the public, to raise awareness and hope to stir up some outrage. The large food corporations have the money to lobby state legislators and

Congress not to pass laws forcing them to be more responsible for the waste from over 500 million chickens raised on the Delmarva Peninsula yearly. We strongly believe that the general public, including those that are part of the process, should have a platform to make their voices heard. Jillian tells me that you're a very quick learner, extremely dedicated, and," he continues, "that you are wasting your time answering phones and the like. What do you think?"

"I think that you have just given me an unbelievable opportunity, opening the door to a whole new type of activism." She dares for the first time to shine her eager eyes into his. "But you must be aware that I have absolutely no experience in journalism. I just finished my first year at Georgetown, and I have no idea what I even want to major in."

"I don't think you need a degree in journalism to do this job. You would, however, have to be very detail-oriented as you learn about all the laws and regulations concerning the Bay and its watershed. That's a tall order right out of the gate since six states are involved, and the laws constantly change. With that in mind, I want to engage in-depth with farmers on both shores of the Bay, state officials, and anyone else with first-hand knowledge and an informed opinion about the issues I just outlined. I need someone I can rely on to help me set up and keep track of these interviews and assist me in putting together articles to submit to *The Ledger* from the research and face-to-face contacts. Do you think you can handle that?"

"If Jillian thinks I'm qualified, and you're willing to give me the chance to prove her right, then I'll certainly do my best!" She extends her hand to meet his, then looks him straight in the eyes again, trying to remain calm and professional. She wills herself not to allow her rising giddiness to burst open, like floodgates holding back an overflowing dam.

• • •

Margot returns to the guest house after a momentous day, one that she continues to relive as a turning point in her summer, if not in her life. She fires up her laptop, wanting to break this news to Sarah. Instead, Margot sees emails from both her parents. She reads her mother's first.

Blah, blah, blah, and by the way, has Sarah been in touch with you recently? I have no idea how long she plans to stay in Ghana, but I think that we should buy her a one-way ticket home, and that's it!

Margot doesn't appreciate being thrust into that uncomfortable place between her sister and her mother. *She sent me a quick email this morning saying that she's been invited to stay as long as she wants. I get the impression that Sarah likes this Daren guy by how she describes him. If that's the case, she won't be in a big hurry to leave.*

Abigail is quick to reply. *Well, I'm glad she confides in someone in this family. I still don't understand why she didn't feel she could discuss her problems with her father and me before gallivanting halfway around the world!*

Margot responds that Sarah made it clear in her first email to them why she left. For whatever reason, her mother doesn't want to accept that as the real answer. Margot is annoyed that Abby keeps trying to drag her into a situation, not of her making, which she has no control over. Instead, she moves on to her father's email from earlier today: *Alors, Pitchoune, comment ça va là-bas,*? How's it going over there? *We miss you. Maybe we could meet up next weekend in Annapolis at a nice place with a view of the Bay, our treat.*

Margot answers: *I miss you, too, Papa. I emailed you and Mom that my current boss has allowed me to change jobs and work with a local reporter. I'm excited about this offer. He's going to pay me more than I was earning with my internship. The person in question needs an assistant to help him research and organize interviews concerning the huge increase in chicken farming in the area and the ensuing rise in pollutants dumped into the Bay.*

Meanwhile, I'd love to meet you and Mom for lunch in Annapolis any weekend we are free. Just let me know if you want me to make a reservation. Gros Bisous, Moi. Lots of Kisses, Me.

Her father's email has made Margot go all fuzzy. She still feels a strong connection to him that she expects will lessen with distance and the passage of time. She isn't that far from DC and Gaithersburg, but she has concluded that her parents belong to another world, one that she has chosen to withdraw from, for now, to follow her calling.

Margot has fewer qualms about pulling away from her mother. All her life, she's heard Abby describe her childhood as a lonely experience of being raised by a withdrawn mother who showered what love she had to give onto her younger brother, David. Abby grew up resenting them both. Instead, she imagined herself to be her father's little darling. Sadly, in reality, he never stepped forward to reassure her, as if he weren't even aware of the lopsided family dynamics. Still, Abby bought into the story that she was difficult and unpredictable as a kid and, therefore, must have deserved the rejection she experienced.

David, Margot's uncle, on the other hand, could do no wrong. As far as his parents knew, he managed to emerge from his childhood and then his adolescence without a hiccup or a blemish. He finished his education with a master's degree in finance and became a CPA and the head of his firm.

Even though she has always been told how much easier she was to raise than her sister, Margot has grown up keenly aware that their mother favored Sarah. Margot's been trying to understand why, since their tenth birthday, when Abby gave Sarah a gold necklace with her initials that she had been wanting, but Margot doesn't remember her mother ever asking her what she might want as a gift. Instead, Margot received an illustrated copy of *Little Women*, exactly like the one her grandmother had already given her the year before. Margot relived that day as a clear message that she was less important to her mother than Sarah.

Maybe I somehow remind Mom of David the Perfect, who I know is certainly not by a long shot. Margot has always felt intimidated by her mother and, to a lesser extent, her sister. Or, maybe, she speculates, her mother is jealous because Michel favors the daughter most like him. For now, at least, she has a reprieve, knowing she doesn't need to compete for her mother's affection as long as she and Sarah both remain away from home.

• • •

When Michel returns home in the evening, he can tell that Abby hasn't had the best of days. Now that she's on her summer break from the law firm where she works part-time, he had hoped his wife would find something enjoyable and productive to do, like taking that yoga class Abby's talked about or recreating a cutting garden filled with bright, colorful annuals, as she does most summers. He would be just as happy if she admitted to being bored and was looking forward to going back to work.

Instead, he finds her sipping her favorite Sauvignon Blanc

from an oversized glass, her face looking slack, a blankness clouding her gray-green eyes, as she pretends to watch the news on TV. She is still in sweatpants, and Michel notices a roll of tummy fat bulging around her middle that wasn't there six months ago. Her curly hair is flopping more than usual across her forehead, indicating to her husband that she has given up on herself again today.

"*Alors, comment vas-tu*?" How are you? Michel inquires a bit sheepishly as he picks up and flips through the mail that sits unopened on the coffee table.

"I've exchanged a few emails with Margot about Sarah," Abby replies indifferently, still facing the TV. Then, she abruptly turns toward him, her eyes livid with animus. "Margot gave me some news because *she* heard from Sarah. Have *you* had any contact with her? She hasn't texted or emailed me directly since she left!"

Michel sits beside her on the sofa, gently takes the glass of wine out of Abby's hand, and then sets it down next to the mail. He kisses her on both cheeks the French way, then looks at her and smiles.

"Have you considered going back to work full-time? It would certainly help with financing two private colleges at once. And," he pauses, "you could fulfill your desire for a more meaningful career."

Abby squints at him, shakes her head a bit dismissively and picks up her wine glass.

"Sarah has sent emails to all of us, including you," Michel knows better than to discuss Abby's career options any further. "Maybe she is more often in touch with Margot than with us, but that's normal. Hey, do I need to do anything about dinner?

I'm pretty hungry. We can do take-out. Do you want me to call the India Palace?"

"I'll have the usual, thanks," Abby replies as if she already knew this was where their supper would come from this evening. Then, she picks up her half-empty glass and takes another long swig of the fruity yellow wine.

"I thought we could take Margot out somewhere this weekend," Michel suggests as he looks up the phone number of the restaurant. "When was the last time she went anywhere with just us? I emailed her about meeting in Annapolis at a nice place on the water."

"Maybe you and I can plan to do something the following weekend," Abby interjects. "We've talked for months about going somewhere during my vacation. What about that place near Charlottesville? The Cliff House?"

"I did like that place, but I also remember it was quite expensive. Besides, unfortunately, I have some out-of-town meetings coming up."

"There's always fucking something," Abby pretends to bemoan as she pulls Michel's face down to hers. "*Mon Michou*," my Michel-cabbage, she coos as she kisses him on the lips. "All that time I lived in France, I never understood how a cabbage could be a term of endearment."

7

THE TRIPS

Early to Mid-June—Kumasi, Accra, Lake Bosumtui, Ghana

Once Sarah recovered from jet lag, she enjoyed seeing more of Kumasi and getting to know Daren's family better, especially his young sisters, Layla and Elia.

That following Sunday, they all participated in *Adae*, and Sarah wore her new skirt and a lacy, white blouse that Daren's mother lent her for the occasion. *Adae* was an amazing spectacle for her, like something out of a movie. When the king appeared surrounded by his entourage, six burly men wearing long robes and animal skins raised him on a bright-red, throne-like chair and carried him through the streets. The women who followed behind were dressed in yards of intricately patterned Kente cloth with matching turbans. Hordes of children in little black suits and puffy white dresses ran alongside. Small bands of drummers, flutists, and men with banjo-like gourds played and chanted as the king went past.

Sarah was especially moved to see how joyful everyone was. At the same time, she felt the loneliness of an outsider, unable to share their sense of community, exuberantly expressed through these ancient rituals that reached back even before any Europeans had ever set foot in Ghana.

• • •

Now, several weeks have passed, and Sarah senses that Daren would like to move on with whatever he might have planned for the rest of the summer. She assumes that he must have friends he would like to see, even if he has had to keep secrets about himself from them.

Sarah was still attracted to him despite, or maybe because of what she's found out. She wonders what it would be like to have sex with someone who is not entirely straight. Then, when out of the blue, Daren offers to take her to Accra, the capital, she's thrilled. Her mind begins to simmer with curiosity about what else, if anything, he could have in mind. She knows that Mr. Owusu owns an apartment there, but Daren has told her that his father would be in Lagos, Nigeria, for at least a week, indicating that they would have the place to themselves. She suspects it is no coincidence that Daren has picked this particular time to take her to Accra.

Whenever she thinks about it, Sarah feels a twist of anticipation stir in her belly as she visualizes a scenario in which Daren flips from believing he is gay into becoming a passionate partner. He and Sarah are both lost souls in their own way, and, if nothing else, she hopes they might be able to provide some support for each other.

Daren has made clear what he wants to get out of this by showing his world that he can have a woman by his side. But Sarah isn't convinced if his conversion could be real or that he is staging this trip to ward off any suspicion his family might have about his sexual proclivity.

Daren has engaged a car and driver to take them to Accra. Not far out of Kumasi, the paved road gives way to dirt, gravel, and broken stone. There are no seatbelts in the back, so she and Daren roll around, colliding with each other as the driver barrels down the road, swerving to avoid the rubble and larger potholes. He hardly slows down as they speed through the jangle of small villages as crowds of people, dogs, and donkeys are trying to cross the main road.

They stop briefly at a gas station with a decent bathroom and lunch counter, then start again as the car races toward the capital. Sarah and Daren start kidding around, exaggerating the car's motion and bumping shoulders harder than necessary. They're like two ten-year-olds, upping the intensity until one of them cries "Uncle"! In the end, Sarah asks Daren to stop. Although she hates losing to a guy unless sheer physical strength determines the outcome, she understands that Daren's ego needs even this very small manly-man victory right now.

When they arrive in Accra, the sun is low on the horizon. The apartment building is in an upscale section of the city that backs up to a private beach, each complex with gated access. Like most of the other buildings in the area, this one is six stories high, and each apartment has a pair of wide, rounded balconies. One balcony faces the ocean at the back, and the other overlooks a well-tended lawn with a variety of shrubs and flowers edging a circular driveway in the front. Sarah is enthralled by the calming view of an orangey-pink sunset over the water, along with the gentle whoosh of the waves as they break and spread out onto the glowing sand.

The apartment has been decorated with sleek, modern furniture offset with brightly colored accessories, wall hangings, and elaborate hand-woven area rugs. Daren mentions to Sarah that when his father is here, a housekeeper and a cook come almost every day, but he would prefer not to deal with them. "We can eat out," he says casually, as if this alternative were the obvious answer.

"I'm not sure I can afford to eat only at restaurants for the next few days. Can't we buy some stuff and cook for ourselves? I don't mind doing the cooking." She opens the fridge and sees quite a few essentials already there.

"Okay," Daren replies through a wide grin, "we'll throw a dinner party later in the week for some of my friends and cousins here, and you can cook the whole thing. A small group. I'll limit it to a dozen."

"Twelve people? That's a lot …but I'd be happy to do something like that as a thank-you."

"I think it would be a blast to present ourselves as a couple to everyone I know."

Sarah stares into his animated face, a devious smile pulling back his lips and showing his gleaming, white teeth. He's obviously in a teasing mode, but she wonders if he is more serious at some level than he seems to pretend. As she picks up her bag and heads for one of the bedrooms, she doesn't even know at this point if she should take herself seriously.

When she crosses the threshold, she sees she is in the wrong room. Some of Mr. Owusu's clothes are folded on a chair, along with a bath towel. She starts to back out of the room and bumps into Daren, right behind her.

"I don't think you want to stay in here, do you?" Sarah turns around, but he doesn't move and blocks the doorway.

"No, I can see I'm in the wrong place. Where should I go?"

He doesn't answer, and instead, he takes Sarah's face in his two wide hands and kisses her full on the mouth.

Sarah is so flabbergasted that she doesn't kiss him back or even close her eyes. When he opens his eyes, she stares at him like a deer in the headlights.

"Oh, God! I'm so sorry!"

"No… no, don't be. I'm the one who should apologize. Almost from day one, I've wanted to change the nature of this relationship. I just didn't think that would happen. Are you playing with me, or do you want something else?" She tries not to sound defensive, but suddenly, she is totally confused. Daren led her to believe he is gay, but now she concludes that this is probably not the whole truth.

"I don't know where that impulse came from, but I'm attracted to you too," he answers. "I've been with women before, but it never quite worked out. I'd like to know if it could be different this time. There are so many things that seem off about me. You probably think I'm crazy, and I wouldn't blame you if you asked me to take you to the airport and send you home."

"That is the *last* thing I want to happen," she whispers as she gazes longingly into his moist, imploring eyes.

Sarah has no idea what the outcome could be, but she doesn't care right now. Instead, she takes Daren's hands that hang dejectedly by his sides and places them on her face again, leans toward him, and offers herself, eyes closed.

• • •

After that first night, Sarah can only conclude that Daren is not exclusively gay. He is thrilled but somewhat confused as he tries to come to terms with his true sexual identity. The first time at least, some of the mechanics of lovemaking hadn't gone as Daren might have wanted—not easy to maintain an erection, causing him to second-guess if he were really able to be with a woman. But the next time, with encouragement from Sarah, remembering all the ways to stimulate sexual desire that she'd heard and read about, he quickly became a very willing partner.

Although Sarah never reached a climax, she loved the intimacy of touching and exploring each other's bodies with fingers and tongues, and then finally the thrust and throb of Daren inside her.

For the next several days, they live in a magical space that exists only for the two of them. Driven by discovery and passion, they quickly learn how to please each other as they spend most of their time locked together in an erotic dance choreographed by the rhythm of the waves crashing onto the beach below.

By the third morning, however, the bubble that had formed around them breaks open enough that they both begin to feel restless. Daren suggests that they hire a car and go to Cape Coast.

"In the mid-1600's, Cape Coast Castle was just a Swedish trading post for mahogany and gold. This whole area was called the 'Gold Coast' before it was Ghana. But it quickly became a marketplace for the slave trade.

"The elaborate white castle we will visit was built for White people—traders, soldiers, priests, and later British Governors and their families. They lived safe, comfortable lives in that castle, in stark contrast to the underground dungeons they had built near the beach that could hold up to 1,500 people at a time who had been captured from all over Ghana.

"The British, after taking over the fort from the Dutch, developed the slave trade to the max. They paid willing chieftains to hunt down people from enemy tribes and bring them to Cape Coast to be shipped to slave markets in Brazil, the Caribbean, and some of the southern colonies in America. The last those unfortunate souls ever saw of their homeland was the *Door of No Return* as they were led out in chains to the beach and put on ships to the New World and a life of slavery."

"That's just horrible! My God, why would some Ghanaians do that to their own people?"

"Why would anyone of any race want to enslave another human being? Power, revenge, money? All of the above."

Sarah can tell it pains Daren to talk about this tragic chapter in Ghana's history, but he wants her to understand how it still affects him. As they drive out of Accra toward Cape Coast, Daren becomes silent and pensive, staring out of the window as if he were seeing the landscape for the very first time. He reminds Sarah of her father at times—so present one minute, then suddenly withdrawing into his solitary world the next.

Eventually, he turns toward her, takes hold of her hand, and looks solemnly into her eyes. "I've been thinking a lot about what will happen after we go back to Kumasi. I'd like you to get to know my family even better and to meet some of my friends. How would you feel about that?"

Sarah imagines how difficult it would be for her and Daren to continue what they started here in Accra. She is aware that he wants to show her off, not as a girl friend, but as a girlfriend to everyone who ever doubted his sexuality. He desperately needs to be accepted as a *real* man by the people who matter to him and believe that all real men are heterosexual.

As she stares back at him, she can feel herself going soft all over. "Of course, I want to meet your friends, but maybe we don't have to stay in Kumasi until mid-August. That's almost two months from now."

"You're the best, Sarah!" Daren replies, his penetrating eyes probing her expression. He is truly grateful to her for putting all her trust in him, for accepting him as he is.

When they arrive at the fort in Cape Coast, it's obvious to Sarah that Daren is on a pilgrimage, even though he has come here many times before. Sarah is shocked by what Daren told her and what she can now observe. They tour the large white castle and then the dungeons where the slaves were stored in such horrendous conditions that by the time they were chained together and then loaded into the bowels of a ship, many of them were already dying.

In less than a century, some six million people from all over West Africa were forced into slavery. The British government outlawed the slave trade on their ships in 1807, but that didn't stop pirates, mercenaries, those who ran the slave markets, and the landowners who purchased the slaves. From the beginning, White traders and slaveowners justified their inhumane trafficking of Black people because they believed God had created the Blacks as an inferior race. Therefore, those involved in the slave trade considered it acceptable to treat those people as a commodity, to be bought and sold like ore and timber.

Africans were also labeled *heathens*, who didn't believe in the Christian God and whose way of life did not conform to what White men considered a civilized society.

Coming face to face with how cruel people can be to one another has shocked Sarah into re-evaluating some of her acquired views about human nature. Now that she is in Africa and has some insight into another culture, she has concluded that people mostly want the same things from life, no matter their race, origin, or religion. The scale might be different, but it is not always about how much a person can acquire, as it is about what a person stands for. What did all those tribal chiefs and British soldiers, those ship captains, and plantation owners stand for? It makes me very sad, Sarah laments.

• • •

The following morning, they leave for Kumasi. As Sarah watches the scruffy roadside brush whiz by, she can't ignore the nagging feeling that she is on the verge of getting herself into something she will not be able to control. She also senses that the erotic aura of their lovemaking is fast losing its intensity with the accumulating distance from Accra. Mostly, though, Sarah worries about what she will do with herself between now and August. The thought of all that pending idleness starts to weigh on her conscience. She had an obligation with the internship to earn money for school. She was supposed to be at basketball practice three days a week.

It occurs to her that maybe, at some level, it would be better for them both if she were to leave Ghana. After all, she has no reason other than Daren to stay through the entire summer. Her shoulders slump and her breathing becomes shallow as she tries to picture herself back home, then back in school.

She continues to stare blankly out of the window at the blur of green and brown when out of nowhere, tidbits of her last trip to France several summers ago drift like sunbeams into her awareness. Sarah remembers visiting Marie-Laure Aubert, her father's cousin. Marie-Laure is a few years older than her parents. She so wholeheartedly welcomed them with her easy-going attitude that Sarah had immediately felt accepted, like a part of her family. Marie-Laure was a professor of art history at one of the Toulouse University extensions before she recently retired to her house near the village of Mervilla, about fifteen miles south of Toulouse.

Marie-Laure never married nor had any children. The more judgmental members of her family gossiped about Marie-Laure's risqué reputation from rumors of some tumultuous love affairs and because she indulged her creative impulses by gallivanting across the world spending much of her leisure time and money viewing and collecting art. After hearing that, Sarah and Margot began to salute her as a role model and a trailblazer.

However, Sarah doesn't want to leave Daren, and anyway, she can't fathom that her parents would be willing to send her a ticket from Accra to Mervilla. But before she sets aside this little glimmer of an idea, she decides to text her sister and ask her if she can find Marie-Laure's email address.

• • •

Sarah and Daren arrived in Kumasi near sunset. Sarah thought that she would be used to seeing all those bats streak across the glowing sky by now. But they still fascinate her in their numbers, wildness, and the speed of their flight. Tonight, they appear to her like a metaphor for life itself—fast and furious and too soon over. She tries to jog herself out of this surge of melancholy as they drive up to the house.

The family gathers outside on the veranda for cocktails. Daren breaks the pensive mood wide open by kissing Sarah lovingly on the cheek, then offering a toast to his 'girlfriend'. Wide, knowing smiles break out on his parents' face as they raise their glasses in unbridled joy at this turn of events. Sarah, however, is embarrassed by what she perceives as being made the central figure in a spectacle staged just for his parents.

After a few minutes, she excuses herself to go upstairs and freshen up. She changes into another sundress she bought for a few cedis at an Accra market and then hurries back downstairs to join them on the veranda. Daren converses with his father, as Sarah sits next to Madam Doctor.

"How did you like seeing more of Ghana?" Daren's mother brightly asks as she observes Sarah through a different lens, now that she has a much tighter connection to her son.

"It's been a wonderful experience being here, then going to Accra and Cape Coast. You've been very kind, letting me stay this long. I wish I could do something for you in return."

"Oh," she replies, all smiles again. "You've done a lot for me. It makes me happy to see Daren so happy. I hope you will stay as long as you wish."

Sarah's eyes sparkle, knowing that she's made such a positive difference in Daren's life. Yet, she is still somewhat unnerved about what will happen next. Why, she admonishes herself, can't I just enjoy what could be a rare idle summer? Soon, I'll be an independent adult having to earn a living. I may never have this opportunity again. She returns Dr. Owusu's smile but can't seem to come up with anything authentic to say.

Mercifully, the maid calls them to supper. The cook has prepared a meal that fills the room with an aroma of pungent spices from roasted chicken in a reddish-brown sauce, root vegetables, rice, and manioc. Between the cocktails and an abundance of wine, Sarah feels herself releasing some of the anxiety that has caused her to feel so edgy, as she gradually loses her fear of saying or doing the wrong thing.

Daren takes her hand under the table, giving it a hard squeeze. She turns toward him, her face glowing with love and desire, expecting to see the same emotions emanating from him as well. Instead, he lets go of her hand. Without even turning back to her with an explanation, Daren becomes totally engaged with his father, talking to him across the table.

A nagging sadness floods her heart as she senses something else more troubling, as if Daren's attraction to her were suddenly oozing away like bubbles from a boiling pot as they evaporate into steam. She tries to convince herself that she's drawing the wrong conclusions, especially considering how they have just spent the past few days together. Still, Darren and his father are seriously talking about going to Nigeria to meet with some of Mr. Owusu's business associates.

Daren never mentioned anything planned for this summer, much less going away with his father on a business trip. Daren doesn't turn back to her during the rest of the meal. As Sarah attempts to reach over to him to get his attention, he and his dad stand up and leave the room. She looks over at his mother for an explanation, but she is talking to her girls. She then rises to leave as well, telling them it's time for their bath. Before leaving the room, she looks back at Sarah to apologize and mutters, "I'm sure Daren will be back shortly."

What the fuck is happening? Sarah almost blurts out. Do they think I haven't heard or noticed anything? I'm sure not waiting here alone like some reject. She rushes up the stairs into her bedroom, then closes and locks the door. "How can this be love?" she demands of the darkened space. And then it hits her. Daren has never told her that he loves her! He probably hasn't even asked himself the question. After all, they've only been together for a very short time. Yet, it is becoming more obvious that all Daren ever wanted was for her to be his proof-positive that he is not gay. Humiliation and anger surge up from deep inside, like waves from the Atlantic, as if she were drowning in her own bile.

On a rash impulse, Sarah pulls out her phone and shoots a quick email to Marie-Laure: *Hi, remember me, Michel's kid, one of the twins? I know you have invited us several times before, so how would you feel about me coming to visit you again? Hugs, Sarah Aubert.*

• • •

In the end, Daren doesn't leave for Lagos. But it has more to do with a disagreement between his dad and him than with Sarah. The following morning, he's waiting for her on the veranda when she comes down to breakfast.

"How're you doing?" he casually asks as he tries to look into her swollen eyes for the answer. But she averts his face as she sits down.

"I'm okay, I guess. You and your father just disappeared, talking about going to Nigeria, as if I wasn't even there at all."

"Yeah, well, Dad and I had a bit of a falling out about that. I don't want to get sucked into his business dealings. Big brother George is getting an MBA in London right now, not me. Still, I might have to go with Dad to Lagos for a couple of days, but only because Dad needs someone he trusts to accompany him to a few of his meetings. If he shows up alone, he looks weak."

"Doesn't your father have other people in his office? Why does it have to be you?"

"I guess because I'm gone most of the year, and he misses me. He probably believes that someday soon, I'll come to my senses and see how exciting it is to be building stuff all over Ghana. I am curious to know how these deals get made—

negotiating with the Chinese and all, and they have their hands into every building project in the country right now."

"When would you leave?"

"Tomorrow or Tuesday. But we have all of today, at least. I've sort of said yes to hanging out with some friends near Lake Bosumtwi. I got an email early this morning from my best friend, Robert, whose family has a weekend house near the lake. You'll like him and a couple of others who might show up. They'd be really glad to meet you."

"Showing me off again?" she says as she tries to keep the sarcasm out of her voice. "Sure. I'll get ready as soon as I finish breakfast."

Sarah puts on a bikini under a sundress and stuffs some underwear and a towel into a bag. When she returns to the veranda, Daren isn't there. As Sarah waits for him to show up, she uses the time to email Margot. Sarah gives a cursory glance at who else has been in touch and sees that Marie-Laure has responded. Daren arrives before she can read the message.

They head out of Kumasi with Daren at the wheel, driving toward the southeast on what quickly becomes an unpaved road. For a while, they both just stare ahead and say nothing. Eventually, Sarah breaks the silence. "Hey, what's up?"

"I was thinking about my friend, Robert. We've stayed in touch, but I haven't seen him since I left for DC almost a year ago. How about you?"

"I'm happy to be able to visit this lake that I hear is so beautiful." But that isn't the whole truth. She's especially happy to be alone with Daren, away from the family and the help. At Daren's home, they are never alone. Sometimes Sarah wonders if all that passion was simply a figment of her imagination. Just thinking about it makes her stomach tighten.

Lake Bosumtwi is a natural crater lake and getting there takes them over a rough mountain road. From the top, they have a picture-perfect view of the pale turquoise water, a calm reflection of the hazy sky and the little settlements grouped around the lake. By the time they weave down the mountain and arrive at Robert's house, it's almost noon.

A picnic lunch has already been set up on the lush emerald lawn, shaded in part by several palm groves stretching from the house down to the narrow beach. Daren introduces Sarah to Robert, who in turn names off the others.

Someone puts a fruity drink into Sarah's hand. She hesitates, then takes a sip. At home, she is underage to consume any alcohol in public. Here, the rules are different. Sarah doesn't want to be a downer or appear rude, so she gulps another, bigger swig. Almost immediately, she experiences a warming sensation spreading throughout her body. Although it tastes mostly like mango and coconut, the drink makes her feel fuzzy. What the hell. Maybe if I relax, I won't feel like the odd-one-out. I'll go into the water with everyone else, and I'll enjoy myself.

And that's what happens. One hour in, thankfully, with some food in her stomach to absorb some of the alcohol, Sarah feels quite mellow. She swims and plays around in the lake with everyone else, but afterward, she is the only one to ask if she could shower. A woman named Zulla or Tulla escorts her to a cabana with a lounging area and a bathroom.

As she steps into the shower, she hears the door open, and the next thing she knows, Daren is in the stall with her, naked, semi-erect, and all over her. Sarah loses all inhibitions between the drinks, the flowing water, and the heady atmosphere.

Rationally, she knows that someone could walk in at any minute, and anyway, it would be obvious to everyone what they are doing.

After a few moments, they leave the shower, water still running and flop soaking wet and already intertwined onto the day bed. Then their bodies lock together, rocking back and forth, building urgently to a frenzied climax. For a few magical moments, Sarah feels that she and Daren are one inseparable person. Then, an overwhelming urge to fall asleep in his arms overcomes her, and, as Daren gets back into the shower, Sarah is powerless to move.

The sun is low on the horizon when Daren awakens her, saying they should head back to Kumasi. Sarah takes a quick, cold shower to revive herself, then returns to the lawn to make her last round of thank-yous and good-byes. As they climb into the car and head out on the narrow road back up the mountain, Sarah is sure that she's never been happier in her life.

8

LE DÉNOUEMENT, THE OUTCOME

Late June, Early July—Kumasi, Accra, Ghana

After Daren left to join his father in Lagos, Sarah finally re-opened her email and scrolled down to retrieve Marie-Laure's message. *Of course, I remember you, silly goose. I would love it if you could come to Mervilla. I've been putting off having some much-needed back surgery because I have no one to take over the house, garden, and animals while in the hospital and then rehab.* She even offers to pay for Sarah's ticket, although Marie-Laure doesn't yet know she is not in Maryland.

Sarah wonders how she would even get from Kumasi to Mervilla. Then, she stops herself. Aren't I in love with Daren? Can I bear to be away from him for a month or two? But what Marie-Laure is proposing would most likely be for longer than that. Even taking Daren out of the equation, Sarah realizes that if she accepts Marie-Laure's invitation, she wouldn't be home in time to start school. She experiences a rush of relief, thinking that this could be the answer to her problems—a solid plan that her parents would probably approve of. She might even be able to do an online class.

She starts to contemplate how such a decision might affect Daren; they obviously cannot be a couple here. Although she likes Ghana and Daren's family, she is aware that she doesn't fit in. The fact that Marie-Laure's offer is so appealing throws her into a quandary about how solid her relationship with Daren even is. She knows for sure that if he plans to travel with his dad, she will not want to remain in Kumasi without him.

Sarah fled to Ghana so she wouldn't have to figure out how to deal with her parents and their expectations. Now she is being offered a deal that would involve a commitment. Marie-Laure is presenting her a chance to be useful, even indispensable, proving to herself and her parents that she isn't just some flighty, impulsive child anymore.

Sarah responds by telling Marie-Laure briefly what's been going on in her life this past year, leaving out the intimate details about her and Daren. Each time she thinks about him, the same rush of desire flows like a bubbling-hot whirlpool throughout her body. This has been her first love affair, and she cherishes all of it—the urgency, the abandonment, the physical closeness, even the messiness. But is this love? she asks herself. Do I honestly know what love is? She thought so, but right this minute, when she allows her imagination to wander into the future, she is already packing for Mervilla.

More than anything, Sarah wishes Margot were here or that she could have a heart-to-heart with her. Instead, she composes an email to bring her sister up to date. Sarah hopes that by seeing her thoughts take shape visibly on the screen, she will be able to trust that what she's about to write is what she honestly believes.

Hey, Sis, I hope you are getting along well in your new job. Papa sent me some background info and said you've relocated to Annapolis and are now working for a journalist on something you care about. I envy that you've found a cause you feel so dedicated to, instead of just hanging out all summer doing nothing much, like me. I feel shitty about all this, as things aren't working out the way I was hoping. I haven't said anything to the parents, but you could probably guess when I asked you for Marie-Laure's email that something here had to be going off the rails.

Daren acted like he couldn't bear to be away from me—until he picked up and left for Nigeria to work with his dad. I think the bottom line for him is that it ain't gonna work out. The way I feel about him makes it hard to accept, but I've pretty much decided to spend some time in Mervilla—if I can find a way to get there. I guess Marie-Laure will work that out with Papa—once I've told the parents about all this. She's going to have back surgery in mid-July, and she'd like me to come and help out.

Anyway, no matter how much I care about Daren, I don't see how I can stay here if he's away. It's humiliating and boring. I wish I could click my heels together like Dorothy in The Wizard of Oz and be with you in Annapolis for a while. But right now, my gut is telling me that anything would be better than staying in Kumasi – except going home. I hope you miss me as much as I miss you! Gros Bisous, Sarah

• • •

Sarah finally hears from Daren, who is "so sorry" he wasn't "able" to be in touch sooner. Sarah asks herself what "able" means. Wasn't there an internet connection in his hotel? The bottom line is that now he will remain in Accra for a few more days to help his dad wrap up loose ends on some project or another.

Sarah composes an email to Marie-Laure expressing her

thanks for the invite and explaining that she's pretty much on her own doing not much of anything here in Kumasi. Contrarily, she hopes to be very useful in Mervilla. As Sarah re-reads the email, she feels panicky about going through with this plan, especially since her parents would also have to agree. If Sarah hits *Send*, she'll be setting in motion events that will quickly spin out of her control. At the last minute, she saves her email to *Draft* and writes to Margot instead.

Within a few minutes, Margot responds. *Sarah—if you truly love the guy, you wouldn't even think about leaving. Your impulse to go is more reality-based than wishful thinking about uncertain outcomes in the future. I've never been in the type of relationship you're describing, but I get the feeling that your gut is telling you to go to Mervilla. The parents would probably be okay with it as well. Bonne chance et gros bisous, Margot.*

That is so Margot, Sarah reacts as she shakes her head, 'uncertain outcomes in the future.' It sounds like something from an Econ textbook.

• • •

The following evening Daren returns from Accra with his father. At dinner, they talk about their meetings and the contracts Mr. Owusu was able to sign for a construction project with a Chinese firm. He praises Daren for his ability to negotiate and brags how proud he is that his son will continue working with others from his company to launch this new enterprise. Sarah almost falls out of her chair! What was all the bullshit about Daren not wanting a career in business?

This last salvo convinces Sarah that Daren has used her to prove to himself and his family that he is straight. Now that all the uncertainty has been put to rest, he doesn't need her anymore. Before she has a complete meltdown in front of everyone, she excuses herself, mumbling something about a splitting headache.

After fifteen minutes of sobbing into her pillow, after she's cried herself into a real splitting headache, she hears a knock at the door. Without waiting for an answer, Daren comes in, sits on the bed, and puts his arms around her. She buries her head against his shoulder and starts to dissolve all over again. Between sobs, Sarah manages to tell him that she will probably leave for France as soon as possible. She says *probably* because she still clings to some infinitesimal hope that he will beg her not to go, that he will kiss away her silly tears and dispel all her fears with a declaration of undying love.

Instead, he rubs her back, and without looking at her at all, he mumbles, "I care very much for you, Sarah…" and then she almost can't take in the rest. He talks about how his desire for her was genuine. BUT... Daren still has feelings for Robert, that they were more than just friends in high school. Since he hooked up with her, he thought he was past all that, but he isn't. He goes on like this for a while, as if he's trying to convince himself rather than her. Hurt and anger flared up in her like a pair of Roman candles. As Sarah withdraws from what she knows will be the last time she will find any comfort in his arms, and even before he leaves the room, she grabs her phone, opens the *Draft* she saved earlier to Marie-Laure, and hits *Send.*

9

TURBULENCE

Late June—Gaithersburg, Maryland

June has been slipping away, and so has Abby's time off from work. She has procrastinated about carrying through with plans to visit her mother in Sarasota, Florida. However, since she'll be returning to work right after the July 4th holiday, her window to follow through is fast closing.

Abby's father passed away suddenly less than a year ago, and she understands that her mother is lonely. But whenever she pictures herself at her mother's house, she experiences a resurgence of anguish dating back to childhood that still sends a charge of anxiety through her body, as if she'd touched a live wire.

Abby's mother, Bella Herschel, had a terrible start in life. Her teenage mother gave her up when she was three months old. Bella was adopted by a well-off family who treated her more like a beautiful object than a child. She has drummed into Abigail throughout her life that she has never been able to trust women. As a result, Abby is still convinced that if she had been a better daughter, her mother might have forgiven her for being a girl.

Abby has an ongoing internal battle between resenting her mother and feeling guilty about it. She understands that Bella didn't just wake up one morning and decide to stop parenting her. Still, Abby allows this tangle of charged emotions to follow her around in life. She believes that this negativity is, at least in part, responsible for a destructive pattern of hers to renege on commitments she's made in earnest at the time—to friends, to family and especially to herself. How often has she backed out of plans to be with her female friends, promised one of the girls to help her with her homework but then stayed late at work, binged on wine and sweets after losing weight until she's gained all of it back and more?

Abby worries that she could fall into this pattern at work—which so far, she has managed to either avoid altogether or to cover up and rectify. It's as if a malicious, alternative self were pulling levers that activate uncontrollable impulses to sabotage her better self—as a lawyer, a friend, a mother, and now as a daughter. She still clings to memories of herself as a dependent child, a defenseless victim of her mother's frequent criticism that shamed her then and still does. Abby's insecurities have fueled her excuses for not wanting to work full-time and therefore not risking what she has already accomplished by possibly failing at a more ambitious career.

Before admitting to her mother that she has not taken any action to come down in a week, she calls her brother, David, to see if they could commit to going to Florida together later in the summer. He is an accountant with his own business and rarely answers any of his calls immediately. As she leaves a message, she reminds herself that it would be so much easier to visit her mother now while still on vacation. She goes online to check flights and is surprised that the prices have already spiked so high, probably anticipating the upcoming holiday. Good excuse—or just bad planning. She's sure her mother would say, "Well, why didn't you get the tickets when you said you would?"

While she is still online, she checks her *Inbox*. A chain of emails between Sarah and Marie-Laure has been *CC'd* to her and Michel. Margot has also written to them both. Abby opens Sarah's first. It takes her a couple of read-throughs before she grasps what is happening. Maybe she's confided other details to Marie-Laure, but the takeaway for Abby is that Sarah was having a lovely time in Kumasi until she suddenly wanted to leave. No real explanation! Abby tries to work out a plausible reason for all this turmoil. She suspects that Sarah has had a go with her 'just-a-friend,' and now the relationship has soured. But why not just come home? What is there about being here that is not an option for her right now?

Abigail revisits her interpretation of Sarah's freshman year at college. Sarah was always very positive about basketball and her sorority, but maybe less about her classes. Abby wonders if perhaps Sarah was signaling some distress, and she just wasn't paying attention. During the spring semester, Sarah didn't come home much on weekends. Abby wanted to believe that it was because she had so many other things to do. Now she speculates that Sarah might have been afraid of how her parents would react if she told them the truth about what was keeping her away.

Abby blames herself as a teary lump forms in her throat, thinking that she and Sarah were moving past each other all year and that she, the mother, didn't suspect anything. Abby fears that now a chasm was hollowed out between her daughter and her that will not be easily bridged.

She hits *Reply All* to Sarah's email: *I'm sorry you are having these problems, and as soon as Papa and I have had a chance to talk, we'll be in touch.* Then, she opens Margot's message, hoping to have better news.

Hi, Mom & Papa. I have started my new job with Steve, and I feel I can contribute something useful to the work we've been doing. He and Jillian want me to stay on at least through September. I know this will compromise returning to Georgetown for the fall semester, but we can discuss this when we meet on Sunday. It's complicated, and it would be better to talk in person. Bisous, Margot.

Is it something in the water, or what? Abby asks herself as frustration starts to smolder like lava from a simmering volcano. What is this – payback time? I thought the girls were fairly easy to raise compared to the kids of some of my friends. All of a sudden, they get a little taste of freedom and pow! Let's reshuffle all the cards and see what happens!

By now, however, it has occurred to her that in both cases, neither of them can afford to do what they want without their parents' support. At the same time, Abby recognizes that the girls will be twenty in October, and they have a right, up to a point, to take their life in different directions from what she and Michel might have preferred.

Abby wants to wash away all this disappointment, but instead of wallowing in a hot bubble bath as she had planned, she opens a bottle of Sauvignon and pours almost half into the largest glass she can find. Before she mellows out completely, she gathers up all the fixings in the fridge to make a summer salad.

As she opens a tin of sardines, she hears the garage door go up. Michel greets her with a kiss, washes his hands, and sets the table. She pours what is left in the bottle into another glass and hands it to Michel. All this occurs in near silence as if both of them dread any mention of the upheaval surrounding their girls. They are twins, after all, Abby reflects, and although their situations are different, it may not be a coincidence that they're each going through a crisis simultaneously.

Abby fears that she and Michel are about to get sucked into a swirl of turmoil as an eddy of dry leaves is pushed around in a summer storm. But then she sees the laser-sharp glint in Michel's dark eyes as he radiates a sense of firmness and confidence that they can be there for their daughters but still set boundaries. The harder part might be to agree on what those boundaries should look like.

"Well," Abby breaks the silence, "what are we going to do with this pair?"

"They're each at an important juncture. Maybe they've been stuck for too long inside the protective cocoon we've created around them. They both need to get out in the wider world and start to fend for themselves. Right now, though, they require our financial help. Sarah, unhappily, continues to lurch from one thing to another. On the other hand, Margot acts like someone who has given her next move a lot of thought. We'll see her Sunday, find out the facts, and take it from there.

"Sarah wants to go to Mervilla, and Marie-Laure needs her. But it's not in Sarah's nature to hide away in the country with no friends and not much structure. I'm convinced that she'll get bored and come home within a couple of months. She can take a leave of absence from GW and return next spring. She will undoubtedly lose her scholarship, but if Margot takes a semester off as well, it will probably work out. The question is, what parameters will we decide to put around our support for each of them? What do you think?"

"I think this whole cocoon comparison is a poetic way of sugar-coating the facts. What we've been doing is called responsible parenting; what they're doing feels like acts of defiance to me. Yes, they have to find their path at some point, but I don't think they're ready—especially Sarah." Abigail sits down heavily on a stool at the kitchen counter. She wraps both her hands around the thick stem of her glass as if it could otherwise tip over and spill the wine, like her daughters who have metaphorically jumped overboard and are being swept away in a gush.

"*Voyons*, look, Abbs. Come down off your raincloud. Margot is going to be fine. She's found something that grabs her, and she wants to run with it. We've all been there at one time or another. It's called growing up, and we both know it doesn't happen in a straight line. Sarah is a bit of a lost puppy right now. But she'll be with Marie-Laure—who's a lot like her in many ways.

"We always thought of our dear cousin as eccentric, to put it kindly. But she had a successful career; she's traveled, and now she's quite happy in her little world in the country. Sarah will become bilingual, hopefully, and she'll have to learn how to make a go of a very different lifestyle from what she's used to. Either she'll find her way, or she won't, but the experience will be better than being in Ghana, where she's outstayed her welcome."

"Just like a scientist to see right through all the chaos to a logical outcome. I just hope that their wishful thinking, dashed hopes, or unrequited passions don't interfere with your beautiful equation."

10

CATCHING A BREAK

Late June, Early July—
Annapolis, Somerset County, Maryland

Steve has set up a meeting in Somerset County, the southernmost county in Maryland, with a chicken farmer, Willard Grassley, whom he interviewed for an article published last year in *The Ledger*. That interview focused on issues that Mr. Grassley and other concerned farmers were having with LaLue Foods, the integrator for whom they worked. Steve wants to interview Mr. Grassley again to focus on unfair zoning laws, which haven't been updated in fifty years. These laws lump huge factory farms, officially called concentrated animal feeding operations (CAFOs), into the same category as smaller, family farms. There have been many complaints to state regulators by the family farmers who want the CAFOs to be reclassified as industrial operations, forcing them to comply with a different set of regulations. So far, state regulators and the courts have not taken any action.

Margot is excited about her first trip to Somerset County since working with Steve. She wonders if the lack of a zoning change is due to willful ignorance or something more nefarious, such as the exciting sound of money jingling around in the right pockets, perhaps in the form of generous PAC contributions.

In his previous interview, Willard Grassley came down hard on the large integrators, questioning whether they were doing everything possible to deal with the inevitable increase in chicken waste. Steve and Margot plan to meet him on Friday for lunch at Swanson's Tavern, about fifteen miles from the Grassley farm.

On Friday morning, they arrive early at the restaurant. As they exit the car, Steve explains how he hopes this meeting will play out. "Willard Grassley gave us some valuable information when we first interviewed him last September. Since that article was published, I know that he's had problems with his employer, LaLue, and several people on the city council. I'm hoping he can update us on those issues and the ongoing problems with factory farms."

Once inside, Steve asks if they could be seated so that when their "elderly uncle" arrives, he won't have to wait in line. The hostess looks them up and down and then replies, "Sure. Just grab a table in the back."

Margot secures a booth near the window and scoots over toward the wall. Within five minutes, she recognizes Steve's sandy curls above Mr. Grassley's balding head and raises her hand. She stands up to greet them, but Mr. Grassley signals her to sit back down as he sits opposite her. When Steve slides in next to Margo, his bare knee grazes against her calf while settling in. Margot is instantly aware of a sharp and tingly jolt that shoots up her leg and then comes to rest in the pit of her stomach. She draws in a deep breath, wondering why now, for the first time since 'He' laid hands on her, does she feel a sexual attraction to this man?

Margot tries to refocus all her attention on Willard Grassley instead of Steve's warm, hard knee. Mr. Grassley looks ancient to her, his skin the texture of tanned leather. What's left of his hair is colorless, and his hands and fingers are gnarled, like old tree branches. But his gray eyes are as sharp as polished silver, he projects a reassuring smile, and, as he begins to talk, it's obvious that his mind is focused and deliberate.

Steve reaches into his backpack and pulls out a small voice recorder. As soon as Grassley sees it, he signals an emphatic "No way!"

"Let me say what I come here to tell y'all—off the record. Your paper ran my story last year, and I get that they would be interested in doing a follow-up. But I have a granddaughter in school in Princess Anne. My daughter's a nurse and midwife in town. I have to think of them and the problems I've caused by speaking out once already.

"Let me refresh your memory about our family farm. My grandfather bought the land in the early 1940s, as the economy rebounded from The Great Depression. My father raised chickens and signed on with Roger's Farms, which was bought out by LaLue Foods in the mid-1970s, a few years after they opened their first processing plant in Salisbury. Dad expanded our land holdings, and things worked well for us until the 2008 financial disaster.

"People in this area, like everywhere else, lost jobs, couldn't pay their mortgages, and many had to give up their farms. LaLue started playing hardball with us farmers because of the demand for cheaper food. They required us to cram more birds into overcrowded spaces or build more chicken houses. We were forced to fatten the birds younger by putting a cocktail of chemicals into the feed. But they refused to be held responsible financially for the extra waste. I've always believed that if ya take care of your birds and don't get too greedy, chicken farming is a vital and honorable business. When ya start to abuse the land, the animals, the environment, then, if ya care about them things, you have to choose. For a while, I went along to get along, but I can't do that no more.

"Anyway, I did speak up about all this, and LaLue assured me and other farmers that they were in the process of changing their practices and addressing our concerns. One positive is that they stopped putting certain hormones and antibiotics into the feed. They're also looking into building a plant that can convert manure into electricity.

"But right now, I suspect—I know—some hanky-panky's going on between a few of the agricultural inspectors and the smaller farmers who're having trouble stickin' to their voluntary dumping limits. Them inspectors have caught on and are threatenin' to expose this and any other illegal practices they can invent—unless... You fill in the blank. That's all I'm gonna say, and if you quote me on any of it but the facts, I'll deny it."

During lunch, they discuss the plight of family-run farms as they struggle to compete with the CAFOs that are better able to comply with new dumping regulations that hit the profit margins of the smaller farms much harder. As they prepare to part ways, Willard leans toward Margot and Steve and says in a low voice, "Y'all be careful, the both of ya. There's people around here who stand to lose a lot if any of what I told you about the ag inspectors comes out. They could get pretty resentful and want to take that out on somebody." And with that, he stands up and heads for the door.

"Wow!" Margot remarks. "That felt like a well-prepared statement, and he appeared to have kept to his script. I think he's brave to even meet with us, given the stakes."

"Well, it's not going to be easy finding out the identities of the farmers and the ag inspectors involved. I wish we could spend more time in Princess Anne and dig around. Meanwhile, we can begin by looking into the state registries online and in Annapolis to see if we can find the names of some of those inspectors."

While they wait for the check, Margot asks to be excused.

"Can you let me out so I can use the bathroom?"

"Sure – you 'go' and I'll pay."

"Very funny."

She expects a line in the ladies' room, but there is no one. A moment or two after she enters one of the stalls, however, the door opens, and a gravelly sounding voice asks, "That you, Millie, Hon? I thought I recognized ya with your grandpa out there."

Margot hardly has time to register what's happening, but her instinct tells her to play along. "Yeah," she mutters, hoping the hum of the AC will muffle her voice enough so that the woman doesn't get suspicious.

"You okay, Millie? It don't sound like you. You got a cold or somethin'?"

"Yeah," she repeats as she flushes the toilet.

"That ag man botherin' you agin? He done the same thing to my niece, Samantha. I told your mom about it. Didn't she say nothin' to ya?"

"Yeah …but…"

"Oh, I know. What's his name? Larry? Jerry? I cain't 'member. You keep away from him if ya can. He's a mean ole so-and-so. A real bully. He's been hittin' on my nephew, too, so's not to report him for somethin' he ain't even done!"

As Margot hears her push the lock on the other stall door, she decides to make her getaway.

"Hey, Millie," the woman calls after her as she pulls back the door, "tell your mama that Ruby Stiller says hi, ya' hear?"

"Yes 'um," she calls back as she exits the bathroom and makes a beeline for Steve, who is just putting away his wallet.

"Let's get outta here, ASAP! I'll explain in the car!"

Steve gives Margot a what-the-hell look, but they jump into the car and pull out of the parking lot before anyone else leaves the restaurant.

"A woman came into the bathroom just after I went into one of the stalls and started talking to me. She apparently mistook me for Willard Grassley's granddaughter, but she sure recognized him. She started asking me if I was okay, telling me her niece was being exposed to what sounded like some sort of harassment—probably sexual—by an agricultural inspector named Jerry or Larry—and insinuating that Millie Grassley is dealing with some harassment as well. She said her nephew is being 'hit up' by this guy, and I guess she means demanding money to not accuse him of something he hasn't done or report him for something he has. She even told me to say 'hi' to my 'mom' from her. Her name is Ruby Stiller."

"Holy Moses, that's incredible! Do you have any idea how critical this is? Now we have several really important facts we can use as a starting point. Good work!"

"Hey, all I did was play along. But now what? This info is

about people who all live somewhere in this area, but that's a big space if we don't know where to look."

"Well, we can start in Annapolis and work our way back down here again if need be. We've got something to go on, and we have to be willing to follow the facts wherever they lead us."

• • •

A week after learning that both her girls had decided to throw commitments to the wind and not return home in time to start their sophomore year, Abby is still ruminating about what feels like abandonment from both of them. To overcome her resentment, she decides to do something useful by giving each of their bedrooms a good cleaning.

Sarah's personal space is a jumble of bedding and dirty clothes that Abby puts into a hamper to be washed. She leaves the remains of scattered jewelry, makeup, and hair paraphernalia for another day. Despite the heat that seeps in from outdoors, she opens a window, replacing the stale air as if she didn't want anything as personal as even a trace of Sarah's body odor to remain.

Abby only intended to straighten and clean, but then she has an urge to search through Sarah's drawers and closet, hoping to find some concrete clues as to why she left as she did. For now, however, as she surveys the chaotic room, she decides she'd look for clues later when she has the energy to put things away.

Margot's room is tidier, so there isn't much for Abby to do except strip the bed and arrange the books and folders Margot has left scattered on her desk. Abby takes a moment to flip through a notebook or two, curious to know what Margot was working on at the end of the school year. As she is straightening a stack of papers, she notices a smaller journal-like booklet at the bottom of the pile that turns out to be just that. Abby is surprised that Margot even kept a diary and wonders, as she rifles through some of the pages, just how long she's been doing so.

Abby opens the journal in her hand; it's dated from January through December, 2014. She concludes that Margot has the one for 2015 with her, but what about others? Abby decides to look around in the desk drawers, on closet shelves and in shoeboxes on the floor, but she comes up empty. She sits down on Margot's bed and starts to read a few pages, written in tight script, some days carried over to the next, and others skipped altogether. As Abby skims the pages, one theme strikes her as particularly troubling and important to Margot: sex and the predatory nature of men in general and one man in particular, whom she doesn't name. She calls him 'He,' who has done something to upset her enough that she wrote about her fear of dating and the inevitable pressures of having a relationship with any man.

Abby can only conclude that Margot must have experienced some sort of abuse or even an attempted date rape while she was still in high school. But without the earlier journals, she can't verify her suppositions. A knot of anguish throbs in Abby's chest as she suddenly becomes aware that no matter what happened and when, Margot never uttered a word of it to her. Maybe she's talked to Sarah, but if so, whatever they may have discussed has remained between them. Abby knows there is no way to ask Sarah, whom she hasn't spoken to since she left for Ghana. Her only recourse is to find the other journals.

Aside from giving the room a quick vacuuming and then starting a wash, Abby spends the rest of the morning searching the house for Margot's diaries. She is about to give up when she remembers the tiny closet at the end of the upstairs hallway that leads to a small attic above the girls' bedrooms. The only things stored there are suitcases and some boxes of Michel's papers and published articles. The attic is sweaty hot, and Abby has to bend over because of the low ceiling. Fortunately, Michel's boxes are marked and dated, but one unmarked box is off in a corner under the eaves. Abby has to practically crawl to reach it, but she is able to drag the box out of the attic and into the hallway.

She kneels on the floor and opens the top flaps that were folded but not sealed. Inside are three booklets in Margot's handwriting in neat, carefully composed diaries from 2010, when Margot was thirteen, until two years ago. Abby takes the journals then returns the box to the attic. She hides the three diaries in the bottom drawer of her dresser under a pile of scarves that she rarely wears anymore.

• • •

Even though Annapolis will still be crowded with tourists this 4th of July weekend, Margot was able to make a reservation at O'Henry's Grille, an upscale restaurant away from the main downtown area. When her parents arrive, she is waiting for them outside. She requested a table by a window so they have a view across the Bay, dappled with countless sailboats like gaggles of geese as they buffet the choppy water.

Margot quickly sits in the chair opposite Michel. Abby observes with a jab of jealousy that Margot always gravitates more toward him. She looks like him, and she thinks like him, too. As proof of her mother's reflections, Margot gets right to the point. "I hope you will allow me to stay here in Annapolis a few more months. I've been on the Georgetown website, and I can take a leave of absence but still get credit for classes from another school. I've worked out the living arrangements, I'm hoping to find a second-hand car, and I'm looking into some online classes at the University of Maryland University College.

"Last week, my new boss, Steve Rich, and I went to Somerset County to interview a chicken farmer who had filed a complaint last year against LaLue Foods. Many of these farmers are often unable to dispose of their ever-increasing amount of chicken waste legally. Yet, the huge corporations they work for are far more concerned about coughing up more money than trying to help them manage the waste. The Bay is in so much trouble, and I want to do something about it!"

"It's all good, Margot, as long as you keep the option open to go back to Georgetown for the spring semester," Michel is quick to intervene. "Otherwise, you know we will help you financially. Your mother and I want to give you a chance to see how this crusade you want to dedicate your life to can become a feasible career path for you."

Abby is surprised to hear Michel use words like 'crusade' and 'path'. She weighs whether he is being sincere or sarcastic. But Margot is on a path she feels passionate about and has conveyed that idea to her parents.

"It's a huge privilege to attend a school like Georgetown. But I can't be in two places at once. Right now, I know what turns me on, what makes me excited to get out of bed in the morning."

Abby hasn't said much since they sat down, but neither Margot nor Michel seems to notice. She has read Margot's diaries, but she knows this isn't the time nor the place to discuss what she discovered. Abby rarely allows a troubling thought to go unexpressed, especially concerning something this distressing.

Instead, her head and chest sink, and her shoulders tense up to the point of pain. Abby takes a deep breath, straightens her back and flashes a forced smile directly at her daughter.

"Your father and I are very proud of you," she manages to say. "Not everyone your age can focus so clearly on what they might want to do in life. Some people never get there, and others, like your father, are born gifted and are directed by it from a young age to fulfill their potential."

The food arrives before anyone can respond, but Margot's broad smile is full of gratitude and relief. Mission accomplished! She wishes she could give each of her parents a big hug right now, but instead, she picks up her fork and begins to eat the delicious-smelling food just placed in front of her.

11

BIENVENUE À MERVILLA, WELCOME TO MERVILLA

Early July—Kumasi, Ghana; Mervilla, France

Now that everything is out in the open, Sarah has been desperately trying to cope with her disillusionment. The bubble has burst, and she is left with the sensation of falling helplessly, endlessly until she finally lands in a messy pile of self-pity. But in the end, surprisingly, she does not break apart.

This morning, she eats breakfast late, hoping that Daren and his parents are no longer home. The sun is high and strong, a white, searing disk almost blinding her as she sits on the veranda. Since summer is the rainy season, there will undoubtedly be an afternoon downpour. It occurs to Sarah that the back and forth between gloom and hope is a lot like the weather, and sometimes life feels like nothing more than a struggle to adapt to its vicissitudes.

As she sips her coffee and nibbles at the dry toast, she takes a cursory look at her unread emails. They are mostly part of the chain she started three days ago when she sent everyone her SOS to go to Mervilla. Her parents are okay with it but certainly not delighted, and they insist on paying for the tickets.

Sarah interprets this as an unstated expectation that she will do whatever is needed to support Marie-Laure during her recovery from surgery.

While waiting for these plans to go into effect, Sarah tries to keep to herself. Daren avoids her by spending as much time as possible with his father before they return to Accra. It crosses her mind that if their dates correspond to her leaving, she could hitch a ride with them to the airport.

When everyone returns home from work or wherever they have been all day, Sarah greets them, eyes clear, a smile on her face. However, Dr. Owusu looks at her with worried wrinkles creasing her forehead. She has observed that the relationship with Daren has taken a sudden U-turn. Sarah wants to lighten his mother's concerns, so she walks over to Daren and forces herself to take his hand. He's startled, but then he squeezes it and holds on so Sarah can't let go right away. She is on the verge of blowing her attempt to remain sanguine, but raw determination buoys her up like a sudden puff of wind that fills a sagging sail enough so the boat can tack to shore.

They have dinner at the usual time. However, this evening, Sarah sits with Daren's sisters rather than next to him. Even though she hasn't spent much time with them since coming to Ghana, she enjoys telling them stories about herself and her twin sister when they were eight or nine years old. Dr. Owusu also follows the conversation as she laughs along with Sarah and her daughters. It's obvious, though, that Daren's mother is troubled. Her expression changes as soon as the conversation ends, and her jovial smile melts away. Her lips droop, and her eyes seek out Sarah's as they exchange wistful glances. They had shared the same hopes and dreams concerning Daren's sexual identity, but it is not his fault that things didn't turn out that way.

When Sarah returns to her room and checks her email, she is very relieved to see that her parents have purchased her tickets from Accra to Paris and Paris to Toulouse. Margot has also sent an email full of support and sympathy. Sarah knows she will mourn the loss of her first love, but perhaps even more, she will have to find a way to nurse the implosion of her convictions—or were they illusions about love itself? She's convinced, though, that by changing countries, languages, and focus, she will eventually be able to look back on this trip, not just as a painful memory but also, hopefully, as a valuable learning experience.

After some hesitation, Sarah texts Daren, and five minutes later, she hears a knock at the door. He appears as dejected as she is, and she recognizes that he is genuinely sorry to have hurt her. He starts to go through the whole apology thing again, but Sarah stops him. "You are who you are. We both understand that this is the only honest way you can live your life."

Mr. Owusu has arranged to leave for Accra the day after tomorrow, and Daren will also come. Sarah's flight doesn't depart until almost midnight, so they'll drive her to the airport well in time to catch her plane. In a little over forty-eight hours, she will be out of Daren's life, perhaps for good.

• • •

The Air France Boeing 777 from Accra to Paris taxies to the runway. It pivots and then comes to a standstill, revs up the enormous turbofans under each wing just before it accelerates forward, roaring down the runway, pushing Sarah back in her seat. She closes her eyes in deep exhaustion now that her turbulent stay in Ghana has finally ended. As the plane lifts off, a sob rises from within her chest and into her throat. As they ride through the cloud cover and into the starry night, tears roll down her cheeks, along her jaw, and drip in a steady trickle down her neck. She's afraid that if she reaches down to search her bag for some tissues, the intensity of her hiccupping sobs will grow louder and louder until they drown out the engines' throb.

She glances over at the person sitting next to her, but he has already fallen asleep. Nobody notices her or cares about her problems. She mops up her face and neck, then puts on her earphones and activates the screen in front of her. The PA system comes on with the captain welcoming them on board, followed by a safety video with young, perky women dressed up like dolls doing some exaggerated impressions of jubilant passengers putting on their seatbelts and helping a smiley kid adjust her oxygen mask. Who is going to go all giggly if anyone would ever need to put on an oxygen mask? Sarah wonders.

When the video ends, Sarah scrolls through the list of movies. She settles on a French comedy called *Bienvenue à Marly-Gomont*. (The African Doctor.) The movie tells the true story, written by the son of Dr. Seyolo Zantoko. Originally from Zaire/Congo, Dr. Zantoko has just completed his medical degree in France and wants to remain there. The mayor of a small town in Picardie near the Belgium border recruits him. No White, French doctor wants to set up a practice there because the job is in a traditional, rural, rainy part of France, known colloquially as *La France Profonde*. Most people have never had contact with a person of color, but Dr. Zantoko is more determined to make a go of it than the villagers are to drive him away. However, his practice starts to fail as people prefer to consult with the White doctor in another town. After attempting to fit in by hanging out regularly at the local pub, some townspeople eventually accept him—especially after he is called upon in an emergency to deliver a baby under very difficult circumstances. Along the way, he also learns to accept who he is, no matter what others think of him.

Although Sarah can identify with his story as the ex-pat trying to gain a foothold in a foreign country, compared to Dr. Zantoko, she feels small and inadequate, with nothing to offer anyone except a willingness to try.

At some point, Sarah dozes off. She's awakened by the lights coming on in the cabin, carts passing in the aisles, then the rustling of plastic wrap being torn open as everyone scarfs down a typically tasteless airplane breakfast. Soon the PA system instructs the crew to prepare for landing.

• • •

Sarah feels headachy and stiff, but she is also aware of a profound sense of relief. Now I'm on my own, she recognizes with a shiver of trepidation, quickly followed by the thrill of embarking on a new adventure. As she passes through immigration control, Sarah gives the border patrol lady a big smile as she receives her passport and chirps, "*Je suis très heureuse d'être en France!*" I'm very happy to be in France!

There is a four-hour layover, and Sarah doesn't have much money—only enough for a coffee or two and a croissant. She settles herself into a seat at the gate for Toulouse, dozing off for a few minutes.

Eventually, she decides to find the bathroom so she can freshen up. She splashes water on her face and rinses out her mouth. As she looks at her exhausted, rumpled self in the mirror, she promises the person staring back at her that she will take care of her, along with Marie-Laure, her house, the garden, and all the animals. As she tries to untangle her disheveled hair and put on some lipstick, she remembers the needlepoint wall-hanging her grandmother Bella made for her mom when she lived in France: *Grow Where You Are Planted*. Good advice!

Finally, her flight to Toulouse is called for boarding. Sarah sits in her window seat then curls her tall frame into as much of a fetal position as this narrow space will allow, feeling totally alone and thoroughly scared. An hour after takeoff, the plane is taxiing on the runway at Toulouse Blagnac Airport.

Sarah retrieves her suitcase, then sails through the door and into the terminal. She and Marie-Laure recognize each other immediately. A moment later, Marie-Laure enfolds Sarah in her strong arms, kisses her twice on each cheek, and then holds Sarah at arm's length so she can look at her full-on.

"Oh, you poor dear! You must be exhausted and hungry! Did you have a good trip? Do you want to go to the loo? My house is about a forty-five-minute drive from here."

As they exit the terminal and walk toward the parking garage, Sarah observes Marie-Laure more closely. She has a sturdy build, typical of many people in this part of France. A mass of dark curls streaked with gray float around her shoulders, setting off her round face and ivory skin. A prominent nose divides her wide, blue eyes from her infectious smile. Sarah is particularly captivated, however, by Marie-Laure's special energy that radiates like a beam of light, drawing in anyone who catches her glance into her sphere.

Marie-Laure drapes one arm around Sarah's shoulder and leads them to her little two-door Renault Twingo.

"Do you know how to drive a stick-shift," she asks as Sarah

tries to maneuver her suitcase into the trunk.

"No, I've never had a reason to learn."

"Well, tomorrow afternoon, I'll take you down some country roads and teach you."

Marie-Laure shines a warm, encouraging smile at Sarah that causes her to believe she can do anything. She chats away with a sing-songy rhythm and flat vowels, giving every word, even *Oui*, at least two syllables: *Oui-eh*. It's the way people speak in the southern part of France.

When they arrive, Marie-Laure exits the car and opens the gate to the dirt driveway leading up a short hill to the house. Three mongrel-looking dogs start playing tag with the car, tails bobbing, tongues hanging out. As they inch along, a sensation of pure joy flows through Sarah like the taste of birthday cake. For the first time in seven weeks, she senses what it must feel like to be home.

12

THE CRUSH

Early July—Annapolis, Deale, Maryland

After Margot and her parents part company, she calls Steve, anxious to tell him that her parents have agreed to help her stay in Annapolis. She feels effervescent, knowing she will continue working with him. To her disappointment, Steve doesn't answer, so she leaves a message.

Margot decides to get some exercise and fresh air after an eventful weekend, much of it lived indoors. She takes a walk by the beach. A steady breeze blows off the Bay, and sails are trimmed so the boats can skim over the whitecaps as they speed through the choppy water.

Steve calls during her walk back to the house. They briefly discuss plans to return to Somerset at the end of next week. Margot is about to hang up when he invites her to have an early dinner at a café in Deale, a local fishing village about a twenty-minute drive from the guest house. Margot very much wants to say "yes" but she hesitates. Steve picks up on the pause and asks, "Are you okay? Because if you're too tired, we can do it another time. However, I'd like to discuss our strategy for the trip to

Somerset and how we're going to prepare this week."

Margot thinks all too often of the sensation that riveted through her when his leg brushed against hers at the restaurant last week. Despite her many trepidations, she accepts his invitation, hoping to move further away from an earlier trauma that seeps into anything having to do with feeling comfortable around men—even one she is attracted to. "No, I'm fine, thanks. Just give me a half-hour, and I'll be ready."

As they drive toward Deale and the Westshore Bar & Grill, an awkward silence fills the space between them.

"How was your weekend?" she finally asks. "Did you go home to see your folks?"

"My 'folks' live in Pennsylvania, so no; I had a few things to catch up on in Baltimore. Also, I worked on organizing our research and interviews to dig deeper into what Willard Grassley told us about some extortion schemes. Seems there's a real backstory somewhere in all this, and my gut tells me it's imperative that we start to follow the leads we have. I mean, look what you were able to find out from that woman at Swanson's."

"Yes, but only because I happened to be in the restroom at the same time she came in."

"I'd say it was more because she thought you were Willard's granddaughter. She followed you in, and I was impressed that you played along, like you had a gut feeling she had something important for us to know." He beams at her more intensely than simply giving a compliment to a bright assistant.

As they exit the car and walk toward the restaurant, Margot says, "Well, I'm very flattered you feel that way." Despite her intention of keeping some detachment, she flashes him an eager smile.

Once seated, he orders a beer, a Coke for her, and a pizza. When their drinks arrive, Steve raises up his bottle as if he expects her to clink her glass.

"So, what are we celebrating?" Margot asks a bit coyly.

"That we are officially an investigative team. How does that sound?"

"Pretty damn good!" Now she is beaming—overjoyed but still somewhat afraid of sending the wrong signals.

Steve smiles back warmly at her enthusiasm. As they eat the pizza, all talk turns to how they plan to set up the week ahead. Still, Margot feels herself being pulled along by a budding attraction to him. For the first time in over five years, she is less queasy at the idea that a man would touch her and want to have sex with her, and especially that she would want to reciprocate.

• • •

As soon as Steve drops her off at the guest house, Margot immediately wants to contact Sarah. But she doesn't act on this impulse. She's never told anyone what happened when she and Sarah were thirteen and just beginning to blossom. The family had gathered for Passover that April, and their uncle, David, had trapped her in the hallway coming out of the bathroom, pushing her up against the wall, and running his hands all over her body, including under her dress and inside her underpants.

Margot still remembers something hard pushing up against her lower abdomen while David covered her mouth with his parted lips as his breath became fast and raspy. Then suddenly, he released her and locked himself into the bathroom she had just vacated. Margot was so shocked that she couldn't move, as if her feet were nailed to the parquet floor. She was too stunned even to scream or cry. Instead, Margot forced herself to return to the dinner table where her relatives were seated as the Seder meal was being served. She remembers sitting there like a ghost—unable to speak or eat or even look anyone in the eye.

She refused to participate in the reading of a portion of the service, but everyone attributed her aloof behavior to a teenage-mood thing and gave her a pass. Margot couldn't imagine what she had done to bring on such an attack, but she was sure that somehow it was her fault. David was a married man, the father of two young children. In what universe would he do something so heinous unless she had somehow signaled to him that such behavior would be okay with her? After almost a year of being dumbstruck by shame and guilt, Margot began reading about these types of situations. She quickly discovered that she was far from alone, as she learned that many young girls are abused by someone they know. Most of the advice she read suggested seeking professional help. Since she was incapable of telling even her twin sister, Margot decided instead to record her seething emotions in a diary. She bought a journal with her allowance and began to write.

• • •

After a few hours of fitful sleep, Margot hears a ping on her phone, signaling a text message. It's from Steve. *Had to go in early to see my boss. Will join you at the office at 10:00. Jillian knows and will give you a ride.*

Feelings of excitement and self-doubt pull Margot in opposite directions until she feels dizzy. She is now a part of a team that consults with people like Jillian, who have important positions in environmental activism. But I'm just a novice. What can I possibly contribute at this stage?

Quickly, she regains control as she forces herself not to

over-dramatize. She is about to take the next step into this venture, assisting a man she cares about and admires, who has told her he has confidence in her abilities. For now, she allows herself to give in to the eagerness. Her apprehension shrinks until nothing is left of it but a slight flutter in her chest, a speck of a dark cloud on the horizon that could later grow into a cloudburst or simply fade away.

13

A FRESH START

Early to Mid-July—Mervilla, France

Marie-Laure has made good on her promise to teach Sarah how to drive a stick shift. Yesterday, they headed out with Sarah at the wheel on some of the back roads that circled up and around the hilly terrain surrounding Mervilla. The lesson went well except when Sarah tried to put the gear into reverse. They will try again every day until they both have enough confidence for Sarah to debut on the main road linking Mervilla to the other villages along the way into Toulouse.

Marie-Laure's surgery is scheduled for July 10th, less than a week away. Not only must Sarah quickly become a skilled driver, but she also needs to learn the basics of tending a large kitchen garden and caring for several very different species of animals. Marie-Laure hired a high-school student, Bernard Sarmac, to help Sarah while she is away.

When Sarah awakens the following morning, she is eager to meet Bernard, who will arrive within the hour. She throws on some shorts and a T-shirt and heads downstairs to the kitchen. The backdoor is open, and she sees some of the garden from where she is standing. She steps outside and inhales a deep breath of the soft, clear air. In the distance, the morning haze obscures the outlines of the rolling hills and scattered farms into a panorama of tranquil beauty. Sarah savors a sense of wellbeing that she has not experienced in a long time.

Marie-Laure is hanging the wash on a clothesline so that it will quickly dry as the sun burns off any lingering haze. Sarah takes her mug of coffee and walks down the short path to join her.

"*Bien dormi*? Sleep well? Marie-Laure brightly asks as she continues to hang some table linens. "Let me," Sarah offers.

"Thanks, I am in some pain this morning. Bernard will arrive soon. High-school kids here don't get summer jobs as they do in the states, and they work with their parents or sometimes go camping. If they're lucky and well-off, they're sent to England, Canada, or the United States to learn English. Since Bernard isn't able to do that, his mother volunteered him to help us out in exchange for you speaking English to him."

"Um," Sarah stammered, "then, how am *I* going to learn French?"

"Trust me, you will sound like a Toulouse native in no time!" She pronounces it *Too-lose-ah*, drawing out all of the syllables. "Bernard's horizons are pretty limited, and I think you could be a good influence on him. His father left them last year, and his older brother joined the military and is serving in Mali. His compass isn't finding north right now.

"Bernard's mother has to work this month, and she's afraid he'll get into trouble if he stays home alone. He'll be a big help to you, and if nothing else, he knows how to drive; he just isn't old enough to get his license yet."

They return to the house together. Sarah goes back to her room and prepares to take a shower. She closes the shutters and then pushes them up using the sidebars that convert them into a sloped shield against the sun. Thin stripes of gold and purple ripple across the bed and floor, reminding her of the wide awning at home that overhangs part of the backyard patio. Sarah is surprised that she doesn't miss the house, friends, or parents much. Instead, she is enthralled by how restful it is to be away from the traffic, the noise, and the overwrought sense of always being in a rush. Marie-Laure never seems to be in a hurry. Instead, she projects a soothing optimism that, in the end, things will most likely work out for the best. Sarah is keenly aware that all is not yet settled in her world—far from it. But she senses that if she could go with the flow, she would eventually begin to heal.

The dogs announce Bernard's arrival with excited yelps even before he knocks at the front door. Marie-Laure never locks the door during the day, and she calls out "*Entre*!" Come in. Sarah looks up to see a gangly boy of about sixteen with shaggy blondish-brown hair that forms a curtain across his face. He hesitates, eyes cast downward at his dusty sneakers, before extending his hand toward Sarah. He then bends down to Marie-Laure so she can kiss him on both cheeks twice, as is their ritual. It's one kiss on each cheek in some places, and for others, it's three kisses altogether. Only after you've banged your nose on someone's jaw by not anticipating how many *bises* are the norm, that you learn what is customary.

Marie-Laure offers Bernard a glass of fresh-squeezed orange juice and asks Sarah to toast the rest of the baguette for him. "Thawnkyoo," he said shyly to Sarah, who has to stifle a chuckle at his accent. As she follows him to the chicken coop to explain to her how to take care of six hens and a rooster, Sarah wonders just how much of a language they might have in common.

Marie-Laure has told Sarah that she lets all the chickens out of the coop for a few hours most mornings. She has named all seven of them, and she knows which are which on sight. Sarah only made their acquaintance a few days ago, and other than the fact that three are reddish-brown and three are white, she can't tell the hens apart. The rooster's name is Coq – which means rooster. At least his name is easy to remember.

Bernard opens the latch to the coop and pushes back the wooden door. The hens squawk and rush out onto the sandy stubble along the path to the clothesline, pecking around and stretching their wings. Some soon wander into the grassy side yard shaded by a huge cedar that appears to be as old as the surrounding hills. Sarah is surprised there is no fence to keep the chickens from leaving the property altogether and wandering off into the woods. Sarah wonders if the rooster acts like a border collie and rounds them up if they go too far. Bernard is in the coop now, raking the smelly straw covering the floor. He puts it all into a wheelbarrow, walks down a short slope at the back, and dumps it into a pile at the edge of the woods about 100 yards away.

Sarah joins him when Bernard starts back up the hill toward the coop. She asks him in rapid English, which sounds to Bernard like pops from a bee-bee gun, when and how much to feed the chickens and the rooster. He stops in his tracks and focuses on her with all his being as if he were expecting to find the answers written across her forehead. When Sarah tries to repeat the question in French, she is stymied by her lack of pertinent vocabulary, thoroughly confusing Bernard. He drops his head, puts the rake up against the side of the coop, and starts to walk toward the house. Sarah calls after him, then follows at a trot. But the faster she goes, the faster he moves, quickly breaking into a run. She arrives at the house in time to see him open the gate, jump on his bike, and pedal away. She is flummoxed about what she might have done to cause Bernard to flee like this.

"Marie-Laure, Marie-Laure," she calls out in a semi-panic as she runs around the back toward the garden.

Marie-Laure hears Sarah's call of distress. A moment later, she appears at the kitchen door. "*Qu'est-ce qui se passe?*" What's going on?

"I tried to ask Bernard a couple of questions, first in English; then in French, only I didn't have the vocabulary to say it properly. He just up and left on his bike. I'm so sorry. I'm not entirely sure what I did wrong."

"It's okay, my dear." She comes outside and takes Sarah's hand. "Bernard is very shy, very unsure of himself. He's a reliable worker and never questions anything I tell him to do. But he doesn't talk much, even in French. I think he was just embarrassed. I'll call him and see if I can get him to come back."

"I would feel the same way in his shoes. My French isn't so great, but at least I've used it enough outside the classroom to usually get by, but not this time."

"What was he doing when this happened?"

"He was about to put down fresh straw in the chicken coop. I can do that if you tell me where to find it."

"Some bales are in the shed behind the coop, and the

chicken feed is in there as well. If you bring out the bag, I'll tell you how to feed them." Marie-Laure says this with such warmth in her voice, as if she were providing a meal for friends. Sarah gives her a loving smile and then laughs. "Most chickens end up as a meal for humans. But these are providing food for us. I guess the gratitude is mutual."

• • •

Bernard did come back that first day and has since become indispensable to Sarah. They have since fallen into a pattern: she speaks to him in English, and Bernard responds in French. They more or less do the same things every day, so after a while, they have each mastered enough of a barnyard vocabulary to get said what is necessary.

Sarah would like to talk about other things, such as music, sports, and whatever else Bernard might want to share. From the little he has said about himself, she realizes that his life is very different from hers. Sarah has been told since childhood that she can become whatever she wants, and she is confident that her parents will do all they can to help her achieve her goals. After staying with a wealthy family in Ghana, she knows it's also a given that their children will be assured of a first-rate education.

She understands that globally, it can be much more difficult for young people to have these same opportunities. Although education in France is free even through university, getting there was not always an option for many kids who are filtered out for various reasons early in high school and encouraged to learn a trade instead. Bernard's mother wants him to learn English, an encouraging sign that she will push him to expand his horizons.

• • •

July 10th arrives, the day of Marie-Laure's back surgery. Both she and Sarah are nearly silent as they each go about getting ready to leave for the hospital. Once in the car, Sarah tries to reassure Marie-Laure that everything will go smoothly for her and that she and Bernard know what they need to do while she is gone. Marie-Laure is still quite anxious, and her only reaction is a weak smile.

After arriving at the Hôpital Purpan in Toulouse, a nurse takes Marie-Laure to be prepped for the surgery. Sarah is shown into a special waiting room for family members. Only two other people are in the room. One is dozing, and the other is reading a book. Sarah sits on a lumpy settee and leafs through a pile of donated magazines scattered haphazardly on a large metal coffee table. Sometime during the third hour, she wanders into the hall to find a bathroom and hopefully a vending machine. Finally, a nurse enters and indicates that Sarah should follow her to the recovery area where Marie-Laure has been taken. Sarah follows the nurse through a series of corridors, down some stairs, and into a large ward with curtains separating one bed from another. The nurse pulls back one of the curtains, and there is Marie-Laure, still groggy but who has come through the operation like a champ. Sarah sits with Marie-Laure briefly until an orderly arrives to move her into her room. Then, Sarah kisses her delicately on one cheek and leaves.

As she exits the hospital, Sarah doesn't recognize anything. There is no outdoor lot like the one where she parked this morning. She concludes that she must be on a different side of the building from where she entered this morning. But finding the car in this maze of a facility turns into a frantic search. Near the edge of an outright panic attack, Sarah ends up instead succumbing to a *fou rire*, uncontrollable laughing about something that usually isn't that funny to begin with. She is still giggling as she trots back through the hospital lobby for the second time and out yet another door, tears streaming down her face.

Finally, she spots the car several aisles away, at the back of the lot. As she gets in, the sheer relief of having found the car sends her into another spasm. "I'd almost forgotten how liberating laughter can be!" She wipes away the last of her tears and then drives out of the hospital parking lot.

• • •

When Sarah finally awakens the next morning, she decides not to visit Marie-Laure until much later in the day. She does her chores, then takes a break for lunch and makes a salad with fresh vegetables and herbs from the garden, then toasts the leftover baguette and smears it with fresh goat cheese. She also pours herself a glass of local red table wine, the color of garnets. She raises her glass to Marie-Laure's recovery, but also to her kindness, her integrity, her optimism—qualities Sarah hopes to cultivate in herself.

Sarah would love to have a conversation with Marie-Laure about how she arrived at the important choices she's made. All the stories she's told Sarah about herself describe a deliberately chosen life. She never married, but surely, she had the opportunity. Her vision of how she wanted to construct her life never included a husband and children. Sarah recognizes that she has no idea how her own life might unfold, but as long as she remains in Mervilla, things will likely stay pretty much the same. And that's perfectly fine with her.

After lunch, Sarah piles all the dirty clothes into the washing machine, later to be hung outside to dry. She loves how the clothes smell after drying in the sun, even though some become as stiff as if they were dipped in cornstarch. Meanwhile, Sarah decides to do some general cleaning. She starts upstairs in her room; then, she tackles the two rooms at the other end of the hall. The doors are kept closed when the rooms are not in use, and she's never had a reason to open them until now.

When she enters the room on the right, it's dark and musty smelling since the windows and the shutters have remained closed throughout the summer. She opens them wide to air out the room while she cleans. Along the wall to the right is a trundle daybed with a faded Chintz coverlet and a few hand-embroidered throw pillows. A matching slipper chair sits lonely in the corner, and a walnut dresser is centered on the opposite wall.

Marie-Laure's home is filled with art objects and paintings, and this room is no exception. Sarah is immediately drawn to a painting hanging above the dresser. It's a portrait of a seated woman looking partially away from the artist as if she were encapsulated in her world. She is nude from her upper body to her lap, covered with a dark purple cloth. The colors were applied in broad washes, not entirely within the lines, and appear to have faded over the years. The piece is signed S.A. "What a coincidence," Sarah says to the woman in the painting "My initials are the same as yours. Is it possible that we could be related?"

After giving the room a quick dusting, Sarah is about to move on when she again glances at the painting. The model is young, almost child-like; her head droops toward the right with strands of hair slightly obscuring her left eye. Those soft, downcast ovals are exaggerated in size, and the direction of their gaze leads to her hands, folded one over the other in her lap. Her torso is slumped, and her overall posture depicts a sense of deep dejection. Sarah stands before the painting and tries to imagine why she was posed this way. There is a sense that something ominous is about to take place. Sarah slowly exits the room, gently pulling the door closed as she backs away from a scene that she knows instinctively had to have ended badly.

The second room appears to be Marie-Laure's office. A beaten-up wooden desk is blanketed with papers, a laptop off to one side. Along the opposing wall are four teak bookshelves overflowing with so many books that some were stacked on the floor. An imposing black metal filing cabinet stands like a sentinel between two shuttered windows. This scene of the disrupted organization suggests that Marie-Laure gave up at some point trying to keep everything in its rightful place. Sarah feels like an intruder, and she vacuums quickly and then leaves.

She cleans the downstairs rooms, tidies up the kitchen, then returns to the clotheslines outside to take down the dry laundry. She had intended to iron, but now she is tired. The wide hammock suspended between two elm trees was too inviting to pass up. She backs into it, sinks into its strong, enveloping hold, closes her eyes, and instantly falls into a deep sleep.

When Sarah awakens, she has no idea what time it could be. It's hard to keep track in the summer because the sun doesn't set until well after 10:00 p.m. In any event, visiting hours at the hospital are over. She calls Marie-Laure to apologize, but Marie- Laure tells Sarah that she has been in pain most of the day, so it was just as well. Sarah promises to come tomorrow if Marie Laure is up to having visitors.

After eating some leftovers, Sarah turns on the TV and flips through the channels. As she tunes in to a movie already in progress, she is aware that she understands more of the French dialogue than she did just two weeks ago. With her accent and frequent errors in French, she often thinks of herself as a walking, talking sore thumb. But with time, she has become more confident she will soon speak French well enough to stop feeling like a perpetual misfit.

Around 9:30, Sarah retires to her room, intent on answering some emails. Instead, she turns off the light, opens the shutters to let in the cooling night breeze, and lies on top of the light coverlet on her bed, the soft night air flowing over her. She can't help but think of Daren as she wonders if he'll be going back to GW in another month. She curls up into her sleeping position, glad not to be in the same city as Daren come fall. She knows there is no possibility of ever being with him again as they were for that brief, magical time in Ghana. If nothing else, she sighs; he opened wide the doors to my libido that cannot be closed again. In that respect, I did come of age this summer, and I don't regret it.

14

DIGGING DEEPER

Early to Mid-July—Annapolis, Maryland

Abby has read Margot's journals, but she couldn't bring herself to talk about them in front of Michel when they had lunch together with Margot in Annapolis. Abby was shocked and disturbed about what she had discovered. If what Margot has been writing about for the past five years were true, then the fact that she chose to take a leave of absence from Georgetown makes more sense somehow.

Abby is determined to find a way to confront Margot, preferably in Annapolis, without Michel. The more she thinks about it, the more Abby is skeptical that her brother could have done what Margot has accused him of. After all, she was so young—hardly budding, still just a child with very little prior knowledge of what sexual abuse even looked like. Brushing too close to someone exiting a bathroom is not abuse; it was probably an accident. But if Abby were honest with herself, this wouldn't be the first time David had been accused of inappropriate behavior with a younger teenage girl who was not yet in high school, when he was a senior. David has always claimed they didn't have intercourse and that everything else was consensual.

• • •

Margot and Steve spend most days in Annapolis or traveling to the Eastern Shore. As a follow-up to the explosive information Willard Grassley dropped into their lap in early July, they are trying to document rumors concerning agricultural inspectors, kickbacks, and illegal dumping.

When they are in close contact like this at the guest house, despite her nagging fears on so many levels, Margot senses that Steve has feelings for her beyond their working relationship. She would love to test her ability to tolerate and even come to enjoy physical contact with him. Margot has corresponded with Sarah about her feelings for Steve, avoiding the reasons holding her back. Sarah, the more experienced sister, has pushed her beyond her rigidly professional demeanor to gently signal her attraction. But for now, Margot chooses to compartmentalize her feelings, setting aside her simmering crush in favor of getting on with their mission. Anything else could upend their professional collaboration with Margot losing her job.

• • •

During their trip last week to Princess Anne in Somerset County, Steve suggests they split up. He explains that he wants to contact some farmers who might be entangled in this alleged extortion web. Margo's task is to meet with several state officials overseeing regulations for chicken-waste disposal and prod them to discuss further efforts to curb illegal dumping. The prevailing attitude toward her is that it's nobody else's business outside this small but influential community of decision-makers.

Margot is aware that an important part of her job is to dig

and uncover facts to bridge the gap between what she and Steve think they know and what is provable. However, unearthing those links to the truth has been extremely difficult. She decides to go back to Googling the State of Maryland's website and navigating her way through the laws, regulations, permits, and procedures concerning chicken farming, chicken waste, runoff, dumping, and other actions that pollute the Bay and its watershed. One keyword leads to another until the whole picture resembles an elaborate spider web, where Margot is the fly caught in the middle.

Ruby Stiller, on the other hand, dropped into the mix like magic, as if Fate herself were guiding their quest to find and call out those who thwarted the rules for profit. The more she thinks about it, the more her gut tells her they have to start with Ruby. When Steve calls her later, Margot doesn't mention any of her frustrations but reports instead what she can verify, which admittedly is not much. Then, she pushes her idea that the entryway into going much deeper has to begin with Ruby Stiller.

"That's the Margot I'm counting on, the one who finds a logical, systemic way to tackle problems."

Margot is a little taken aback. Is Steve serious? she asks herself. Or is he chiding me for giving up on the original plan in favor of involving someone who might derail the whole project?

"Ruby Stiller has a bone to pick with the ag guy in question," Steve remarks, "so she might be persuaded that helping us is one way she can protect her family. I think you should do a White Pages search for any Ruby Stiller who lives in Somerset or nearby counties and is in the age range of forty-nine and up. If you find anyone meeting these criteria, present yourself as a journalist working for *The State Capital Ledger* on a story about illegal dumping, and then let Ruby do the talking."

"I think I might recognize her husky voice, assuming there is only one Ruby who's a middle-aged smoker."

When Margot searches the White Pages website, she finds three Ruby Stillers. However, the closer she looks at the information, the more they appear to be the same person. All three have lived in Somerset County, albeit at different addresses. They have frequently changed jobs, and two were divorced. Margot assumes that Stiller is Ruby's maiden name since two of them use 'S' as the middle initial, each with a different last name. Only the third goes by simply Ruby Stiller.

With some trepidation, Margot calls the number for Ruby Stiller #3. No one picks up, and the answering machine has a computer-generated voice greeting. She tries a second time, leaving a brief message about having information concerning the agricultural inspector for Ruby's area, hoping to entice her to respond. Then, she texts Steve to let him know she has at least tried.

While waiting to hear back from Ruby, Margot decides to reach out to her mother. The call goes into voicemail, and immediately, she hangs up. Abigail has only answered one of Margot's emails, rambling about what she was doing and not addressing what Margot had written. Since leaving home in June, Margot suspects that Abby has lost some interest in her. She believes it's her mother's way of letting her know she is not a child anymore and that the details of how she lives her life are no longer worthy of her special attention. This realization seems harsh but somehow true.

Margot understands that both her parents are still disappointed with Sarah. However, she resents being thrown into a basket for wayward daughters when, in fact, she is doing something she cares deeply about while expanding her horizons. She is also making an effort to be as frugal with her meager salary as possible so as not to cause her parents any financial stress.

In the midst of her mulling over these concerns, her phone buzzes, and it's her mother calling back. Margot is tempted to let the call go into voicemail, but she relents at the last minute.

"Hi, Mom, I guess you saw I called. I didn't want to bother you, so...."

"It's fine, Sweet Pea. I've wanted to get in touch with you as well, and I'd like to come to Annapolis this week and take you to lunch, just the two of us."

"But haven't you gone back to work?"

"Yes, but you know I job-share. I'm free on Tuesdays, Thursdays, and every other Friday. This Friday would be good for me. Everyone will be going toward the Bay in the afternoon, so the Beltway coming back later should be a piece of cake. Can you manage to take a half-day off on Friday?"

Margot is silent as she begins to sense some sort of a trap. *If Mom wanted to be in touch, she could have at least answered my emails.*

"Let me talk to Steve, and I'll get back to you as soon as I can. Are you sure you want to drive all this way? Maybe I could arrange to come home for a long weekend toward the end of the month."

"No, no. I would enjoy being near the water and seeing you simultaneously. There are too many distractions at home."

"It seems like you wanted to talk to me about something specific. Are you still upset that I'm staying in Annapolis through the fall semester?"

Abby dodges the question entirely. "Let me know about Friday. Love you, bye." Click.

Margot is befuddled and annoyed that her mother has waded back into her private little pond so unexpectedly. She never calls me "Sweet Pea" anymore. Something's going on.

As she continues to speculate about what has brought on this sudden interest, she receives a call from Steve. "I'd like to come by later if that's ok. We can try Ruby again when I get there, and I'll bring some beer. What have you got in the fridge?"

"I have some ham slices and enough salad to make it a meal, and I think I even have an unopened bag of chips. By the way, my mom wants to meet up with me on Friday and spend part of the afternoon. Would that be okay with you?"

After a short hesitation, he answers, "Sure. We can work around it."

Steve arrives around 8:00. He opens a pair of beers and hands one to Margot as they sit down to eat. Margot smiles to herself about Steve giving her a beer. The last time he gave her a drink, it was a Coke while he drank a beer. So, he must have upgraded her adult status, she thinks with a wry smile.

"Ruby hasn't called me back, but I wasn't clear about why I was calling in the first place. I said I had some information about the ag agent, but in reality, I haven't even been able to verify if his first name is Larry or Jerry, much less obtain his last name. I think you should be the one who calls her now."

Steve agrees and taps in her number. After four rings, the answering machine picks up. Steve leaves a short message about who he is, the organization he works for, and how he is trying to access information Ruby might have. He leaves his number with a request that she call him back. Just like that. No dancing around, no games. Margot has just learned a valuable lesson: don't bullshit the people whose trust you will need to get what you want.

Then, suddenly, Steve's phone vibrates against the table. He glances over, and his expression changes as he sees the caller's number. He picks up the phone and hands it to Margot as he hits *Accept*.

"It's Ruby Stiller."

Margot's mouth drops open as she puts the phone to her ear and says, "Steve Rich's line, Margot speaking. How can I help you?"

"Did someone from this number call me just now? What's this about?"

"Yes, Mr. Rich tried to contact you a few minutes ago. I'm his assistant. Mr. Rich is a reporter with *The State Capital Ledger*. We're working on a follow-up story about the expansion of chicken farming in your area, and we're hoping you can help us."

"How'd ya git my name?"

"Do you own or work on a chicken farm or have a relative who does?"

"Yeah, but that don't explain how ya got my name."

"You would have to talk to Mr. Rich about that. We're looking into how farmers have been affected by the spread of concentrated animal feeding operations."

"My nephew has a farm with four chicken houses. Contracts with LaLue. Nothin' big like them other operations taking over the place. They zoned 'em wrong, and now we cain't hardly make a living."

"You sound pretty upset about that, Ms. Stiller. Some of

your neighbors have already complained to the state about these laws and about the smell from the extra manure no one can get rid of."

"How do I know you are who you say you are? I know people who spoke before to the press, and they got into a heap of trouble for it. too."

"Why would they get into trouble for telling the truth?" Margot asks with more urgency. Steve jots down some words on a napkin and shows them to her: *Set up a meeting for tomorrow.*

"Look, Ms. Stiller. We would like to talk to you and your nephew in person so you can see we're honest people who know how hard it is for you to make your farms profitable."

"Well, now, I dunno. Some of them people are also my neighbors. But lots of them owners of the really big farms don't even live in the county. The ag man don't take too kindly to our problems, neither. Given' us grief about all them regulations what costs us more to follow. But I'd have to talk to Jake since he's the one owns the farm. I don't want to say nothing that would git him in trouble."

"Well, I understand that very well, Ms. Stiller. Do you think we could drop by his farm tomorrow afternoon?"

"Lemme call him, and I'll call you back."

Click!

Steve reaches over, grabs Margot's hand, and gives it a big, hard squeeze. He beams an excited smile at her, reflecting what must be written across her own face. Then Steve lifts Margot's arm over her head in a gesture of triumph. "What'd I tell you?" he says proudly. "You're a natural."

"Well, I guess I said the right things since she didn't just say no way and hang up. But we still don't have an interview yet, so let's not count our chickens, ha, ha, pun intended."

As he lowers her arm and releases her hand, which has become all sweaty, Margot leans across the table toward him, and for a moment, their eyes catch and lock. Then his phone vibrates its way toward her, and he nods at her to answer it.

"Mr. Rich's line, Margot speaking."

"Yeah, hullo. This is Jake Wheeler, Ruby Stiller's nephew. Just who are you, anyway? My aunt was too wound up to tell me straight what you want."

"What we want, Mr. Wheeler, is to find out the truth about the CAFOs that are popping up all over Somerset County and how they are affecting family farms such as yours. Mr. Rich and I work for *The State Capital Ledger*, an online and print publication in Annapolis. Last year we did a series on chicken farming and waste management throughout the state but focused mostly on Somerset County. We interviewed several of your neighbors who work for LaLue Foods. We understand there's a lot of pressure on the smaller farmers to compete with a growing number of factory farms and then legally dispose of the resulting manure. Mr. Rich and I would like to talk to you in person about your situation and how your business is faring. Would tomorrow work for you?"

"Whoa, I don't even know who you folks are, and I got enough troubles without exposing myself, my family, and my business to more."

"We don't want to cause you any trouble. We just want folks to know how old zoning laws make it possible for these CAFOs to exist alongside traditional family farms and how your operation handles all that manure without going over your TMDL."

"Well, it sounds like you know what you're talkin' bout. But you cain't come to my farm. Can we meet somewheres else? I know of a diner near Venton called Zeek's. I'm not sure my aunt will be with me, but we could meet there for coffee around 1:00 tomorrow?"

"We'd like to invite you and your aunt for a bite to eat. Would 12:30 work for you?"

"Yeah, I guess so. But I don't want to be beholden to you about lunch, and I ain't really got that much time."

"We'll do whatever works best for you, but it's our pleasure to share a meal with you. Just a sandwich. You won't be beholden, I promise."

"Where you coming from anyway?"

"Annapolis."

"Jesus, that's a ways up. Well, call me when you turn off the main road to head toward Venton. We don't live that far."

"Okay, see you tomorrow around 12:30." But he'd already hung up.

"What was all that about lunch?" Steve inquires. "He could have just as easily said 'no' to any of it and hung up."

"But he didn't, did he? I was raised in a French family. Eating together creates bonds. My grandma Marguerite used to say that you can't hold a grudge against someone and still break bread with them."

"Are you sure it's the food and not the wine that mellows people out?" he suggests with a playful smile. Margot lowers her gaze to keep from staring back into his shiny eyes that animate his quick sense of humor.

"I admit it's both."

Steve suddenly changes the subject as his face assumes a more serious demeanor. "I'd like you to work on a background article for next week's *Ledger* online feature story about the alleged pay-to-play schemes we've been trying to verify. We can ask for comments from the public and try to stir up some outrage. Once we've met with Jake Wheeler and Ruby, we'll hopefully have more to go on. Can you write up a preliminary report for Janet, the online editor, by tomorrow morning before we leave for Venton? That way, I'll have time to edit it and email it to her over the weekend."

Margot stares back at Steve, then takes a deep breath and lets out a slow sigh.

"What's that about? C'mon, that's not the Margot I know!"

"We really don't have much to go on yet. Will you help me?" That comes out more sheepishly than she would have liked. "I've never written anything like this before, and it's pretty important to get it right."

"Sure, but only if you let me share the byline."

15

BASTILLE DAY

Mid-July—Mervilla, Toulouse, Carcassonne, France

Sarah reflects on what she has learned about *Le Quatorze Juillet,* July 14, Bastille Day, and how it changed the course of French history. On July 14, 1789, starving, penniless commoners, with nothing else to lose, stormed the Bastille fortress and prison, leading to an important turning point in the French Revolution.

In 1792 the monarchy was abolished, and in 1793 the Declaration of the Rights of Man and the Citizen was adopted ahead of the First Republic that established a constitution allowing all adult males to vote. Napoleon Bonaparte staged a coup in 1799 and changed the form of government to an autocracy when he had himself crowned emperor in 1804. Napoleon conquered much of Europe until the British finally defeated him at the Battle of Waterloo in 1815. For seventy-five years, various factions ruled as constitutional monarchies or republics.

In 1940, Germany invaded France and set up the collaborative Vichy regime in the northern part of the country. During World War II, Charles de Gaulle headed the French

Résistance from London, and after the war, he became the Provisional Republic leader. In 1958, he established the Fifth Republic, which is still France's system of government.

Knowing more about French history, which mirrors and then radically differs from American history, has helped Sarah appreciate how these two cultures have informed her parents' beliefs and attitudes toward a host of situations. The French national motto is *Liberté, Egalité, Fraternité*, Liberty, Equality, Brotherhood, whereas the U.S. motto is E Pluribus Unum, One Out of Many.

As far as Sarah is concerned, the French live their motto with less overt patriotism but more commitment to its principles than do Americans. France believes in a society with a wide safety net. In the United States, people in need receive some help from the government but are then expected to somehow pull themselves up by their bootstraps. How can these people associate themselves with the 'many,' Sarah asks herself if they can't participate in America's prosperity?

• • •

When Sarah calls the hospital, Marie-Laure answers with a clear, strong voice. "I'll be at the hospital when visiting hours start around 2:00," Sarah promises.

In the meantime, she spends the morning watering the garden and caring for the animals, including Charlotte, the goat. Goats are herd animals and like company. Sarah allows Charlotte to follow her around the property as she picks some periwinkle hydrangeas, a few Black-eyed Susans, and a handful of pink daisies to make a colorful bouquet for Marie-Laure.

When she arrives at the hospital, Sarah is eager to present her bouquet and to see for herself how much progress her dear cousin has made since her last visit. As she barges into the room and looks around, she is surprised that, instead of Marie-Laure, she is confronted with the backside of a large, shapeless man bending over the bed and gurgling in a sugary, sing-songy voice: "*Ah, ma poule, comme je suis heureux d'être enfin avec toi.*" Ah, my little hen, I'm so happy to be with you at last.

The man realizes someone else is in the room and turns around. Before Sarah can say anything, he flashes her a welcoming smile, like he's known her all her life. He strides toward her and extends his hand.

Marie-Laure chirps from the bed with no awkwardness in her voice, "*Ah, Sarah, te voilà! Je te présente mon ami, Jean Lebrun.* Sarah immediately deciphers the double meaning and assumes that '*ami*' in this case means lover. "Jean is an antique dealer in the old city and my traveling companion."

OMG! Sarah gasps: Marie-Laure has a boyfriend, a love interest, with whom she has sex! Sarah's face turns beet red as Marie-Laure and Jean both laugh. Jean fetches another chair and invites Sarah to sit down. He takes the flowers from her and leaves the room, searching for a vase.

"You look shocked, my dear. Is it because we are not so young or maybe because you've never visualized your parents having sex?" Marie-Laure says this to tease her, but her questions are as disturbing to Sarah as is the truth that these things happen.

"I'm happy for you." is all she manages to say.

Jean returns with the flowers and sets the vase down on the windowsill. Sarah notices another bouquet there, too, with a dozen lipstick-red roses that scintillate in the midday sunlight flowing in through the open window.

"Thanks, Sarah. These flowers are lovely."

"Oh, you're welcome. I've been watering the garden every day, just like you told me. You've only been gone a few days, but Charlotte misses you. She followed me all around this morning and didn't want to go back into her enclosure."

"She never wants to go back there. Her fondest dream is to be let loose with the garden gate left open."

Marie-Laure laughs again as Jean beams at her. Even in bed and only several days after surgery, she projects a vitality so captivating that it was easy to see why this man, or any other man she could accept, would be in love with her.

"I'm going to leave now," he announces as he bends toward her again to give her the requisite four cheek kisses. He holds the last one a little longer. "I promised my son I would help him set up for their barbecue later today. You know, they always have a big gathering on July 14. I'll come back tomorrow."

"Yes, of course. And can you sneak some leftovers in for me? The food here leaves a lot to be desired."

"I will do my best."

Sarah rises and extends her hand to say goodbye, but instead, Jean gently takes her shoulders and softly touches his cheeks to hers. "I hope to see you again soon, Sarah. I'm so happy Marie-Laure has you to take care of her and that 'household' of hers."

"*Oui, bien sûr,*" Yes, of course, she mumbles. But when she glances up at him again, he has a twinkle in his expressive brown eyes and an affectionate smile.

Marie-Laure is pleased that Sarah and Jean have met. She tells Sarah that she has known him for many years and that they had an affair ten years or so ago when he was still married. He wanted to try to make his chaotic marriage work, but eventually and inevitably, that fell apart. Then he got back in touch with her, and now they are together again. He prefers his apartment in the city, and Marie-Laure loves her farm in the country. "We are that much happier to see each other this way," she remarks with a meaningful smile.

Sarah would like to ask her about the painting she discovered upstairs while cleaning the house. However, she hesitates, thinking she might have intruded into off-limit rooms. Instead, she stands up and says, "I think I should leave too. You look tired."

"What do you plan to do this evening? If you want to see fireworks, you will do well to stay in town."

"But they won't start until at least 10:00 pm at the earliest."

"You're right, but it's too bad. The city does a good job. However, if you want to see great fireworks, you should go to Carcassonne and watch them from just outside the citadel along the Aude River. That's something special to see. I'm so sorry I can't take you there myself. Maybe next year."

While she contemplates the idea of driving sixty miles south to this massive fortress, dating back to Roman times, Sarah decides to stay in town for now and explore the old city. She parks just outside the twist of narrow streets in the heart of *Vieux Toulouse*, near the Saint-Étienne Cathedral. Most of the little specialty shops are closed, and many have a protective metal shutter rolled down over the door and display window.

As she starts back up the Rue Fermât toward the car, she passes by an art gallery with several paintings visible in the window. One of the smaller pieces closely resembles the young woman's portrait Sarah saw at her cousin's home, except this time she is looking straight at the viewer. Sarah tries to make out a signature and a price, but the boutique is dark, as that side of the street is in shadow. She taps the name and address of the shop into her phone and walks on. That would be an amazing coincidence, and I will ask Marie-Laure about it on my next visit, she promises herself.

Since Mervilla is on the south side of Toulouse, not far from the highway that extends down to Carcassonne, Sarah decides to go home first, then head there later. She remembers visiting *la Cité* once during one of their family's trips and discovering a whole town inside those yard-thick stone walls where people live and work all year round. As Marie-Laure instructed, she plans to leave as early as 6:00, hoping to find parking near the Aude River.

Sarah rests for an hour in the hammock, then packs a sandwich and some water into her backpack. She drives along the back roads to see the scenery and the other walled towns along the way. The route is tightly lined with tall plane trees on either side, like sentinels holding leafy green parasols. Small farmhouses and vast fields of wheat, corn, and sunflowers are scattered on the hilly terrain as far as the eye can see.

She drives through several villages along the way, some dating back to the Middle Ages—Villenouvelle, Villefranche-de-Lauragais, and Castelnaudary. They, too, were fortified, built as high on their chosen hill as possible. Constant battles erupted between kings and noblemen throughout medieval times, each trying to amass as much territory as possible. In Carcassonne itself, bloody religious wars occurred to expel Muslim invaders and later between the Catholic Church and the Cathars, a popular sect that loyalists to the Catholics eventually obliterated.

Marie-Laure has told Sarah that some people in this region, even today, have never forgiven the Church because of the horrors it inflicted on the Cathars six centuries ago. When the French bear a grudge, they hang onto it forever; her father, for instance, still resents the British for what they did to Joan of Arc and Napoleon, even though the latter probably deserved it.

Sarah approaches the northwest side of the modern city of Carcassonne around 7:30. Traffic that was heavy out of Castelnaudary on this strip of the road has come to a near halt some four miles outside of town. Sarah is afraid that she is arriving too late to find parking on the eastern side of the citadel, nearer the river.

Now that she's come all this way, though, she's disinclined to give up so soon. She turns off the main road at the next intersection and drives along an alley bordering a scraggly stretch of woods. After a quarter-mile, Sarah finally spots a space created by two cars with enough distance between them so she can maneuver the Twingo into the gap. She puts on her backpack and walks back toward the main road, hoping to find a city bus or a special shuttle to take her into town.

When she returns to the intersection where she turned left, on the right is a large square with a crowd of people walking in several different directions. She stops a few of them to inquire about public transportation into town, but no one seems to know where, or even if, such services exist at this location. Sarah stands in the middle of the square trying to decide whether to give up and go back home when she spots three girls about her age who appear just to be milling around. If they brush me off, I'll leave, and if not, well, I'll see.

"*Bonsoir*, Good evening. Are you here to see the fireworks?" Sarah asks. The girls look her up and down, then laugh, as if she had asked them to count from 100 backward by threes.

Sarah turns and starts to walk away when one of them stops her, "Sorry! We weren't laughing at you, honestly. Are you lost? You aren't from around here, are you?"

"Well, no. I'm staying in Mervilla, outside Toulouse. I drove here like everyone else to see the fireworks. I guess I'm on the wrong side of town, and now I'm going to miss everything."

She notices the girl's crooked grin that could be a smirk until she looks at Sarah full-on. Her lips quickly lift and part into an infectious smile as she stares at Sarah with mesmerizing, pale-blue eyes the color of a hazy summer sky. The other two girls project curious glances at her and don't say anything. All three are wearing denim shorts and halter tops, similar to how Sarah dressed that first embarrassing evening in Kumasi. "Where did you want to go?" asks the first girl, who was still smiling. She is the perkiest of the three and appears to be the leader. Her eyes sparkle, and her long blonde hair, straight as corn silk, dances across her back in the evening breeze.

"I was told the best place to view the fireworks is near the Aude River. Is it too far to walk there from here?"

All three burst out laughing again. Sarah is tempted to walk away for good this time, but then one of the other girls, who had not spoken yet, asks in accented English, "Are you British or American?"

"Does it matter?" Sarah retorts in English, "Isn't my French good enough for you?"

"*Ne te fâches pas*!" Don't be angry; the leader intervenes and takes Sarah's arm. "We love Americans! You are American, I hope, because we aren't too partial to Brits." They all laugh again, and then, so does Sarah.

"Yes," she replies in English, "I'm American from Washington,

DC." Then, she switches back to French "I was born in Toulouse. I'm staying with my cousin for the summer. Do you all live around here?"

"Unfortunately, yes," the third girl answers. "I've never been out of France before. Are Americans really like what you see on TV—either very thin or very fat, and if you're Black, you live in a ghetto and are usually poor?"

"Good God, is that what you think? I could say the same about the French and their attitude toward Africans and Muslims."

"*Calme-toi.* Relax. I'm teasing you. Hey, what's your name anyway? I'm Nadine, and she's Julie, pointing to the girl who had spoken to her in English.

"And I'm Sophie," the leader laughs again, "but my true friends call me *La Princesse.*"

"Seriously?" Sarah asks, wondering how she got that moniker. "My name is Sarah. But really, do any of you know where I can go to see the fireworks? Otherwise, as much as I'm enjoying your company, I think I'll head for home before everyone else gets back on the road."

"No, please stay with us," Sophie insists as she flashes her irresistible smile back at Sarah. "Do you have a car? Because if you do, there's a pull-off about five or six miles up the highway toward Toulouse. You can't hear the music, but you can still see everything. Anyway, we live near Castelnaudary, so it's on your way home—sort of." Sophie grabs Sarah's hand, then draws her lips into a slight pout. "Let's go if you don't want to miss anything."

They start back to where Sarah parked the Twingo. Nadine and Julie squeeze into the back seat, as if Sophie would naturally sit in front. Although the road is still crowded, traffic is moving.

Soon signs for the autoroute going north lead them to the rest stop. Along the way, Sophie softens the mood by asking Sarah some questions about her family and then talking about her own. She's the only child of an older couple, and her father owns and operates a winery that's been in his family for many generations. They live in a chateau built in the mid-1800s, a summer house for Prince Philippe, *Count de Paris*, the grandson of Louis-Philippe, the last king of France, which is why Sophie's friends refer to her as *La Princesse*.

When they arrive at the turn-off, they all scramble out of the car and walk to the edge of a bluff that drops off into a chasm of blackness, except for the twinkling headlights from the highway far below. Sophie pulls out of her purse what looks like a cigarette but is really marijuana. The girls sit on the grass and pass the joint around. Within minutes, Sarah begins to relax, as her mood mirrors the calm of the purple sky and a waning moon that sheds a subtle glow on the rolling farmland in the distance. She is beginning not to care that much about the fireworks when, at exactly 10:30 by her watch, an explosion of blue, white, and red erupts over the citadel, kindling the sky above it for a few seconds. Then, another rocket shoots up and bursts into a shower of color just before the last sparkles of the prior display fade into the night.

Their chatter quiets to whispers as they marveled at the spectacle. The rush of vehicles speeding along the autoroute fades into the background of Sarah's awareness, as she enjoys the warm night air, sharing this experience with Sophie and her friends.

At the end of the show, Sarah drives them back to Sophie's 'estate'. It's hard to make out the size of her house and the extent of the property in the dark, but before they separate, Sophie plants a quick peck on each of Sarah's cheeks, then presses a piece of paper into her hand with her phone number on it.

"We should try to meet up again. I often drive up to Toulouse, and I'll start back to university there in October. Will you still be around by then?"

"A lot of things would have to fall into place for me to be able to stay, but I'm hoping to. I'd love to get together with you before then. I'll be in touch."

16

IT'S COMPLICATED

Mid-July—Annapolis, Maryland

Steve and Margot spend the rest of the following day at the guest house working on the article for *The Ledger*. Margot realizes that if she could tell a wider story, citing people Steve has interviewed as examples, the piece would be more engaging than writing about generalizations and abstract facts.

She settles down at the kitchen counter with Steve's laptop, his voice recorder, and his notes, hoping she will be able to write an engaging, well-sourced story. She wants so much to impress him or at least not to let him down. Maybe this is a test, she worries, like the SATs or a final exam. C'mon, Margot, as Steve likes to say, enough of that! You know more than you think you do. Eventually, Steve approaches and looks over her shoulder to see her progress.

"I guess this is a pretty tall order since we don't have much yet to go on," he remarks. "Just get down the basic facts from your research, and we can finish it after our trip tomorrow. I hope we will get enough information from Jake Wheeler that the article will write itself."

Margot breathes an audible sigh of relief. "That's more than fine with me. Besides, I'm hungry. Aren't you?" He looks at her and turns on his 'older-brother' smile. He thinks I'm a kid, not even old enough to drink a beer in public, still too inexperienced to be anything to him other than a promising assistant. Margot fears this bout of self-doubt could lead to tears, so she excuses herself and retreats to her room upstairs. She washes her face in cold water, then peers at herself in the bathroom mirror. Instead of seeing a discombobulated kid, Margot is surprised at the reflection of an attractive young woman with bright eyes and a hesitant smile shining back at her.

When she returns downstairs, Steve is talking to someone, and she hears him laugh softly into the phone. When he notices she is there, he wraps up the call. "Let's go, Kiddo. I'm starving!"

"Kiddo?" Margot says it before she can stop herself. "Is that how you think of me? And here I thought …."

Steve places his hands on her shoulders, then gathers her into his arms and just holds her there. Her first inclination is to panic, but instead, she throws her arms around his neck and lifts her face to his. He bends slightly forward as his lips brush across hers. Then, abruptly, he pulls away. Margot can't pretend anymore; her shoulders start to shudder as tears of disappointment flood down her face.

"Aw, Margot, don't. I can't bear to hurt you. I think you're terrific, and you know how much I … respect you. But you're so young, and you've got a whole world of men out there who are going to…"

"To what? Love me? Have sex with me? I think I'm in love with you. I've been afraid of this moment ever since I was a kid, but now I want you to be the first to make love to me."

Steve bows his head then directs at her an expression of regret. Or is it pity? She concludes that he probably didn't understand what she meant about mingling her fear with a confession of love. Still, she is overwhelmed by this rejection and cannot bear to look at him. He reaches over to take her hand then sits her down on the couch.

"Listen," he says, as his expression saddens, "You need to know this. I'm coming off a serious relationship that ended badly, at least for me. I thought I had met the woman I wanted to spend my life with. In the end, she turned me down and broke it off. I, too, am not ready to be with anyone yet. And anyway, if we were to give in to our impulses now, it would turn our working relationship into something untenable. I would never compromise that or you by going down a path I wasn't sure about and taking this in a direction that could end up hurting us both in ways more than sex could ever make up for."

"I've ruined everything, haven't I? How can we work together after what just happened?" Margot wants to flee, to weep until she is empty, and then to somehow wipe away the last ten minutes, just like she has fought to escape the traumatic aftermath of David's abuse.

"Please don't think that! I'm serious. I'm very flattered that you care about me. I care about you, too, just not in the way you want—right now. Give it and yourself some time. I can almost promise you that in the end, it will be you who changes your mind. You have your whole life ahead of you, and I hope to be there watching how it unfolds. Now, let's go out and get some grub, okay?"

They drive back to the Westshore in Deale. In the car, Steve talks about his career plans, as if everything between them has returned to being as natural as seeing a rainbow after a sun shower. He hopes to expand upon what they are working on for *The Ledger* as a springboard toward a wider audience. Margot makes an effort to focus on what he is telling her. The painful lump of humiliation still lodged in her chest begins to dissolve slowly, and soon she can breathe deeply again.

Although Steve said she is too young, Margot understands that it's not just about age. It's also about the maturity that comes from being out in the world, facing adversities, and figuring out how to advance toward a chosen direction in life. It means giving up illusions and finding a way to deal with the pain that follows that loss. Margot has already gone down a part of this road at an even younger age, and she survived. The whole process reminds her of a butterfly, struggling to break out of its chrysalis until it finally emerges as a fully formed adult, then unfolds its wings and can finally fly away.

• • •

Margot dozes fitfully off and on throughout the night when a distant buzzing sound suddenly arouses her. She's sure it's still early as she bounds out of bed and hunts around for her phone, grabbing it just before the call goes into voicemail. "Up and at 'em. We need to go!" Steve says urgently. "I'm on my way over there right now."

How is it possible that she completely forgot they are supposed to meet Ruby Stiller and Jake Wheeler today in Venton? She throws some water on her face, brushes her teeth, and grabs the same clothes she wore yesterday. She hears a knock at the door before she barely has time to comb her hair.

He glances at her and remarks, "Yeah, I had a hard time sleeping, too."

"Do I look that crummy? I did a lot of thinking about what you said yesterday. I know you're right. I just really want to stay on this project, and I…"

"Margot, it's okay. I know you do, and I want to work with you, too. So, nothing more needs to be said. We have a big day ahead, and we need to get on the road. I'm hoping this Jake guy doesn't bail on us. But I have his number in my phone, so this won't be our last contact with him, regardless. I read your piece—twice. I like how you emphasized that many of the problems happening in Somerset can probably be documented all over the Delmarva Peninsula. Good work! Let's see what we find out today, and then I'll do a little editing. We can email it to Janet by this evening."

During the drive south toward Zeeks, their brief exchanges of chit-chatty trivialities grate on Margot, as the trip seems to take forever. They arrive a little early, but within ten minutes, a young man wearing a UVA Cavaliers' baseball cap walks in and glances around like he, too, is waiting for someone. Steve approaches him and asks, "Jake Wheeler?"

He nods but fidgets like he is not entirely comfortable. As he follows them to a table near the kitchen, away from the other patrons, Jake announces, "My aunt ain't coming. She's really not involved, and I'd appreciate it if you wouldn't contact her again. She gets all emotional about stuff she can't do nothin' about. Your call really upset her, and that's partly why I came—'cuz I figured you'd just keep botherin' her."

"Look, I'm sorry about that," Steve replies, "but there're some real problems with how factory chicken farming is taking over this entire area. If no one says anything about it, nothing will ever change. And why are you so afraid of coming forward? Has someone threatened you in any way?"

"Hey, that's my affair. I don't know as I can trust you, and I sure don't trust the government to do anything 'bout it. But I know you're right. The problem is like it always is. The big guys call the shots and give money to the politicians to make sure they look the other way. Otherwise, some of their laws woulda changed by now. There's all kinds of rules on the books about how we're supposed to deal with the litter, but there's even more pressure to raise as many birds as we can, fatten 'em up as quick as we can so's they cain't hardly stand up on their own, and then git 'em to the broiler houses as young as possible. The biggest problem is the waste. I get fined if I go over my limits and get found out. I contract with LaLue, and they do have a composting facility nearby, but it ain't enough."

"I heard rumors you guys are getting a lot of pressure from some of the ag inspectors. Is that right? Are they harassing you?" Steve stares straight into Jake's eyes when he asks this question. Given the look on Jake's face, it's obvious that Steve has hit a nerve.

"Who the hell told you that?" he shoots back, his eyes ablaze. "Why would you even bring that up? I ain't never made no complaints!"

Both Steve and Margot remain silent, and then Steve looks at her and nods.

"Your aunt told me, only she thought I was someone else. I played along, so please don't blame her. But there is no way anything will ever change unless someone is brave enough to come forward."

"What the.... When did this happen? She goes running her mouth and blabbing stuff that's gonna get us in a heap of trouble. That's why I didn't want her to come with me today."

"She thought I was a friend of your daughter's from school, and I let her believe it. She's upset that your daughter and other girls are apparently being harassed."

Clearly, Jake is furious and scared. "Look. Ain't none of your business! You got no idea what goes on, and I'm just tryin' to survive best I can. I got to feed my family and protect 'em. It's gettin' harder and harder to do. Now I'm gonna walk out that door, and if you ever try to contact me or Aunt Ruby again, I'll go to the police!" He starts to get up, but Steve grabs hold of his arm.

"No, you won't because that would open up the whole can of worms, and you wouldn't be able to control what happens next. As I've already said, we're not here to do anything that might harm you or your family. On the contrary, I want to help you. If your daughter is being harassed to get to you, don't you think someone has to try to put a stop to it? Even if you're going over your waste limits, that still doesn't give some asshole the right to threaten you and your family. And I'll bet you aren't the only one. It's your choice, but I don't see how you're going to solve this on your own." Steve lets go of Jake's sleeve. Jake glares at him with a horrified look, then hurries away.

Margot can't help herself; as disappointed as they both are, she says, "That went well!"

Steve cracks a sardonic smile. "I think this isn't the last we'll hear from Jake Wheeler. Let's grab a quick bite and then get going. I'll drop you off at the Sinclair's, and then I have to go back to Baltimore."

Margot and Steve both feel deflated during the drive back as they each retreat into their protective bubble of silence. Margot glances dolefully back at him when he drops her off, then walks slowly toward the guest house.

Margot promised herself that on her return, she would delve into the tedious process of signing up for an online class, yet to be determined and then to do some research on what criteria she should prioritize when buying a pre-owned car. Instead, Margot is slowly beginning to recognize that, despite her letdown from Steve's rejection, somewhere in all this, a breakthrough is becoming apparent. As disheartening as it was with Steve yesterday, Margot dares to believe she is entering a new phase of how she views men and sex; that some decent men don't jump at the chance to take advantage of a confused teenager, one who could have easily been persuaded to go along.

Although she isn't ready to discuss any of the events leading to these profound insights, Margot emails Sarah.

Hey, Sis, how's it going? God, I wish you were here! I have so many emotions spinning around in my head and heart right now, and all my attempts at cold reasoning aren't getting me anywhere! Instead, I'm inclined to follow my intuition, loosen up a bit and be more impulsive, like you. It's scary as hell. Oh, and btw, Mom is coming to Annapolis on Friday to take me to lunch! It feels like a set-up, but maybe she just misses us both. Gros bisous, Lots of kisses, Margot.

17

DISCOVERIES

Late July—Mervilla, France

Sarah and Sophie have been frequently in touch and have become good friends, as if they've known each other since childhood. Sarah recounted her trip to Ghana, although not all the details concerning Daren. In the fall, Sophie will be starting her second year at Jean-Jaurès University, studying hotel and restaurant management. If Sarah remains in France, she will already have a friend who can help her as she tackles the difficulties of attending college-level classes in another language.

Sarah would like to return to the gallery in Old Toulouse, where she saw the painting on Bastille Day, and the girls have planned to meet there later today. Sarah has developed an emotional connection to the young woman in the painting upstairs, whom she visits regularly. She is curious to know more about the origin of the painting since she is convinced that the artist or the model is related to her.

Sarah plans to visit Marie-Laure later at the hospital, but first, she heads into town to meet up with Sophie. She loves exploring Old Toulouse's pedestrian streets, with eclectic little shops and restaurants. After finally securing a parking space on the lowest level of the nearest parking structure, she makes her way to the address of the shop she noted when she discovered the painting in their window on Bastille Day.

Sophie is there waiting and greets Sarah with a beaming smile and a double kiss on either cheek. As they turn toward the shop window, however, Sarah notices that the painting is no longer there, and the door is locked. They decide to grab a coffee nearby, as she tells Sophie about the portrait at home and why she is anxious to know what has become of the one she had seen there on display.

When they return, the owner is unlocking the door, and he switches the 'Closed' sign around, then inquires how he could help them.

"I happened to see a painting in the window of your shop about a month ago, and I'm interested in buying it," Sarah lies with a sincere smile. "It's a portrait of a young woman who looks exactly like the one in another painting at my cousin's, and I wanted to offer it to her as a gift. The one at home is signed S.A."

"So sorry, but that piece was sold just last week."

"Oh," Sarah utters, her eyes searching desperately around the gallery as if she could somehow conjure up the missing canvas. "I think my family might be related to the artist. Our surname is Aubert."

"Well, yes, that is possible, although Aubert is not an uncommon name. That painting is a self-portrait by Suzanne Aubert. She was a model and mistress of Yann Bayard from Montauban, who rose to prominence in this region between the two World Wars. She took up painting under Bayard's tutelage and produced a small but interesting body of work. Her art didn't sell much at the time. When Bayard denied he was the father of her child and moved on, Suzanne became destitute and was eventually committed to an institution. There has been some recent interest in her work, but I don't know where you can find any more of it."

"Oh," Sarah says again, focusing her disappointment on the gallery owner. "That's such a tragic story. Is there any chance you could tell me who purchased the piece? Perhaps he or she could help me find more of Suzanne's work."

"No, I'm sorry I am unable to share that information. If I can't be of any more help, please excuse me. I have an exhibit to prepare."

"Yes, I understand. Just one more question, if you please. Do you know what became of her child?"

"The artists' rumor mill has it that she gave birth to a daughter somewhere near Montaubon and that when Suzanne was committed to an institution, the child was sent to an orphanage run by Carmelite nuns. I don't know anything about your inquiry beyond that."

"Not even a name?"

"You might be able to find a reference if you research the life of Yann Bayard. Good luck, Miss."

"Yann Bayard!" exclaimed Sophie as they left the shop. "That's amazing! We have a number of his paintings at the house, mostly landscapes, though. My mother loves his work, and I think her grandmother or a great aunt was a student of his. Do you think you could be related to his model?"

Sophie is excited that she and Sarah might have this connection. Sarah can't help noticing again how beautiful she is. Sophie's blue eyes are as round as marbles, her shiny, blonde hair dappled by the sun that is filtering through the plane trees that line the street as they make their way toward the parking lot. Yet despite her exceptional looks and her privileged family, Sarah senses that Sophie is lonely.

"It's lucky for both of us that we've met," she gushes as they prepare to part ways. "I'm going to talk to Mother and set a day for you to come over for dinner. We can look at all the artwork throughout the house if you're interested."

"That sounds like a wonderful plan," Sarah replies, "My cousin, Marie-Laure, was an art-history professor at Jean-Jaurès before she retired. Maybe she would allow me to bring Suzanne Aubert's self-portrait, and I'd love to show it to your mother. Right now, though, I have to leave for the hospital. Call me!"

• • •

"Ah, my favorite cousin!" Marie-Laure exclaims as Sarah enters her room.

"You look so much better than even twenty-four hours ago," Sarah remarks as she bends over the chair where Marie-Laure is sitting and plants the requisite number of kisses on her plump cheeks. This ritual is becoming automatic, Sarah observes with some pride.

"I do feel so much better, and I'm looking forward to getting out of here and starting rehab. How are things working out between you and Bernard these days? You haven't mentioned him recently."

"That's because he took part of the week off to visit his grandmother. But he'll be back tomorrow. I've been doing fine on my own, but I am looking forward to having him around again. He sure has been a help to me, and in more ways than just mucking out the chicken coop."

"Really. How so?" Marie-Laure acts somewhat surprised, although Sarah suspects she really isn't.

"Well, I've never known anyone like Bernard with a background that, on the surface, seems so different from my own. It turns out, though, he and I have more in common than I thought."

"Such as...?"

"Such as..." Sarah hesitates as she tries to articulate what their commonalities might be. "I guess it's hard to put into words. I feel a connection that I hope isn't based on pity because he doesn't have many of the same options. Maybe I feel sorry for him, as opposed to feeling like we are on the same level. That's pretty lame, isn't it?"

"No, Sarah, that's not lame unless you treat him as somehow less than... I think your willingness to work with him linguistically and to receive something from him in return is enough to have brought you together as friends."

"Yeah! You're right. I just wish we could talk about other things."

"Have you tried? Even though he's shy around people he doesn't know, I'm pretty sure by now you can talk to him in French about anything you want. And maybe he has a wider vocabulary in English than you think. If not, he would probably welcome speaking in French to you about whatever you ask him. Perhaps he would like to think he's helped you linguistically this summer as well."

Sarah glances at Marie-Laure, then looks down at her lap in shame. "Maybe I have been treating Bernard like a dolt all this time. OMG, what a snob he must think I am."

"Are you still in touch with those girls you met in Carcassonne?" Marie-Laure is kind enough to change the subject. "You haven't mentioned them recently either."

"I don't know about the other two, but I've become good friends with one whose name is Sophie Delacourt. Her parents have a vineyard not too far from Castelnaudary. They live in an old chateau, where the coach house and stables have been converted into a boutique hotel. We met today for coffee in Old Toulouse just before coming here. She said she's going to invite me to dinner sometime soon. Her great-grandmother may have studied art with Yann Bayard. They have quite a few of his landscapes, and her mother may know something about Suzanne Aubert. I was cleaning upstairs last week and saw the portrait signed S.A. in the other guest room."

"What did you think of it?" Marie-Laure inquires as if she expected Sarah to discover it sooner or later.

"I'm fascinated by it. The model appears so dejected, like she was about to collapse from something that would tear her apart. I wish I could know what that was. Are we related to her?"

"Yes, she was my grandfather's first cousin. She died just after the war ended. Apparently, she left behind a daughter, who might have been adopted by one of her uncles. There was so much chaos and lack of even the bare necessities in some areas that no one I know in the family ever tried to follow up."

• • •

For the past week, a harsh, dusty wind called *le vent d'autan* has been blowing up from the Mediterranean toward Toulouse. It can blow laundry clean off the clotheslines and supposedly makes everyone feel irritable.

Coincidentally, Sarah has been waking up every morning

feeling queasy, but she doubts it's because of the weather. Marie-Laure is supposed to come home from rehab later in the week, and Sarah keeps hoping that her symptoms will pass so she can get on with straightening up the house and going grocery shopping.

This morning, Bernard returned to his regular chores, but Sarah didn't feel well enough to do any language work today. His comprehension has improved, and she doesn't want to let their regular conversations lag too much for fear he will forget some of the vocabulary he has acquired. But for now, she's just trying to get through the day.

Meanwhile, the strong and steady wind has blown itself out, and cumulus clouds approach Mervilla from the west. The radio predicts an almost 100 percent chance of strong storms by tomorrow afternoon. Sarah remembers the day she left for Ghana, dancing around the driveway in the middle of another gusty thunderstorm. She was so excited, knowing she was about to be liberated from a summer of work and basketball, that she couldn't contain herself.

Now, two-plus months later, that day seems like it happened ages ago, almost to another person. In retrospect, she realizes she has changed for the better, as she has embraced a different culture and lifestyle that has helped her put her turbulent summer in perspective. At the same time, she fears that the carefree, risk-taking part of being young is slipping away much faster than she had anticipated.

When Sarah awakes early the following morning, she is so nauseous that she can't set foot in the kitchen without feeling like she might puke. She is supposed to pick up Marie-Laure from rehab later and bring her home, but instead, she calls her to tell her she seems to be in the throes of a stomach virus.

"I'm so sorry to hear this, Sarah. I'm sure Jean will be happy to be my taxi, and hopefully, he will be able to stay at the house until you feel better. Just go to bed, rest, and don't worry about anything. And anyway, I'm not an invalid anymore."

"I know, but I wanted to make sure everything was okay before you came back," Sarah manages to choke out between sobs.

Then, she hangs up. Her head is pounding, and she can't seem to stop crying. Why would I be having a meltdown now unless I'm very sick? she worries. She wanders into the kitchen, wanting to make herself a cup of tea to take up to her room. As she starts the electric kettle, a wave of nausea hits her so hard that she barely makes it to the toilet before the heaves overcome her.

Once it passes, Sarah staggers upstairs, closes the door and drops into bed. She falls back to sleep and feels much better when she awakes. Sarah hopes that whatever the illness, it has finally run its course. But suddenly, she starts to think—I never got my period this month, and my last period was in Ghana. Holy, holy, holy fuck. Could I be preggo? She desperately tries to calculate when that period was before she and Daren had sex together at the lake. Definitely, not enough time to have been ovulating that day! she concludes, but then doubts flood back. Oh, shit, but what if…what if?

She climbs out of bed and opens the shutters. The sky is beginning to bubble with storm clouds. Some are so dark they look like they were injected with ink. The wind has picked up, pushing the leading edge of a storm fast toward Mervilla. Sarah wonders if Bernard ever showed up today and if the animals have been cared for. She throws on her robe and runs outside to see if he is around, but she can't find him anywhere. She calls him on his cell phone, and, when he doesn't answer, she leaves a message: "If you haven't left home yet, better not come today."

Sarah notices that the dogs are pacing around and panting, but they'll take shelter under the shed as soon as it starts to rain. She heads toward the chicken coop to ensure there is enough food until tomorrow, gathering up today's eggs. She also wants to check on Charlotte. I'm worried about a blinding storm and Marie-Laure coming home in the middle of it. I'm worried Bernard could be on his way and get caught in a downpour. OMG! I'm turning into Margot!

Within the time it takes her to check on all the animals, a series of lightning bolts cuts through the air, followed by loud claps of thunder. Sarah rushes back inside the house moments before hail starts to pop off the roof tiles and against the windows. She hurries around the house, trying to close all the shutters as heavy rain and hailstones as big as marbles slap against her face and arms. Marie-Laure calls to say she and Jean are on their way, but they've had to pull off the road for now.

A few minutes later, she hears a hard knock at the front door. Bernard and his bicycle appear to have crossed a lake. Sarah helps him and the bicycle into the house, then shuts and locks the door. A puddle forms around him within seconds and spreads across the floor.

"Oh, Bernard, you're soaked! Hey, you and I are almost the same size. I'll get you some jeans and a sweatshirt." He frowns at the idea but still follows her upstairs. Sarah grabs a towel from the hall closet and hands him some dry clothes.

Bernard soon joins Sarah in the kitchen when suddenly they see a wide streak of lightning right in front of the window, followed by a loud crack and then the explosive impact of breaking glass. The noise seems to be coming from the bedroom upstairs at the end of the hall. A poplar tree has been struck by lightning, and a large limb has fallen against the window, shattering the glass. Branches from the tree push through a gaping hole as rainwater and debris scatter over the floor. Sarah and Bernard rush downstairs to find rags and more towels when the doorbell rings.

"*Et merde*," Sarah shouts out loud, "Marie-Laure must not have her key."

She almost reaches the front door when the lock turns, and Jean pushes it open, ushering Marie-Laure into the foyer.

"Oh my God," she groans as she removes her sopping jacket. "It's a mess out there. Trees are down, and these back roads are flooding everywhere."

Sarah grabs Marie-Laure and gives her an emotional hug, and hands them each a dry towel. Then she takes Mari-Laure and Jean upstairs to see for themselves the damage the storm has caused. She feels somehow responsible since she hadn't managed to close the shutters in this room before the tree fell.

By some miracle, they never lose electricity, and, in the time it takes Marie-Laure and Jean to change into dry clothing, the storm has mostly abated.

Sarah wonders if any plants are still standing upright in the garden and how the animals weathered the storm. But regardless of the outcome, she knows that she cannot change anything. A searing pain rises through Sarah's chest and into her throat as she's confronted by a strong urge to open the front door and run as far and as fast as she can. Instead, she releases the shutters in the living room and peers outside. The light of the full moon has just begun to penetrate the few remaining storm clouds. Soon, a steadier glow illuminates the summer night as Sarah opens the front door and steps outside, followed by Marie-Laure, Jean, and finally Bernard. They crowd together on the narrow stoop and watch the moon sail free of the clouds into her own space.

"*Regardez la belle lune.*" Marie-Laure whispers. Look at the beautiful moon.

She glances back at Sarah, who weakly returns her smile. There's a hole in the house and a hole in Sarah's heart as she contemplates what she will have to face if she's pregnant. She stares up again at the sky, watching the moon weave in and out of the thinning clouds, casting a pearly glow through the silhouettes of the backlit trees. Witnessing the moon continue to rise has captivated Sarah's attention, and she breathes deeply into a momentary harbor of serenity, reassured that everyone is safe and that they are all here together, caring for one another, just like family.

18

STEPPING UP TO THE PLATE

Late July—Gaithersburg, Maryland; Washington, DC

When Abby and Margot meet for lunch on Friday, both women are jittery. At first, neither wants to look directly at the other, and they both shy away from anything but the most mundane of small talk. Abby orders a glass of wine, and only after a long drink does she try to establish eye contact with her daughter.

Margot does her best to avoid her mother's stare. She senses that whatever she has to say will put Margot at a disadvantage. It doesn't take long for her to suspect that Abby has rummaged through her room and found her journal from 2014. Margot surmises that her mother now knows what happened to her but isn't sure who the perpetrator could have been, since she only referred to David as 'He.' Unless Mom searched the house and found the box in the attic. In my first entry, I called out David by name. Holy shit! I'll bet that's it! And if so, I'm furious—this would be a new low, even for Mom!

As if Abby could penetrate not just Margot's past secrets but also her current thoughts, she blurts out, "I don't know how else to say this, Margot, but I found one of your journals straightening up your bedroom after you left and then the others in the attic. I know what you thought happened to you that Passover with David."

"What do you mean, *thought*? If you have violated my privacy enough to read all my diaries, how can you possibly believe that I made up any of it? He abused me, but I was too young at the time to realize it. I was terrified, and worse, I believed it was somehow my fault!" Tears flood down Margot's cheeks as she buries her head in her hands.

"Please try to get ahold of yourself. Something may have happened, but surely David didn't do anything so drastic that you could call it abuse. Given your age and the fact that he was married with kids, I simply can't imagine that he would want to risk all that by futzing around with a thirteen-year-old. You were barely mature enough to have anything he might have wanted."

Margot reaches for her purse and then leaves the table for the restroom as the waitress approaches. She runs cold water over a handful of paper towels and plasters them to her red, swollen eyes. No way am I going back in there, Margot vows. She eventually exits the bathroom and walks hurriedly toward the door when her mother stands up and catches her arm.

"Please, Margot. I'm sorry. I didn't mean to be so harsh, and you're right. I can't protect David and pretend nothing happened. We need to talk about this, just the two of us."

"Reread my journals first, and then we'll see. I've tried so hard to work with this trauma all on my own. I never even told Sarah. I can't go through this anguish again right now." Margot fights back another rush of tears that prick her downcast eyes as she strides hurriedly through the door and disappears around the corner.

Abby pays and then leaves, both plates on the table still untouched. As Abby drives back toward the Beltway, she cannot process what has just happened. She's afraid of completely becoming overwhelmed with rage as she tries to come to terms with the probability that her brother did do something inappropriate to Margot. He has never had to account for any of his behavior since everyone in the family thinks of him as Mr. Perfect!

Abby remembers ruminating from time to time that throughout the four years of high school, Margot never talked about having a boyfriend or even showed much interest in dating. Both her parents just assumed she was too caught up in her studies, aiming to go to a prestigious college. It had even vaguely occurred to Abby that Margot might be gay.

When she arrives home, the first thing Abby wants to do is to pour herself a glass of wine and try to chill out on the back porch, focusing on the hydrangeas that are coming into bloom. As Abby is about to head out the kitchen door, the front hall phone rings. Abby is sure it's her mother since she is the only person who systematically calls on the landline. She would rather let the call go to the answering machine, but she reluctantly picks up.

"Hi, Mom. How are you? I've meant to call, but I've been very busy at work. I just got home. I've been trying to get in touch with David to see if he and I can come down together for Labor Day. I called him yesterday to talk about it, but he never answers his phone, and he hasn't called me back yet."

"Oh, for God's sake, Abigail. You know your brother is too busy to travel."

"He usually takes some time off around then. Labor Day

weekend should be good for him."

"Well, you'll see. I called because I wanted to tell you that Sarah rang me from France! You never told me she was in France!"

Despite a sharp stab of jealousy that Sarah hasn't spoken directly to her since she left, Abby manages to come up with an answer. "It was kind of last minute. Michel's cousin had back surgery, and Sarah offered to go and help her out."

"That's nice, but didn't she have a job this summer?"

"Just an internship. It ended."

Her mother quickly drops this line of conversation. "My friend, Irene Sobel, and I are getting tickets for a concert series at the Van Wezel. She's the only person I know who is still willing to drive at night."

"That's great, Mom. I'm glad you're getting out and doing things you and Dad used to enjoy together."

"I hope you never have to experience what it's like to lose your husband. But, yes, it will be lovely to attend live performances again of the beautiful music we both loved."

It occurs to Abby that if she never becomes a widow, it will be because she died first. "Mom, I've got to rush out to the store to pick up something for dinner. As soon as I speak to David, I'll call you back. It might not be until over the weekend, though. Love you. Bye."

"Bye, Dear. I love you, too."

This time, Abby can almost hear a smile in her voice, instead of the judgmental downbeat that often signals the end of their phone calls. Some guilt ruffles Abby's conscience since she just lied multiple times to her mother throughout a two-minute phone call. But now that she's committed to visiting her, she promises herself she will try to work something out with her brother.

Just thinking about David pulls Abby back into the emotional vortex concerning him and Margot that she had temporarily managed to set aside. She has no idea how she might approach her brother about what probably transpired between them five years ago. Yet, as a mother, she has no choice. Those noxious twin intruders, Shame and Guilt, surge once again through her body and form a clog in her chest around her heart.

• • •

When Abby was hired into the law firm where she currently works, she decided to job-share, purposely keeping a fairly low profile, researching and writing reports and briefs. However, after returning to the office in July, Abby spoke to her supervisor, Jim Lerner, about becoming more directly involved with the firm's clients. He assigned her to his team, working with Ayer Homes, a privately owned development company that plans to build a subdivision of 1,000 townhouses in Frederick County, Maryland, along the Monocacy River.

Too many businesses expose themselves to lawsuits due to overreach or deliberately sidestepping State and local regulations. Ayer Homes hired the firm of Harris, Quincy, & Golden as advisers concerning the environmental aspects of their enterprise to avoid legal challenges as the project advanced. Abby is now tasked with reviewing Ayer's ambitious operation, including hiring practices, third-party contracts, and marketing materials, and will present at their next meeting.

The Clean Water Action Project has cited The Monocacy, the largest tributary to the Potomac River, as one of the most polluted rivers in Maryland. Despite this worsening situation, landowners whose property abuts the river are fighting to stop the City of Frederick from creating a 300-foot buffer zone, preventing any building or agricultural activity within that space. Ayer Homes has already agreed to respect the proposed limits. However, the scope of their project would still endanger the waterways due to runoff from construction, increased traffic, and the long-term use of herbicides and pesticides. Most of Ayer's permits have already been approved, but some Frederick officials and outside environmental organizations have expressed concern over the scope of their plans.

These issues will be discussed in a future meeting with Charles Ayer and his staff to convince them to reduce their footprint. Ayer's attorney, Roger Norton, of Chisholm, Bristol, & Norton (CB&N), has informed Jim that he will push Ayer to double down and not accept any modifications to their original business plan.

Abby is painfully aware of CB&Ns image as very WASPy, very conservative. Their tentacles are in all types of businesses throughout the DC area, and their reputation is to push their clients to skirt as many regulations as possible. They despise Obama's environmental programs, executive orders, and the EPA's tighter regulations.

Abby is very concerned because climate change is happening—as well as run-away development, factory farming, and increasing air and water pollution. In Maryland, most voters approve and re-elect candidates supportive of a cleaner environment regardless of party, and, according to polling, much of Ayer's client demographic also supports environmentally friendly construction practices. Abby hopes to persuade the

Ayer group that building green is a critical piece for the success of their venture.

Meanwhile, Abby spends the rest of the day developing the talking points for her presentation. She's seen the mock-ups of Ayer Homes' marketing campaign, including the images for the website of young professionals of various ethnicities standing in front of brand new, faux-colonial townhouses or participating in outdoor activities in a rural setting with the easternmost foothills of the Blue Ridge mountains far in the background. Words describing respect for the environment abound. All this material hopefully reflects Ayer's true desire to preserve the natural surroundings by agreeing to reduce the number of units Ayer will build.

• • •

When she awakes Wednesday morning, Abby feels optimistic. She arrives at the office a little sweaty but soon cools down inside the chilly conference room. About twenty minutes later, Charles Ayer enters with his VP, his head attorney, Roger Norton, the firm's accountant, Leonard Costa, and Anthony Pierson, the architect. Abby is delighted to see that the VP is an African American woman, Ingrid Jameson. She is tall, full-figured, and impeccably dressed. A pair of large, hammered-silver earrings draw attention to her probing eyes and inviting smile. Abby breathes a sigh of relief as she immediately senses that Ingrid could be a supportive player as they try to persuade Ayer to modify his ambitions.

Abby's boss, Jim, begins the meeting by summarizing the most important issues to be discussed. Then he introduces Abigail, who turns toward Charles Ayer and to Ingrid as she starts her talk.

"I want to assure you that as clients, our team will do all we can to promote a version of the project that safely remains within the boundaries of the laws. Building near the City of Frederick is a good choice, given your target customer base, many of whom work down I-270 near Rockville or off I-70 in and around Baltimore. These two cities form a triangle with Frederick that makes the area a perfect place for families to live who may find it harder to afford this type of housing nearer to their workplace or who purposely choose to live closer to nature.

"On your website and in all of your marketing materials, you refer to the surrounding countryside, with mountains to the west and various local waterways that provide beauty and recreation, further enhancing the desirability of moving into your subdivision. However, 1,000 units in these surroundings are not only destructive to the environment in terms of how many trees and natural habitats will have to be destroyed, but in my view, a community of this magnitude contradicts the impression you profess to create. As your environmental consultants, we highly urge you to consider reducing the number of units from 1000 to a number closer to 750."

Abby flashes her most radiant smile at Ingrid as she sits down. Everyone remains silent for a few moments. Then, Roger stands up and trumpets dismissively that any change of plans is out of the question. "They can say whatever they want, Charles, but in the end, none of them have a legal leg to stand on since your permits have already been approved. We should leave now and forget all this BS about some pretty pictures in a brochure."

Then Charles speaks. He understands both sides of the argument, but he is almost ready to break ground. "Why didn't the county and the state bring this up before?" he grumbles.

Both Jim and Abby acknowledge his point. However, Jim alerts Charles again that several organizations are ready to launch lawsuits, like the CBLAC and possibly the State of Maryland, although it granted some of the permits only a few months ago. Should they go forward, these suits will be costly and could tie up the entire project far beyond Ayer's target groundbreaking date. By then, the state will surely up the ante concerning the company's responsibility for runoff, and the county could propose more onerous building restrictions than simply a 300-foot buffer zone.

"I'd like to express my opinion, Charles," Ingrid says. "I think Abigail and Jim have raised some good points that bear discussing back at the office. Instead of building 1,000 units, we build fewer and use the additional land for recreational purposes, adding value to the entire project. We might even be able to charge more per unit and come out ahead."

Tony Pierson echoes what Ingrid has proposed. "Since we haven't begun any digging, we can rework the underground portion of the plans and then see how to arrange the units. Having more green space would certainly enhance the overall appeal, given the surroundings, and Ingrid knows how I feel about that."

"Those are very good ideas," chimes in the accountant, Leonard Costa, who, until now, has kept a low profile. "We need to put all the numbers into the spreadsheet again and see what we get. But provoking a multi-pronged lawsuit in a state like Maryland that keeps adding new water protection laws to the books every year is not fiscally advisable, in my opinion."

"Okay, then," Charles replies as he rises to leave and extends his hand to Jim and then to Abby. "We have our work cut out for us. I'm a businessman, and I don't want to piss people off who could make my life difficult and end up turning my customers against me. But I'm not a nonprofit, either. Let's go back and rerun the numbers. I'll be in touch when I've made a decision."

And with that, he strides out of the room. As Ingrid prepares to follow him out, she extends her hand to Jim and Abby, giving hers an extra squeeze. Is she letting me know she is on our side? Abby speculates. If so, it's because it makes good business sense first and foremost. And then, hopefully, it's also because Ingrid wants Ayer Homes to be on the right side of a growing consensus that taking steps now to mitigate climate change could avert irreparable harm later and especially ward off the delays and hassles from lawsuits that could eventually sink the entire project.

19

SITTING ON THE BENCH

Mid-August, Annapolis, Maryland

August is half gone, and Margot has not yet signed up for a class or seriously looked into buying a car. She feels stuck. Every time she has tried to piece together the puzzle of what should come next, a tightness in her chest and shortness of breath causes a bout of anxiety.

Maybe Jillian and Steve were wrong about me, Margot speculates, and my sense of determination was only a fleeting burst of enthusiasm, wanting others to think well of me. Margot is vaguely aware that she'll miss the signup deadline for classes if she doesn't act soon. She vows that if nothing else, she'll take care of it today, but right now, she wants to nap.

She lays down on the couch but is unable to sleep. Finally, she gives up and goes into the kitchen, sits at the counter, and opens her laptop. She logs onto the University of Maryland website and types in 'General Studies, year 2'. In addition to the requisite STEM subjects, she notes classes in professional writing, analytical reasoning, and oral communication.

Margot's eyes brighten, and a semi-smile animates her

otherwise dejected expression. No matter what she will do later in life, these classes offer training in skills she will need. She begins the process by tackling the tedious admin forms she has to fill out. But first, she submits a request from Georgetown to send her transcripts to the UMUC admissions office. Forty-five minutes later, she has finished filling out all the forms. Satisfied that she has completed a process that she's been resisting, Margot lays down on the couch, and this time she does fall asleep.

Scarcely an hour later, her cell phone rings, jarring her awake. Steve has left a message that he will stay in Baltimore overnight and will check in with her tomorrow. For now, nothing more seems to be happening, after all that driving back and forth to Somerset County. And Steve…he is so far out of reach for her in the way she would like. Her first serious desire to become intimate with a man has fizzled from rejection, and that part was even more painful than the fear of becoming involved in the first place. She has the impression that now she's bumping up against a locked door to which she will never have the key.

Margot slips on her flip-flops and heads for the beach behind Sinclair's property that has become her go-to place when she's in the throes of some depression. She ambles along the sandy shoreline between the calm water and that fearfully chaotic and frustrating place called the Outside World. The lapping of the wavelets and the glow on the wet sand from the receding sun are soothing and reassuring. This endless natural cycle of time and the tides reminds her that, although most people seem resigned to the cliché that life is short, it can stretch out to feel quite lengthy when lived one day at a time. She's not even twenty, so time is reassuringly on her side. She inhales a long breath of air, warm from the August sun, damp and tangy.

I wish Sarah was here with me right now, Margot sighs wistfully. As she climbs the incline up from the beach toward the house, she tries to imagine Sarah at Marie-Laure's, speaking fluent French, taking care of a goat and chickens. She thinks of Sarah as the twin who always appeared to float on a cloud of insouciance. Margot is the one who worries about how her actions might affect others, especially their parents. Now the tables have turned. Sarah has become the do-gooder, and Margot wants to run off-leash until she collides with a surge of motivation and purpose that will shake her to her core.

• • •

Steve and Margot are planning to try again with Jake Wheeler and are willing to return to Somerset County if need be. Meanwhile, they see less of each other, and Margot speculates that this is partly due to her gloomy outlook. She is struggling with a sense of isolation—not truly part of the organization she works for and unable to meet new people, especially without a car. She spends some time searching online again at the local car dealerships. A 2009 Toyota Corolla with 70,000 miles is more than $10,000, and the price rises to over $12,000 for a slightly newer Honda Civic with lower mileage.

She rethinks the car solution by trying to find a sell-by-owner deal, but she's afraid of being a victim of price-gouging because she's a young woman who knows virtually nothing about automobiles. She would like Steve to help her, but she doesn't want him to feel obligated. In the end, she decides to text him about it anyway, since he can always decline. To her surprise, he responds right away that he would be happy to help her find a car, which is the best news Margot's has had about anything in a week!

Fifteen minutes later, her phone jingles. It's Steve. "Hey, my Friend, what are you doing right now?"

"I'm still looking up used cars online. What about you? Where are you? I can hear road noise in the background."

"I'm on my way back from Baltimore. You'll never guess who called me as I was leaving."

"Jake?"

"You're close, but no. It was Ruby who wanted to talk to you but wouldn't tell me anything. She's probably got a good heart under all that toughness, but she's unbelievably suspicious and extremely stubborn. Here's her number. Got something to write with? 443-555-6721. Now you can deal with her. I think something else is going on besides Jake being threatened with some reprisal from this ag guy, Jerry. She wouldn't tell me his last name. Maybe she doesn't know herself. But regardless—for her to reach out to us—it has to be something that's frightened her."

"Wow! Let me collect my thoughts, and I'll give her a call. Meanwhile, I want to thank you for offering to help me find a car. All that research about make, and mileage, and year, but once I looked them up online, they're all over 10K at a dealers."

"That's because Annapolis is expensive. I'll look for you in the Baltimore area. It's not that far, and there are potentially a lot more offers there than near you."

"Okay, good idea. Thanks."

Margot knows her parents are willing to help her buy a car, and she is very grateful for their support. She realizes that many young adults her age don't have anyone to help them, and they have to make it all happen independently. This insight strikes Margot that, when that time comes, one isn't a kid anymore. She is also aware that how well each person deals with finally taking full responsibility for one's life determines how that life is likely to turn out.

It's like learning to ride a bike without training wheels or swimming without water wings, she imagines, although these are weak similes. Right now, she's not convinced that she has even managed to climb the ladder up to the level of the high diving board, much less summon enough courage to jump off.

20

EXPECT THE UNEXPECTED

Mid-August—Mervilla, France

It's been over a week since the big storm, with all the damage it caused. The debris has been cleaned up, the window replaced, and the tree cut back. Yet Sarah's life has not returned to normal; she has come to the unavoidable conclusion that she is pregnant. Although she can't yet bring herself to share this news with anyone, having weathered the storm together with Bernard, Marie-Laure, and Jean was meaningful to her. She is confident that the four people closest to her, including Sophie, would be there for her if she asked any of them for their support. For now, she is determined to go on with her day-to-day routine as usual.

At the same time, Sarah can't escape a constant, gnawing feeling that sooner rather than later, she's going to have to tell Marie-Laure about her 'circumstances.' She's dreading the moment, though. Even if she could compose herself enough to bare her soul, Marie-Laure hasn't been very available. Sarah expected her to oversee the daily activities in her cheerful way without doing much work. Instead, she acts more like a casual observer—too subdued, distant, and detached.

After lunch, while Marie-Laure is still resting, Sarah finally summons the courage to go upstairs and knock at her closed door. Without waiting for her to answer, she gently pushes the door ajar and asks, "Is it alright if I came in?"

Marie-Laure sits up in bed and looks rather surprised. Her hair is disheveled, and she is only wearing a light dressing gown. "I'm sorry if I woke you," Sarah sheepishly says as she sinks into the slipper chair near the bed. "Since the storm, when Jean was here, and all the cleanup was taking place, I didn't have a chance to speak to you alone."

"My dear," Marie-Laure replies in a soft voice, but when she looks over at Sarah, her eyes are clouded, and her usually reassuring smile is nothing more than a strained line. "Part of my problem is to have discovered that I am not as strong a person as I thought. I expected to be more active by now, but I haven't felt up to it. And dealing with the aftermath of the storm has exhausted me. I feel quite vulnerable all of a sudden. But there it is, you know. We are all human, and pain can sometimes stir up a heap of negative feelings."

"I didn't realize you were in so much pain. Why didn't you say something?"

"Ah," she says as she swings her legs over the side of the bed and pushes herself up, "why didn't you look hard enough to notice?"

These past couple of weeks have been more difficult for Marie-Laure than Sarah anticipated. She realizes that because of trying to hide her symptoms and her growing sense of panic, she has focused primarily on her tasks rather than on Marie-Laure's needs—physical and otherwise.

Sarah knows that she can't say anything yet about her predicament that doesn't even seem real—not until she can tell someone. She wishes she could rush over to Marie-Laure and hug her, but by now, she's taken her clothes from the closet, gone into the bathroom, and shut the door.

"I'll just be downstairs," Sarah calls out to her. When Marie-Laure doesn't respond, she quietly leaves the room. The tears she was holding back now fill her eyes and cloud her vision, realizing that when Marie-Laure needed her the most, Sarah let her down.

Sarah accepts that she can't bring up her troubles until Marie-Laure feels stronger. She is also aware that in France, terminating a pregnancy is almost as easy as having a tooth pulled. At the very least, Sarah decides to consult with a local doctor to have all her questions answered and then make an informed decision. She assumes that she's about eight or nine weeks along.

She promises herself she will talk to Marie-Laure later in the day when they return from her physical therapy session. She's also tempted to email Daren before making any decisions, but she hasn't yet been able to bring herself to do so. She fears that her ability to control her situation could become more difficult if he, and especially his parents, got involved. And then there are her parents who keep asking her when she will come home. Her head tells her to end this pregnancy as soon as possible, but her heart isn't yet on the same page.

• • •

Sophie finally contacts Sarah and still wants to invite her and Marie-Laure to her home. Her parents, however, are extremely busy with the vineyard and the hotel during tourist season.

There's also the run-up to the *vendange*, grape harvesting, that takes place throughout September. But Sophie has spoken to her mother about Suzanne Aubert and has learned a few details about her that could help unravel the mystery of what might have become of her daughter.

Sarah is overjoyed to hear from her friend. Even though she lives far from Toulouse, while Marie-Laure will be in therapy today, Sophie suggests they meet at the same coffee shop as before near the art gallery.

Parking in this part of town is always a problem. The tangle of narrow one-way streets and pedestrian-only alleyways is charming when walking around window-shopping or stopping in one of the cafés, but today it takes Sarah more time to park than she had allowed. When she arrives at the coffee shop, Sophie is seated by the window. The fickle sunlight momentarily lights up her face with a wash of gold that causes Sarah to suck in her breath. Sophie rises out of her chair as they embrace.

"I'm so glad you could make it today, Sarah," Sophie says with some excitement in her voice. "I needed to come into town to register for classes. Have you been able to get your paperwork in order so you can apply to Uni as well? You still have time, but don't wait too long. I want to see you this fall. We can do so much together after classes. My parents have a *pied-à-terre*, a small apartment, not that far from here. You could spend the night sometimes."

"That sounds wonderful, but no, I still don't have all my documents together yet. It's complicated, and I'm not at all sure my parents will agree to let me stay." Sarah would love to have the trust in Sophie and the courage to blurt out that she is pregnant, that she can't imagine attending classes as her belly starts to look more and more like she swallowed a pillow. Instead, she promises Sophie to try and speed up the process.

"Well, get it together, Girl. You simply must stay here forever! Now, let me tell you what I found out about Suzanne Aubert and what might have happened to her baby. Susanne had a brother, Jacques, who was married and had an infant. But my mother remembers her great-aunt lamenting that this baby passed away when it was just a few months old. The two couples had met during the summer of 1944, at a hostel near La Montagne Noire, soon after Jacques' baby had died. That's why my mother remembers hearing about his family. Mother thinks it's probable that Jacques and his wife adopted Suzanne's baby in '45 or '46. She isn't positive, but she seems to recollect her mother telling her a similar story whenever anyone mentioned the War. The older folks talked about the War a lot. Even though this region wasn't part of Vichy France, everyone was traumatized by the scarcity of almost everything and the German soldiers who came this far south. So, isn't it great news? You can thank Mother when you meet her."

Sophie flashes Sarah a triumphant smile, her chin raised, as if she had just been named 'Most Valuable Friend of the Year.'

"Oh my God, that's fantastic! My cousin's boyfriend is into his own family's genealogy. Hopefully, he can help us find out more about that branch of our family. I can't wait to tell Marie-Laure. Surely, she knows something herself about Jacques Aubert.

Sarah glanced at her watch. "Oh, shit, I hate to do this to you, but I have to leave. I parked far from here, and, as it is, I'm going to be late picking up Marie-Laure from physical therapy."

"Wait two seconds. I'll pay, and then we can walk to your car together. I have the rest of the day to do what I need to do."

"*Tu es une vraie copine*! You're a true friend!"

It takes Sarah forever to exit the parking garage, and that and a buildup of traffic cause her to be more than a little late picking up Marie-Laure, who looks annoyed but doesn't say anything. Once more, Sarah decides to hang back bringing up little things, like being pregnant or inquiring about Suzanne Aubert. Even though she has very little money, she invites Marie-Laure to lunch instead.

"You've just spent the past month indoors except to sit in a lounge chair in your backyard. Let's go somewhere on the way home for lunch. My treat."

"Oh, Sarah, you don't have to do that. I know you didn't keep me waiting on purpose. I'm just tired and a little sore after the doctor made me twist and bend so much."

"No, it's not for that reason. Are you too uncomfortable to sit for a half-hour at a brasserie?"

"I guess I'm okay to do that. It would be nice to have a bite and to spend some time away from any medical place." She settles into the passenger seat, a smile tugging at her lips.

They drive south along La Rocade, a freeway that links two major highways on either side of Toulouse. Sarah takes the exit before the one for Mervilla, where there is a shopping mall and several free-standing restaurants.

As they enter a seafood place and are shown to a table, Marie-Laure remarks, "You seem preoccupied. Are you alright? I know having to manage everything has been hard on you, too, and I should be able to be of some help pretty soon."

"No, it's not that. It's me. I'm in some trouble, and I'm having a hard time dealing with it, much less being able to talk about it." Sarah is struggling to hold herself together, as she can feel the sting of tears building up, ready to fall.

"In trouble? What kind of trouble? How could you be in trouble?" Her soft, accepting expression changes to one of genuine concern. Sarah cannot hold back any longer as she buries her head in her hands and sobs.

Marie-Laure moves her chair over next to Sarah and puts her arms around her as best she can. "There, there, *Pitchoune*. It can't be that bad! Oh my God, is it news from home? Is some-one ill or something?"

"No! It's me. I'm pregnant! There! I said it!"

Getting it out in the open is like having a huge, foul tankful of anxiety crack and spill out onto the ground. Sarah suddenly stops crying, and her raspy breathing begins to slow. But then she looks at Marie-Laure, who has remained silent; her captivating blue eyes are turned down as if she can't bear to look at Sarah. "Have you told your parents?" she asks. Not, how far along are you? Who's the father? What are you planning to do about it?

"No, and I'm not going to. My parents would order me to come home, and I don't want to leave—if you will allow me to stay."

"Oh my God, Sarah. Of course, you can stay." Marie-Laure lifts her face and shines a loving smile at Sarah, who fills up with gratitude. "But when did all this happen? It's that boy in Ghana, Daren?"

"Yes, it is. He dumped me for a *man*, Marie-Laure, but his parents don't know. He would love for me to be pregnant, so he could convince them to believe that he's straight. Meanwhile, I guess I'm about eight or nine weeks along."

"And, of course, you haven't been to a doctor. I will make an appointment for you with Dr. Cohen in Saint-Agne. She's my regular doctor, and I think you'll like her as well."

"But Marie-Laure, I don't have any insurance or money except what little my parents send me. And besides, I'm not sure I'm going to go through with this pregnancy."

Another awkward silence follows as they both begin eating their food that arrived ten minutes ago. Then Marie-Laure puts down her fork and reaches across the table to take Sarah's hand. "That's your decision, but if you do decide to keep this baby, I will help you. Your parents would rightfully be very angry with me for this. But I hope you'll consider what I'm offering you, and when I say 'help,' I also mean financially."

"I think I am going to cry again! What did I ever do to deserve such kindness?"

"I have selfish reasons for wanting you to stay, and it gives me something to look forward to. And you! You can do so many things here. Look what you've done for Bernard. You have a natural ability to get along with people, and I could be wrong, but my instincts tell me that you would have more space here to explore your options than in Washington."

"But at some point, though, I'll have to go home. I can't run away from my family forever. I love it here—you know that, but I don't see how I'm going to be able to remain much longer. Every email I get from them contains some reference to when I plan to go back, not if."

'I'll call your father and talk to him about you staying on. I won't mention anything about the pregnancy. We can focus on getting your *carte d'identié*, national identity card, so you can sign up for health insurance and go to the university. Classes don't start until mid-October, and you have a lot of time to get your paperwork together. The school year is over in early May, and by then, your baby will be born. So many expectant mothers—whether it's school or work—accomplish whatever they set their mind to. Pregnancy is not a fatal disease, you know. Look, with any luck, you will have the baby over your spring break! Then, if you choose, you can do the second half of the academic year remotely."

Sarah starts to count out the months on her fingers—the start of summer to the start of spring. "Wait a minute—isn't the break in February? I'll look like a blimp by then, but I won't be due until March. And if I attend the second semester remotely, at least I won't go into labor in the middle of a class!"

21

BALANCING ACTS

Late August—Annapolis, Somerset County, Maryland

When Margot reports back to Steve, she tells him that all she could do about Ruby was to leave another message. He senses that she's going through some doldrums. "Ruby sounded anxious to speak to you," he says encouragingly. "There must be something new involving either Jake or Samantha, and she seems to trust you more than she does me."

Margot has never thought about any trust between her and Ruby Stiller. She never considered that her brief, sporadic contacts with Ruby amounted to anything more than a chance meeting and a couple of phone calls.

Steve tries to cheer Margot up by reassuring her that he's been looking online for cars and has located some interesting deals. He offers to pick her up on Saturday morning and take her to Baltimore to check them out.

This news helps lift Margot's spirits. After ending the call, she opens her laptop to answer some neglected emails when her phone rings. Since she doesn't immediately recognize the number, she almost lets the call go. Then she remembers Ruby.

"Hello. Margot speaking,"

"Uh, hi, it's Ruby Stiller. You tried to get hold of me?"

"Yes. Thanks for calling me back. I'm Steve Rich's assistant, and he told me you wanted to talk to me." Despite her earlier gloominess, new energy percolates as she speaks.

"Jake'ud kill me if he knew I'd be talking to ya. But I cain't just sit back and watch how Sam, my niece, Samantha, is being hit on by that Jerry person. Jerry Mercer's his name—the fellow. Sam come to me yesterd'y and told me he got something on her dad he should be telling his boss, but if she be 'nice,' he won't say nothin'. She's scared to death!

"He knows when she comes back from school or hockey practice and when Jake is away from the house. Sam told me that sometimes he puts his arm around her, and yesterd'y he kissed her on the mouth! She didn't think she had a right to stop him. Jake's around and all, but he says he ain't seen nothin', and Sam said her dad thinks she's makin' it up. That Jerry fellow, he be tellin' Jake, he's gonna have to report him if he keeps goin' over his dumpin' limits. He told him he'll keep quiet if Jake can keep him happy. I think Jake's givin' him money. I cain't go to the police or the ag department. Ain't nobody gonna believe me 'less I can get Sam to swear to somethin' on a Bible. But she said if her dad don't believe her, then who else will? You two are reporters, and I bet you hear stories and then have to see if they're true. I don't know where you live, but I want you to come down here and see if you can find out more about what's goin' on, so then you can tell about it, and people will believe you."

"I'm so sorry, Ms. Stiller. That's a really bad situation! Of course, we'll come down. But how are we going to be able to verify what you're telling me unless Samantha is willing to talk to us herself? I'd be very happy to meet her, but I'm not the one she should be telling. If her father won't believe her, what about her mother?"

"Her ma, Alice, split years ago. Even though Sam sees her regular, they ain't really that close. She don't got nobody but me to talk to. You the ones who's smart. I just thought you might be able to figure somethin' out."

"Yes, you're right. Totally. I'll call you back tomorrow. Ms. Stiller. We're going to do everything we can to help you, I promise."

"Okay, yeah. Goodbye."

Margot replays the conversation in her mind as she hurriedly taps Steve's number into her phone. When he answers, she gets right into it without even saying hello. "Ruby wants us to come down there and for me to somehow cozy up to Samantha—at least somehow gain her trust enough that she'll tell us what is going on with this guy, Jerry Mercer. Ruby said he keeps pushing her to do something with him, definitely sexual."

"Wow! Ruby's revelation is a huge deal for them and us."

"Apparently, Mercer now feels entitled to put his arm around Samantha and even kiss her. According to Ruby, he told Sam he wouldn't report her father for over-dumping if she's 'nice' to him. If what she's telling me is true, then he's potentially abusing a minor and demanding hush money from her father at the same time. Ruby doesn't think anyone will believe her or Sam, especially since Jake doesn't seem to take what she says all that seriously."

"Well, right now, it's a 'he-said-she said' kind of thing. What is needed first and foremost is documented proof!"

"Do you have any doubt that Samantha is telling the truth?

I'm sure Ruby wouldn't have called you in the first place if she didn't know it was true. Maybe Sam hasn't said anything about it until yesterday, but I think Ruby has seen them together and figured it out for herself."

"Yeah, you're probably right. But why would Samantha tell you instead of her parents? They're the ones who need to initiate some sort of action."

"Ruby told me her mother isn't in the picture anymore and that Jake won't challenge Mercer unless he witnesses something first hand. Maybe I do have something to contribute that you 'adults' don't quite get."

Steve doesn't quite understand what Margot is referring to, but if she can persuade Samantha to try and convince one of her parents to go to the authorities, that would be quite a breakthrough.

• • •

Two days pass before Margot and Ruby reconnect. They agree to meet the following week at Zeek's near Venton, where Margot and Steve met Jake in July. Ruby plans to bring Samantha to get acquainted with them both and to be assured that they are squarely on her side. They would like to have enough information to go on so they could reach out to other families who might have been exposed to the same type of harassment—sexual or otherwise. If so, Steve thinks he could convince his boss at *The Ledger* to bring this issue to light.

• • •

Steve picks Margot up on Saturday morning as promised for 'The Big Car Hunt.' He has lined up some appointments in Baltimore that sounded promising. In the end, however, they end up spending half the day going from one place to another, only to discover that, for the most part, these jalopies don't live up to what was advertised. They were all quite cheap compared to the *Blue Book* listings, but the adage, *you get what you pay for*, has certainly proven to be true today.

By 2:00, Margot is exhausted, frustrated, and on the verge of giving up.

Steve suggests they find a used-car dealer. Most of the cars they see there are newer and have less than 100,000 miles on the odometer, but they cost well over $10,000. By prodding the salesman, though, to recheck his inventory, he 'finds' a 2009 white Honda Civic with 120,000 miles that Steve can bargain down to just under $8,000. After setting up a loan and insurance from her father that she promises to pay back over time, Margot drives off the lot in her 'new' car.

• • •

Four days later, they arrive at Zeek's near Venton, taking the same table in the back where they had sat with Jake. When fifteen minutes go by, and Ruby doesn't show, Margot calls her.

"Yeah, yeah, I'm on my way. Tried to get Sam to come, but she won't. I ain't givin' up, though."

"Well, neither are we." Steve sees her dejection and knows at once the reason why.

Ruby starts talking even before she sits down. "Sam was very upset when I told her about you and how you might help her. She's so scared, and anyway, how you gonna prove anything about Mercer less you catch him in the act?"

Ruby looks at Margot as if for the first time. She lowers her eyes so as not to make contact, then glances over at Steve. But Ruby doesn't make the connection with the girl she saw at Swanson's.

They all sit silently for a while, as it has become obvious that the idea of convincing Sam to tell her story to a pair of strangers appears overwhelmingly unlikely. "Realistically, Ruby, is there any way Samantha will allow Margot into her life? Because without her cooperation, there isn't much we can do."

"That's just it. Samantha stays mostly to home when she ain't in school, playin' hockey, or goin' to church. She don't have a car, and she don't go nowhere on her own."

Margot steals a better look at Ruby, who reminds her of pictures she's seen in magazines of old women from the Andes with sunburned, wrinkled faces squashed in around a mouth shaped like an upside-down U. Ruby is a wiry, taut woman, undoubtedly been weathered by a difficult life. Margot admires her, though, for her devotion to her niece that has endowed her with a fierce determination to protect her like a mother bear.

"I ain't gonna give up," Ruby says emphatically. "Somethin' awful gonna happen if we don't stop it. I ain't gonna wait for *that* to happen to Sam."

They all know what she's referring to when she says that, but immediately, there doesn't seem to be anything Margot or Steve can do about it.

"We're going to try to find a way to help Samantha without making the situation worse," Steve tries to assure Ruby. "Now that we have a name, we can run a background check on this Jerry Mercer guy and see what comes up. Probably not the first time he's tried to abuse someone. Although I doubt the state would have hired him as an agricultural inspector if he had a record, he could be very good at hiding or dodging anything illegal."

Ruby agrees. "He knows 'zakly what he's doing when he come

buzzing 'round Sam. Thing is, he ain't never been caught before."

Ruby grabs her purse and starts to get up. "Well, don't be too long about it, 'cuz this son-of-a-bitch just lookin' for a way to do somethin' really bad to Sam." Then, she shows them her back and walks away.

Steve projects a depth of resignation that Margot hasn't seen in him before. "This situation is horrible, and I don't see how we can help unless Jake is told and is willing to cooperate, which is a case for law enforcement or at least for a private detective. I think that's the only way we can be of help. And at this stage, with no provable evidence, I can't imagine that *The Ledger* will get involved.

"Let's talk to Jillian when we get back. She, and her husband in particular, know many people in Maryland's political circles. Maybe they'll be able to hook us into another source of help. I'm afraid that what's happening right now is moving too fast and could get away from us before we even get started. But the bottom line is that we can't step back and do nothing! Sam is in real danger, and we can't undo what we know. Let's see what info we can find about Jerry Mercer now that we know his last name, although we aren't sure whether Jerry is a Jerome or a Jerold."

Steve takes her arm and leads her out of the diner as they continue to talk. Margot stops and takes a long look back at the people, mostly men gathered around the small tables and at the bar. She allows herself to imagine that everyone here is aware of this sleazy situation and has decided to do nothing. Because of her own experience and her urban, liberal, feminist prejudgments, outrage surges up in a whirl of bitterness, and Margot wants to scream obscenities at them all. As she gets into the car and leans over to buckle her seatbelt, she mutters,

"What if other people know about Sam and even other girls and don't think the hassle is worth getting involved? What if attitudes about men and girls and sex and entitlement were just so ingrained that they prefer to look the other way?"

Steve puts the car into park and looks sternly into her eyes, now swimming in tears. "If you're going to let your emotions get the better of you, you won't be able to assess the facts as they come out. I get what you're saying, and I'm pretty sure you're right to some extent. But we have to stay focused. We are journalists, and we cannot allow our preconceptions about what is or how things should be to determine the facts. If you think you can deal with that, we can work together on this. Otherwise, we can't."

Margot sucks in her breath as if she's just been punched in the solar plexus. Before she can stop herself, she blurts out, "I can't help putting myself in Sam's shoes. It's hit me at a deeper level how vulnerable she is."

For a moment, Steve stares into her eyes as if he detects something personal that she is holding back. Margot forces herself to hold his gaze, focusing on the flecks of gold that tint his eyes to a warm green.

After taking a deep breath, she says, "You're right. I know you're right. I'm good. I swear. I also know I am going to play a role in this, and when that time comes, I'll be ready."

22

CONNECTIONS

Late August to Early September—Mervilla, France

Marie-Laure has become a resourceful ally, trying to persuade Michel to allow Sarah to remain in France. She has half-convinced him that Sarah is still needed and will definitely apply to university. Sarah knows her father wants at least one of his girls to become bilingual, and this is her chance to make him proud. In addition to speaking and reading fluently in French, being truly bilingual includes knowing how to write correctly. Without being pushed and challenged, Sarah is certain she would never be motivated enough to learn the many verb tenses or remember the gender of all the nouns.

Sarah also wants to know more about cultural norms—why the French laugh at something she doesn't find funny and why shopkeepers call her out if she doesn't say "*Bonjour*" before asking for help. She's also eager to know more about her papa's ancestors with details on how they lived and loved and died.

Sarah sits outside, shading her eyes from the circle of weakening sunlight still hanging just above the trees. She's worried about what her parents will ultimately decide about letting her remain in France. Sarah is especially concerned about getting through this hassle of submitting her paperwork for an identity card and then applying to a university. It would be harder for her parents to order her back to the States if she could get past those two obstacles. But even that isn't as urgent as having to face the most important decision of her life. I'm not even out of my teens, and here I am with another human being growing in my body! Now, it's just a blob of cells, but if I decide to let it go, I need to do it soon. Or else I won't have the stomach for it. She almost laughs at the double meaning. If I do nothing, I will have a stomach because of it!

Sarah scans the landscape again, watching long, ultramarine shadows spread and darken as the sun slowly disappears behind the distant hilltops. She tends to become emotional witnessing the calm beauty of nightfall. Yes, it is repetitive, but each time is unique and beguiling. This daily cycle of light and darkness is completely indifferent to anything on Earth.

When Sarah reenters the house, Marie-Laure is puttering in the kitchen. "Jean is coming over later; can we stretch the evening meal for one more person?"

"Sure. We have a baguette in the freezer and plenty of cheese. Weren't we just planning to have some pasta with your wonderful pesto sauce?"

"I'll call Jean and tell him to bring a fruit pie. He can get a fresh baguette at the same time."

"That's so French," Sarah laughs. "None of you can bear to eat bread that isn't freshly baked unless it's for croutons or morning toast?"

"*Eh, oui. Tu commences à comprendre.*" Yes, you are beginning to catch on.

Sarah loves this ritual of making a big deal out of eating together. French meals are never a single course, and tonight there will be four—with different plates and perhaps more than one type of wine. They begin with cantaloupe fresh off the vine, cut into thick slices and wrapped in prosciutto, followed by the pasta dish, then cheese. More than an hour and a bottle of Gaillac later, they eat the pie that Jean brought. Sarah asks Marie-Laure about the Aubert family ancestors, but she passes that topic off to Jean, who offers to help her research the family tree.

While Sarah is clearing the table, Jean goes to his car and returns with a grocery bag that he presents to Marie-Laure. Inside is a flattish, rectangular something wrapped up in floral paper and tied with a ribbon.

"*Mon Dieu, Jean. Pour quelle occasion*?" My God, what's the occasion? Marie-Laure is surprised and very pleased.

"I saw this in town a couple of weeks ago and decided it had your name on it."

Marie-Laure takes her time removing the ribbon and opening the paper slowly as she peels back the wrapping. "It's a painting! What a surprise," she coos as she turns the frame over to reveal the image. She holds the canvas up and stares at it as if she were looking at herself in a mirror. Sarah can't see the image, sitting opposite her, but she watches excitedly as Marie-Laure's expression changes from delight to utter amazement.

"How did you ever find this? I had no idea another work by Suzanne even existed anymore. Look, Sarah. It's a self-portrait like the one I have upstairs by Suzanne Aubert!"

Sarah also experiences a jolt when Marie-Laure presents the painting to her. The one she had wanted to buy was purchased not by some stranger whom she could never track down but by

Jean! You can't make this stuff up, she chuckles to herself.

"I told you it had your name on it," Jean quips, very proud of his wittiness and because this gift is bringing so much joy to its new owner. "Unfortunately, Suzanne doesn't look any happier in this piece than in the one upstairs," he remarks. "What happened to her in the end? Wasn't she the model for What's-His-Name—from Montauban?

"Yes, she was," replies Marie-Laure, "until she became pregnant by What's-His-Name, who never admitted to being the father. He pretty much abandoned her after that. She died young, in an asylum of some sort, and her baby was sent to an orphanage. It's very sad because Suzanne wasn't devoid of artistic talent. Her life ended so tragically, and maybe her only real mistake was to trust Yann Bayard—Monsieur What's-His-Name—who made a lot of money painting her and indubitably enjoyed screwing her."

"*O la la*," Jean interjects, "do I detect some feminist ire?"

"Probably," she laughs, "But I love the painting, and I love you." She stands up and embraces him as she clasps her hands around his neck. Sarah feels like an intruder witnessing this intimate moment of them together. She stares deeply into the painting and tries to imagine what Suzanne was experiencing while working on this portrait, as she appears resigned to overwhelming forces beyond her control.

Sarah experiences a surge of gratitude not to be in the same hopeless situation. Yet, something in this portrait moves her to her core. Suzanne needs to be rescued! Sarah quickly calculates how old Suzanne's daughter might be, perhaps around the same age as her grandmother Bella.

"*Allez, fifille*." Hey, girlie," Marie-Laure breaks into Sarah's thoughts. "What are you dreaming about? You seem to have left us for a moment or two."

"My friend, Sophie, told me that Suzanne's daughter could have been adopted by her uncle, Jacques Aubert. What if she still lives somewhere in the region? Wouldn't it be amazing if we could all be reunited?"

"I know that was at least a rumor that got passed around in our family," Marie-Laure confirms, but Sarah can tell by her expression that she doesn't think it carries much weight anymore.

"If only we had her first name," Jean sighs. "At least in France, women keep their maiden name on official documents. Who wants to make a trip to the *Préfecture* in Montauban next week and see what we can find?"

• • •

The following day, Marie-Laure schedules an appointment for Sarah with Dr. Cohen for that afternoon. Sarah wonders whether she would be able to go through with an abortion. Her whole body slumps, thinking back to how quickly she agreed to have sex with Daren without using protection, even though she knew at the time that there could be consequences.

From the day she told Marie-Laure she was pregnant, Sarah concluded that her cousin had never been in this situation. But what if she was at some time in her life? Sarah starts to speculate if it could be true. Maybe that's why she's so anxious for me to keep the baby and to stay on with her so she can help raise it. Oh my God! If it's true, then something horrible had to have happened since she's never mentioned anything about ever being a mother. Wow! How am I going to ask her about a thing like that?

• • •

At 2:30 sharp, Sarah arrives at Dr. Cohen's office in Saint-Agne, a village a few miles north of Mervilla. The waiting room is just big enough for a few chairs and a coffee table strewn with medical pamphlets and a couple of children's books. The walls are a nondescript beige, decorated with several framed photographs of regional landmarks.

Sarah begins to flip through one of the pamphlets when a younger, more energetic woman than she would have expected opens the door to her examination room and shows Sarah in.

"Hello, Mademoiselle Aubert. Please sit down. Tell me, what brings you here today?" She directs her curious brown eyes and an encouraging smile at Sarah, her dark hair bobbing around her shoulders as she nods in anticipation of Sarah's reply.

"I'm close to being three months pregnant, and I'm running out of time to decide what I'm going to do about it. I'm not even twenty years old, and the father lives on another continent and has no idea he could become a father next March. Nobody in my family knows except my cousin. She referred me to you because no matter what I decide, I'll need a doctor."

"I detect an accent. You're American, right?"

"Yes, but I was born in France. I want to stay here indefinitely, and I'm in the process of getting an ID card and hopefully a medical card."

"You know you have to be in France for at least three months to qualify for health insurance. Your time limit to end your pregnancy will expire before you can finalize your paperwork, which should not, however, weigh at all on your decision as to whether to take the pregnancy to term. What matters is if you believe you can cope with becoming a single mother at such a young age."

They allow this sentence to hang heavily between them for a moment. "I didn't actually 'choose' this outcome, but I allowed it to happen, despite knowing better. For me, the other question that is just as important is whether I have the right to end an innocent life because I screwed up."

"Well, you didn't do that alone. Why haven't you told the father? You don't think he has the right to an opinion in the matter, even if you decide not to take it? I'm not saying you should do anything. But I know from experience that many women make emotional decisions that they regret afterward. Some women end up resenting the child and, despite their best intentions, are unable to bond with their baby. Often, women who have other children later, deeply regret having terminated an earlier pregnancy. Still, most never look back and go on with their life with no trauma at all. How can I help you? What do you expect from me, other than having this conversation?"

"I don't know. I'm so torn. Right now, I can't bring myself to have this discussion with my parents and especially with the father. He's more attracted to men, and I think I was the end of an experiment for him. I'm afraid of losing control of the situation if I confide in anyone except Marie-Laure, who has offered her moral and financial support—and you.

"I believe in a woman's right to choose. But I guess I'm thinking of my grandmother, who was adopted. Her mother didn't have that legal option at the time, but if she had terminated her pregnancy, I wouldn't be here right now. But honestly, I can't imagine being able to care for a baby on my own, although I won't be doing this entirely alone, thanks to Marie-Laure."

"There are free classes right here in town that you could

sign up for. Almost all the attendees are first-time mothers. You aren't any different from many, who will also become single mothers. And you know, there is a third option; you could carry the pregnancy to term and give the baby up for adoption. Many families would be very eager to adopt a Caucasian child."

Before Sarah can set the record straight on the racial origins of this baby, Dr. Cohen gets up from behind her desk and indicates the examination table. "Let's have a look at you and verify how far along you are. You still have a little bit of time before you have to commit one way or the other. I understand how difficult this is for you, but this stress affects the fetus. I highly recommend you find a way to release some of your tension. Have you ever practiced yoga or meditation?"

Oh, my God, my whole life is being taken over by this pregnancy. Do this, do that –it's all about the baby. Right now, I'm not in that state of mind, so what the fuck am I going to do?

23

IF IT'S NOT ONE THING, IT'S YOUR MOTHER #1

Late August—Annapolis, Maryland

Steve uses his contacts within the state government to identify the full legal name of the agricultural inspector in question: Jerome Karl Mercer. Margot is tasked with searching online for all the public information she can find about him, as she did when she was trying to identify Ruby Stiller.

Several Jerome Mercers exist in the United States. However, if she adds the 'K' and a filter for ages between thirty and fifty, there are five. Fortunately, only one Jerome K. Mercer lives anywhere close to Somerset County, Maryland. He was born on a military base in Germany but lived in Atlanta and a suburb of Columbia, South Carolina. His most recent address is a P.O. box in New Church, Virginia. Margot also discovers that he was married but is now divorced and that he's never officially been charged with a crime. However, without a subscription to this website, Margot doesn't have access to other facts that could be pertinent. For now, she is convinced that this Jerome K. Mercer and ag-man Jerry Mercer are the same person.

• • •

The next morning, Margot is awakened by rays of sunlight striping through the blinds, indicating that she has overslept. She jumps into a cold, wake-up shower, brews a pot of coffee, then fires up her laptop, planning to email Steve with the meager details she has been able to verify about Jerry Mercer. Instead, she notices an unexpected email from her mother that she opens first.

Dear Margot, is there any possibility you could come home for a few days just before the long Labor Day weekend? I'm thinking about going to Sarasota to visit Grandma, hopefully with David, and I must talk to you before seeing him. I can't know what I do about him and just pretend it never happened. Please try your best to come. Bisous, Mom

Margot is surprised that her mother has decided to accept her side of the story and is willing to confront David. Still, her initial reaction is consternation, knowing that the likely outcome will just cause more family friction rather than opening any new pathway to forgiveness. She is sure David will deny everything and might talk Abby into reverting to her initial reaction, that Margot was either exaggerating or just making it all up. She has journaled about this life-altering incident for almost five years, and, at this point, there is nothing either of them can do to give her back those years of carefree adolescence when she should have felt safe while just beginning to gain awareness about how this part of life evolves.

Instead, Margot reflects at that time with grief, mourning the abrupt demise of the innocent child she was up until the moment when David put his sleazy hands all over her. Even if David admitted to what he did and apologized for his behavior,

Margot knows that his confession would not magically wipe away her vacillating fears surrounding trust and men and sex.

She is on the verge of succumbing to her desire to answer her mother aggressively: that she definitely won't be able to come home before Labor Day, and, anyway, she does not approve of Abby discussing anything with David unless she can be there. Instead, she writes, *Hi, Mom. Can't commit to coming home at that time right now. Will talk to Steve and let you know soon.*

• • •

Meanwhile, Steve has done some further research on ag-man Mercer. He has a degree in agricultural management and owns a chicken farm near Columbia, South Carolina. He's thirty-nine years old, was married in 2005, and divorced in 2012. According to what Steve has found out about him, his ex-wife obtained a restraining order against him before their divorce. Still, charges were never brought for domestic abuse nor blackmail, extortion, or any other form of misconduct.

In addition, Steve is now convinced that it is essential to get in touch with Sam's mother, Alice Wheeler. He has uncovered that she still lives in the area, not far from Princess Anne.

"Does she have any idea what is happening to her daughter?" Margot asks Steve when they are strategizing over the phone. "If she does know, then why hasn't she come forward? Ruby hasn't mentioned her at all, except to tell me that she and Jake separated when Sam was young. Do you think she could be that helpful?"

"We won't know until we find her, but I'm hoping that she would be willing to go all-in with us, especially if we can help her financially so she can hire a private investigator or even a lawyer.

"I think if we can get Alice involved, she might even be able to act as a go-between with Jake. But ultimately, he would have to buy into this plan, too. If he's Sam's legal guardian, it could be difficult for Alice to take any action at all on her own.

"I truly believe that Jerry Mercer has a more sinister past that he's managed to keep off the books and out of easy view on the internet. Even though he owns a chicken farm in South Carolina, he's moved around a lot, and I haven't been able to account for any of his jobs before his current position. And if all he's ever done until recently is to be a chicken farmer, where did he get the money to start a big enough operation to make a living? I've checked his credit score, and it's decent but not perfect. I'm convinced, though, that he's squirreling money away somewhere, especially if he's hitting up other farmers like he is with Jake.

"I know on the surface that Mercer doesn't present like a guy living on the edge. But if what Ruby has told us about Sam and Jake are true, then I believe this sleazy bastard has left his calling card elsewhere along the way. Maybe he's used an alias in the past. Maybe Jerome K. Mercer *is* an alias!" Steve chortles, like someone who just had a brainstorm. "In any event, if we could find enough verifiable evidence, then we could take this to the next level."

For now, they agreed to see what other facts they could uncover before taking any action. Steve will try to contact Alice Wheeler, and Margot will continue to dig up all she can about Mercer, researching Maryland and Virginia case files, for instance, to see if his name ever comes up.

Margot quickly discovers that Mercer has testified several times in court as an expert witness for the State of Maryland during hearings and trials involving one environmental NGO or another that regularly sue the state under the Clean Water

Act. These cases all contend that dumping and runoff laws aren't being enforced, nor are the integrators paying their fair share toward waste management.

Margot also compiles a list of the farmers from this general area involved in similar lawsuits against the integrators. Mercer knows as much as anyone how all this plays out. Not only could the farmers be fined for going over their dumping limits, but they could also be sanctioned by the companies that pay their salaries—the same companies which have legally managed to foist that responsibility back onto them.

After her research, Margot better understands how Mercer is in a position to play head games with whomever he fancies, including the adolescent daughters of the farmers he targets. It stands to reason why Jake is so hypersensitive toward her and Steve as they snoop around, trying to gather enough facts to expose a crime, maybe several crimes that could come back to bite him.

• • •

Margot's online classes began last week, but she's barely had time to do the required reading and research with any consistency. Much to her disappointment, she can't seem to muster enthusiasm about the subject matter. Margot contemplates if, in fact, she has embarked on a path that she believes she *should* be on but is unable to force her heart and then her head to follow. She's much more focused on helping to unravel what is happening to Samantha Wheeler.

Although Mercer is threatening Samantha, on another level, Margot worries that Sam might be flattered by his attention. If this turns out to be the case, she might decide to give herself up to him out of curiosity or some excitement associated with being the love interest of a man twice her age. Just the thought of such a relationship causes Margot's stomach to lurch.

Margot is also keenly aware that she and Steve have temporarily set aside their research project concerning over-the-top chicken farming and the ensuing pollution of the Chesapeake Bay. However, they have discussed how and where these two stories could overlap. As of now, they don't have any proof that even this one agricultural inspector is engaged in extortion and sexual advances toward a minor. Until they have some concrete evidence, they can't draw any general conclusions about what other forms of corruption might be linked to the wider environmental issues they've been researching.

"My gut tells me that Mercer isn't afraid to inflict harm on people who try to cross him," Steve concludes. "Maybe if we could find evidence to suggest he's been in legal jeopardy from past behavior, we might be able to get the authorities involved. I want to find out what the restraining order was about before his divorce. But as reporters, without just cause, we have less access to this type of personal information than a law-enforcement officer or even a private detective. All we can do is dig around, ask questions, and follow up on any leads. See if you can extract any more information from Ruby and let me get on with my research concerning Alice Wheeler."

Margot immediately places a call to Ruby, but she doesn't answer. That woman absolutely never picks up her phone! she laments as she leaves another message. Margot hesitates, then decides to call her mother. She needs to give her an answer about coming home for Labor Day, and she would like her informed opinion concerning Alice Wheeler and her rights to intervene on her daughter's behalf, especially if her ex-husband refuses to do so. Her call goes into voicemail. Just as she starts to leave a message, she hears a few beeps indicating that another call is coming in: it's Ruby.

"Things here got worse since we were last in touch. I seen Sam in Jerry's car! I went to fetch her after hockey practice, and they was sittin' in his car, smokin 'God knows what! I know he brung her a gift—a watch from a nice store with a logo on it. She's acting now like she's got a crush on him. She's a pretty girl and an easy target since she ain't had any experience with men. But I know from Jake that Jerry keeps right on hittin' him up for money, and I think he's payin' it. If he had any idea that Sam was goin' with this guy, he'd tan um both within an inch of their lives!"

"Well, that certainly is *not* good news," Margot replies dejectedly, "I've been concerned that this could happen. If Sam is now seeing Mercer voluntarily, I don't see how we can do much of anything."

"He's still a snake, and he's twice her age. She's still a minor, and there's laws agin' them being together."

"I'm not so sure—not if she consents."

"She's too young to know what she's doin'. Have you and that reporter found out somethin' 'bout Jerry before he come here? Can you pin anythin' on him? He done stuff like this before; I know it, but I cain't prove it. He ain't bad lookin', and she's been sucked in by a pair of blue eyes that belong to an older guy with some money and a car she can brag about to her friends."

"I'm almost certain that legally if she consents to whatever they do together, the law will be on his side. He could only be held libel criminally if he forces himself on her, and then it's his word against hers. Do you think Jake would act then, like filing a complaint with the police?

"Jake ain't gonna do nothin' 'less he seen somethin' with his own eyes."

"Steve and I are still doing some research about Jerry Mercer's past. We've uncovered some things, but nothing that would indicate he's a child molester or an extortionist. The best thing you can do for Sam is to discourage her from encouraging him."

"You think I don't know that! She stopped tellin' me stuff, is why I think she changed her mind about him. It's probably already too late."

Margot hears the desperation in Ruby's voice. Yeah, she surmises; I agree that it's probably too late. But, instead, Margot replies with as much conviction as she can muster, "Don't give up yet, Ruby. Is it okay if I call you Ruby? Steve's likely going to find out something about Mercer that will indicate he's been down this road before. He's already going outside the law by hitting Jake up for money. That's extortion, and it's very much a crime. Just try to get Sam to confide in you again, and please stay in touch." She comes up just short of mentioning Alice Wheeler. And with that, they both click off.

Margot immediately rings Steve. "Ruby just called. She told me that now Samantha is voluntarily going around with Jerry. It's so hard to accept that neither of her parents can protect her. I almost asked Ruby about Alice, but I don't know if she has any clue about what's happening to her daughter. Have you found out anything more?

"I know enough that I can tell you to call Ruby back and ask her what she knows about Sam's mother," Steve said like it's an order. "I've got an idea."

• • •

Margot doesn't want to spend a sleepless night thinking of how their attempt to help Samantha could fall apart, especially if Alice isn't willing to involve herself in this tangle of harassment and abuse that could end up becoming very public. She also ponders how it would help anything to ask Ruby a lot of questions now when she's not exactly sure what she's supposed to be finding out. Instead, she calls Steve.

"I've left three messages for Ruby, but she hasn't called me back. What am I supposed to quiz her about anyway, since I don't know what your 'idea' concerning her and Alice even is?"

"I was thinking that if Alice knew about Jerry and her daughter, she might be willing to rescue Sam by taking her away from the farm to live with her for a while. So, I wonder what the relationship is between Ruby and Alice. If Ruby could be convinced to go along with this plan, maybe she, or even Alice, could influence Jake. If he has full custody, though, I suppose he could prevent Sam from going to stay at her mom's. And anyway, there's the probability that Sam would balk if she's hanging out with Jerry the way Ruby said.

"But before something bad happens, as it inevitably will, Jake and Sam might be scared enough for her to leave the farm. Jerry probably has no idea who her mother is or where she lives. Even though she's kept her married name, Alice doesn't have a landline, and she uses a P.O. box in another town to get her mail. Trust me; she isn't that easy to find."

"Have you been able to get in touch with her yourself?"

"Not yet, but I haven't tried that hard. I need some input from Ruby to know how to approach her."

"Ruby didn't sound too sympathetic when she first told me

about Alice, and she hasn't mentioned her at all since."

"That's where you come in. I think you can convince Ruby to cooperate. She said she would do anything she could to protect Sam, and this could turn out to be that thing."

24

IF IT'S NOT ONE THING, IT'S YOUR MOTHER #2

Late August—Gaithersburg, Maryland; Sarasota, Florida

Abby is keenly aware that Michel would like her to work full-time, and, since she returned to the office in early July, she is seriously considering it. She's been putting in longer hours, and she enjoys the tighter relationships she's been forming with her co-workers. Most of all, Abby relishes the satisfaction of successfully challenging herself professionally by participating in strategy meetings and contributing all the legal knowledge she's accumulated over the years from doing so much research.

Once home, she allows herself to relax, to sink into her recliner in the den with a glass of wine and catch up on the news. Recently, she's noticed that the press can't seem to stop talking about all the hoop-la surrounding Donald Trump since he announced back in June that he's running as the Republican nominee for President.

Abby remembers that even before Obama first ran in 2008, Trump started this 'birther' bullshit, questioning whether Obama was born in the United States. For her, Trump is a corrupt, racist, and dangerous megalomaniac who can't possibly be taken seriously. However, throughout the Obama presidency, she's become aware of the anger seething throughout predominantly White, rural, and small-town America about having a Black man as President. But no matter who the candidate is, if a Republican were to win in 2016, Abby fears a major effort to dismantle regulations President Obama managed to get on the books concerning the environment and climate change. She believes that global warming is a more accurate term, and she's proud that in some small way, by pursuing her purpose and striving toward her goals, she is also helping to raise awareness.

• • •

Uncharacteristically, Abby is running late this morning. When her phone rings, she almost lets it go to voicemail, but instead, she checks to see who the caller might be. It's David! She's taken aback because she can count on one hand the number of times a year David calls her instead of the other way around.

"David? To what do I owe this unexpected honor?" Abby says with some discernible sarcasm in her voice.

"Mom's in the hospital, Abby. She had a sudden, extreme headache that caused her to pass out. Thank God Maria was there and called 911. She's probably had a stroke! I managed to talk to one of the doctors for just a minute. They're doing a CT scan now and will know more in about an hour or so. Is there any chance you could fly down there? I really can't leave town right now, and one of us needs to be there. It's serious, and … oh God…," she can tell he's trying to stifle a sob.

Abby feels a sudden jolt of panic as it registers that in an instant, the resiliency of life can break apart and shatter—that we are all as fragile as spun glass.

"If her condition is that serious, then we should both be

with her. There must be some way you can leave for a couple of days."

"I'll come as soon as I can, probably not tomorrow. Hopefully Thursday."

Abby is on the verge of demanding to know why he can't drop everything like he's asking her to do and just get on a fucking plane. Instead, she says weakly, "It would be so much better if we faced this together. We could probably get on the same flight."

Silence.

"Okay, fine! I'm going to get off the phone and try to get an airline ticket, but I won't be able to get there until tomorrow."

"I'll call the hospital again in a couple of hours if I haven't heard back from them before that. Abby, thanks." Click.

"Yeah," she murmurs into a dead telephone.

Instead of leaving for work, she immediately searches online for early flights the following morning. One-way tickets aren't that expensive, so Abby quickly purchases one from Baltimore to Sarasota. She then texts Michel, telling him what's happening. By now, she's running very late, so she texts Jim to inform him about her mother.

She leaves the house for the Metro station, then hurries onto the platform as a train approaches. As she takes a seat and before they dive underground so deep that her phone connection will be lost, she texts her co-worker, Ava, to see if Ava could cover for her for the rest of the week and possibly most of the next. She also calculates the best way to get to the airport tomorrow. It's expensive to take a cab, but Abby worries that an Uber or Lyft driver might not show up on time, if at all. By now, she regrets making this commitment so willingly in the first place. Maybe her mother's condition isn't as serious as David thinks. She should have waited to see what the doctor has to say. Abby begins to seethe over the fact that her brother has successfully manipulated her into taking on, for now, all the responsibility for whatever might happen with their mother. That is so David. And he'll get a pass from Mom this time, too, because she believes that his work is so much more important than mine. Shit, I believe that too, or I wouldn't have agreed to go without him.

As the train hurtles through the claustrophobic underground tunnels, Abby reminisces about other trips to Sarasota when the girls were younger, and the family would drive down for Christmas.

Even before her dad retired, her parents decided to move to Florida. Once they agreed on where they wanted to live, they bought a nice home with a pool and a backyard that flowed into the sixth fairway of a golf course. Although it is too hot and humid most of the year for Abby's liking, at Christmas, the climate is like Goldilocks's porridge—not too hot and not too cold.

She remembers their drives down to Florida that seemed endless but still fun. They would leave in the evening and drive all night, switching off so each of them could sleep a bit between stints at the wheel. Once over the border from Georgia, they stopped at the first all-night Denny's they came to, ate a ton of pancakes, eggs, and toast, changed into lighter clothing, and arrived in Sarasota around noon.

Abby almost misses her stop, her eyes glistening with unshed tears. As she exits the train and then the station, she continues to brood. Although she maintains that she doesn't get along with her mother, deep down, she knows that they both love each other in their somewhat twisted way. Her mother's illness and possible death could be another big change in our family, Abby surmises, much sooner than I could have imagined.

As she enters the elevator, Abby forces herself to set aside worries about something that hasn't even happened yet. Once she is settled in her office, she calls Ava and leaves a message. Abby sends a quick email to Sarah, letting her know that she is going to Sarasota but doesn't say why. Finally, she calls Margot.

"Hello, Mom."

"Hi, Sweet Pea. Are you busy?"

"I can talk for a few minutes. What's up?"

"Your grandmother had a dizzy spell and fell. She's okay—didn't break anything. But I've decided to hop down there for a few days to see for myself. Could be she'll need some in-home care for a while to keep a closer eye on her."

"Oh, my God, are you sure she's okay?"

"Well, David spoke to her, but of course, he can't leave immediately to go with me. I plan to call them both later. I'm at work now. I just wanted you to know."

"Yeah, well, I'm glad you called. It's really good you're going. When are you leaving?"

"Tomorrow morning. I'll call you later after I get more details. Bye."

Abby feels guilty that she has just lied to Margot, probably because she wanted to spare her daughter any undue worry. But if she's honest with herself, it's more because she needs a way to decompress. Under the circumstances, Abby cannot vent her anger at her brother about her fear that she will be faced with a situation she won't know how to handle.

She connects with Jim and fills him in on her plans for the trip. "Unfortunately, I don't know exactly when I'll be back, but I'm always reachable by phone, email, or Skype."

Despite these reassurances, she can sense that he's peeved. This trip is more disruptive than she feared, and her frustration is bumping up against her need to focus on work.

• • •

In the end, Abby booked a ride to the airport with Uber, and the driver showed up right on time at 5:30 the following morning. When Abby boards the plane, she doesn't feel any sense of pending disaster. David has told her that the doctor said their mother was doing as well as expected. However, she's still pissed at him, who couldn't yet confirm when he would come nor how long he would stay. As she settles into her middle seat, her eyelids droop; the next thing she is aware of is the pilot's voice over the PA system telling the flight attendants to prepare the cabin for landing.

When Abby arrives at her mother's house, the housekeeper, Maria, greets Abby with such emotion that her heart immediately starts to pound. "Maria, what's happened? Have you heard from the hospital? Is my mother alright?"

"I don't know," she wails, a bucket and mop nearby, groceries still in bags on the kitchen counter. "Nobody tells me nothing! I'm just the maid."

Abby drops her purse and gives the young woman a tight hug. "If it makes you feel any better, I don't know much more than you do. I'll call my brother now to let him know I've arrived. Hopefully, he'll have some updated information."

She should have known when David answered her call right away that something was very wrong. He tells Abby in a monotone that he has finally spoken to their mother's attending doctor, who informed him that their mother had a major stroke due to a blood clot. They won't know for several days how much damage has occurred. They could decide to do a coiling and stenting procedure to prevent further bleeding from a probable leaky aneurysm. Abby can visit her for a few minutes in the ICU later today.

Since she doesn't want to upset Maria, Abby says, "Mrs. Herschel is doing better. I can't thank you enough for what you did for her when she passed out. You acted quickly by calling 911, and it probably saved her life." She purposely avoids the words 'stroke' and 'aneurysm.' She doesn't want to talk about surgery or suggest they might have to bring in professional caregivers.

"I'm glad I was here," Maria says with her slight Chicano accent. Abby has no idea what her legal status might be. Maybe she's one of President Obama's 'Dreamers'. And that's another important issue that won't get resolved if a Republican wins the White House next year, Abby laments.

Abby unpacks but is still too riled up to go to the hospital yet. She doesn't want to become too emotional in front of her mother, assuming she is conscious and more alert than David described. After several attempts to get through to the attending doctor, she is transferred to someone at the ICU nurses' station. They inform her that Mrs. Herschel will be getting another CT scan soon, and then the doctor will decide whether surgery is indicated. Abby will need to come to the hospital as soon as possible to sign some papers before the procedure.

She calls David to tell him about this development. When he doesn't pick up, she leaves him an urgent message. Within a minute or two, he calls back.

"Abby, I'm so sorry. I did get your message about Mom's condition and the possible surgery. We must do whatever the doctors think is best—even if there's a risk. As soon as we hang up, I'm going to purchase an airline ticket for tomorrow. The situation is complicated here right now, and not just with the business. I won't book a return flight until we know how things will work out with Mom. I hope that makes you feel better."

"Yes, David, it does. I'm feeling so completely overwhelmed and having you here will help." Abby is suddenly aware of a wrenching sense of abandonment—by David, her boss, the girls, and even her mother. All the worst memories of trips here that eventually soured come flooding back. As she pulls out of the driveway in her dad's old Mercedes, Abby is ashamed to admit that she came because she had to, not because she wanted to.

• • •

Sarasota Memorial Hospital is just off the Tamiami Trail, several miles from downtown. As usual, pockets of stop-and-go traffic cause slowdowns on the narrower stretches of the roadway. Abby becomes agitated, knowing that it's due to a few old folks ahead who poke along at ten miles under the speed limit. She recoils from the whole elderly scene that she perceives not so much as people enjoying their 'golden years' but more as a slow process of withdrawing, of marching in place until the clock runs out.

When Abby arrives at the hospital, she checks in at the Critical Care Unit, then tiptoes into her mother's room. Bella seems to be asleep. Abby is taken aback at how small and frail her mother appears in the oversized hospital bed, hooked up to an IV drip, oxygen, and a monitor that beeps with her every breath. She hardly recognizes this diminished woman as her mother, the person who since childhood has always loomed so large in her life.

She drops into the chair next to the bed and takes her mom's limp hand. It feels cold and unresponsive. She squeezes it anyway to let her know someone is here. At first, Bella doesn't react, but then she slowly turns her head ever so slightly toward her daughter and opens her eyes. Abby leans over and plants a gentle kiss on her mother's forehead, even though she's not sure that Bella recognizes her. A moment later, Bella closes her eyes, then turns her face away again.

Abby can't hold back her tears any longer. She feels she is already in mourning, not because her mother might die from her stroke, but because of her ongoing struggle to make peace with her before that happens. Now, it may be too late! She regrets that they have squandered so much time over so many years pushing each other away. Whenever they got into an argument, Abby was convinced that her mother took pleasure in throwing a bucket full of negative adjectives at her that continue even now to regurgitate their venom: whenever Abby feels that she has screwed up, she can picture her mother saying, I told you so!

Just now, however, seeing Bella so vulnerable, Abby is flooded with remorse at her complicity in their dysfunctional relationship. She understands that Bella had many issues that had nothing to do with her. Anyway, Abby has always given back as good as she got. She gently lifts her mother's hand again and whispers, "I love you, Mom, and I know that you tried to do the best you could. I want so much to forgive us both."

She abruptly stands up, grabs a handful of Kleenex from a

box on the windowsill and flees the room and then the hospital without making eye contact with anyone. She still has not spoken to the doctor. She still doesn't know how her mom's condition might evolve or if they plan to operate.

Abby isolates herself in the car, taking a few moments to recover. She digs around in her purse for her phone, then calls back into the CCU. A nurse informs her that she would be able to see the doctor soon, and then she should go to reception to take care of the paperwork.

When she finally returns to her mother's room, Abby notices that Bella's bed has been raised to a semi-sitting position. She still has a blank expression on her face and does not appear to know that anyone is sitting beside her. A moment later, the door opens, and the doctor strides into the room.

"I'm Dr. Everette – uh, Ms...."

"Abigail Aubert, Mrs. Herschel's daughter. I'm so glad to finally meet you."

"Let's talk a walk, Abigail. Is it okay if I call you Abigail?"

"Of course." She tenses up as she follows him out the door and down the hall. "Won't my mother wonder why we've walked out together without saying anything to her?"

"I'm very sorry to have to tell you that Mrs. Herschel had a major stroke caused by an aneurysm. The good news is that she's still with us, and I think she will recover. However, I cannot predict how well. Right now, she is unable to speak and is also partially paralyzed on her left side.

"We can alleviate some of the inflammation in her brain, and therefore improve her overall condition, by doing what's called an endovascular repair, inserting a coil through a catheter into an artery in her groin that will block blood from flowing into the aneurysm. It's not invasive surgery, and we hope that a few days after the procedure, your mother can be moved to a nursing rehab facility. In her case, she will need extensive care there and eventually at home. Are there any family members who reside in the area?"

"No. Both my brother and I live just outside of Washington, DC. I would like to go back at some point to organize things at work for a longer absence. Could we set up some home care once she comes out of rehab?"

"Well, let's not worry about that right now. I need you to sign some forms, and then we can do the procedure. Most patients do very well."

Within a few minutes after signing the required papers, promising not to sue the hospital if her mother dies while they try to prolong her life, Bella Herschel is wheeled away. An orderly shows Abby a small waiting room. No one else is there, and she phones her boss, Jim. "The good news," she begins, "is that my mother is having a procedure today that is expected to pave the way for some recovery. I'm planning to come back as soon as I can, hopefully by the middle of next week."

"This situation with Ayer Homes is complicated, Abby," Jim replies. "They already have the permits to build 1,000 units, and they don't seem inclined to back off from that number. I'm trying to schedule another in-person meeting with them, but if they persist, I will have to turn the whole thing over to Victor."

Victor Baranski heads the team of litigators. If his group takes over, she and Jim would be off the case completely. Abby is very disappointed that things are turning out this way. She had hoped that Ayer would come around in the end, and she was especially looking forward to working with Ingrid.

• • •

When her mother is brought back to her room, she is still hooked up to all kinds of beeping monitors. Her eyes are still closed. Abby sits in the chair by her bed, wondering how long she needs to be here. She decides to wander out into the hallway to see if she could get more information. As she walks toward the nurse's station, she recognizes Dr. Everette coming toward her.

"The procedure went very well. There is no more leakage into the brain, so I hope we'll see some progress over the next day or two. You would do well to go home, get some rest, but keep your phone nearby, just in case we have to get in touch with you later."

"Thanks. I will. My brother is coming in from DC tomorrow morning. Will we both be allowed to see her then?"

"If your mother is up to it, that's fine. I'll let them know at the nurses' station that two of you will be coming, but you can only stay for a short while."

"I appreciate everything you've done for her, doctor. All we can do now is hope for the best." Abby focuses on his weary face. Worry lines form a V across his forehead, and his hooded eyes tell the story of someone under constant strain. She smiles at him, but he has already looked past her and started back down the hall.

• • •

After a long day, Abby is anxious to go back to the house, open a bottle of wine, and sit in the cool quiet of being the only one there. Since David is coming tomorrow, her fear of being here alone has receded. Hopefully, their mom will start to improve in a few days. As she drives out of the hospital parking lot, she wonders if there is any wine at the house and what might be in the fridge that she would want to eat. She stops at a small strip mall that backs up to Sarasota Bay. The sun hovers over the Bay, crowned by layers of deep rose and gold. The hibiscus is in full bloom, and an onshore breeze ruffles through the Spanish moss dripping from a grove of live oak trees.

Abby buys a roasted chicken, some mixed veggies from the fancy salad bar, and two bottles of her favorite chilled Sauvignon Blanc, seemingly waiting just for her.

Once back at her mother's house and after pouring herself a glass of the soothing wine, she emails Michel and the girls.

Mom had a non-invasive procedure today to stop the bleeding from an aneurysm and is resting comfortably. However, she will have to be in rehab and need some extra help once she comes home. Sarah, since Marie-Laure is much better, I would appreciate it if you would seriously consider returning home. It would be great if you could come down here and spend some time with Gran since it appears that you are determined not to go back to school this fall. Please let me hear from you. I miss you all. Gros Bisous, Moi.

Abby almost erases her directive to Sarah to pull herself together and come home, but then, in a mini snit, she hits *Send*. *Tant pis pour elle*, too bad for her. The hardest part for Abby is knowing that as far as work is concerned, she doesn't have control over any of it. She wants to become more involved with the firm's clients but is helpless to make that happen as long as she is needed here in Sarasota.

25

FAMILY TIES

Late August to Early September—
Annapolis, Maryland; Sarasota, Florida

Margot finally hears back from Ruby the following morning as she is making her way down to the beach. "I ain't had time to call ya yesterd'y. I've been trackin' Sam like you was supposed to do —followin' her and Mercer all the way to New Church! He took her to his house! They were there over an hour, 'fore he drove her back home. She ain't returnin' my calls, but I know somethin' nasty happened there. I know it like I knew my second husband was cheatin' on me!"

"Oh my God, Ruby! You've got to find out what happened! Can you go to the farm later and try to get her to talk to you? Steve is also trying to get in touch with Alice."

"Alice Wheeler? Why would he want to do that?"

"Because Steve knows that she and Sam are in touch and that they see each other from time to time. If Alice never gave up her parental rights, then there's no reason for her not to be involved—is there?"

"Well, I ain't heard nothin' 'bout that! Jake wouldn't let that happen."

"Why not? We need all the help we can get right now. If you can find out what went on at that house and Sam is willing to tell her mother, too, then Alice might be able to go to the authorities."

"I ain't sure it'll work. Jake ain't gonna allow Alice to do nothin' he don't agree to. But I'll try agin to talk to Sam."

"Good, Ruby. Let me know what happens. Bye."

When Margot gets to the beach, she removes her flip-flops and strolls barefoot across the hot sand, listening to the swoosh of lazy waves and the distant cry of gulls swirling between the Bay and the beach. She feels helpless to aid Samantha in any way, but she fears even more that no matter the outcome, there would most likely be all kinds of negative consequences for Sam but probably none for Jerry Mercer. Margot is struck by seething resentment that David never had to pay any price for his behavior. She is more determined now that Samantha should have her day in court.

After spending time contemplating all the ugliness of Sam's situation and her inability to prevent anything more from befalling her, Margot marches briskly back up to the guest house, wanting to call Steve and recount what Ruby has told her about yesterday. Once home, she hurries into the shower. Fifteen minutes later, she sees that Steve has called and left a voice message: *Please call me when you get this. I have some important news regarding Alice Wheeler.*

Margot hesitates momentarily, then hits *Call Back.* Steve goes right to the point. "I've been able to get in touch with Alice Wheeler. She's agreed to help, and she's spoken to Sam. Have you been able to talk to Ruby?"

"Yes. She told me yesterday that she followed Mercer and

Sam to his house in New Church. They were there for over an hour. She's been trying to get in touch with Sam, but apparently, she won't return her calls."

"We've got to find out what happened yesterday. If Mercer abused her in any way..."

"Of course, that's what we are all thinking, but if Sam won't tell anyone about it, what can we do?"

"I'm supposed to meet with Alice at Zeeks at 11:00. If you can get in your car right now and come down here, I can put the meeting off for an hour or so. I think, of all those involved, you're the best person to convince Alice how urgent it is for her to intervene on Sam's behalf. She told me that Jake had physical custody but not full legal custody, so she can engage a private investigator or even go to the cops."

"I'm on my way."

Margot hurries to her car and speeds away. A little over an hour later, she parks in the lot at the diner and rushes inside. Margot spots Steve, and a woman she presumes is Alice at a table in the back, ordering something. "I'll have some ice tea with lemon, please," she tells the waiter as she squeezes into the small booth next to Steve.

At first glance across the table, Alice presents as a mousey-looking, middle-aged woman with short, reddish-brown hair, dull eyes, and a sallow complexion, someone you wouldn't notice if you passed her in the street. However, when she extends her hand to Margot, her eyes brighten, and an engaging smile spreads across her lips, as her whole demeanor suddenly becomes more animated.

"I'm so pleased to meet you," Alice says sincerely. Instead of just shaking Margot's hand politely, she holds it tight as if they were already friends. "Your colleague here has told me about your commitment to helping my daughter. I'm so very grateful."

When she lets go of Margot's hand, Alice's smile fades as she looks forlornly from her to Steve. "Jake and I don't see eye-to-eye on how to handle almost any situation involving Samantha. It's one reason we split up. I got a steady job working for a doctor in Princess Anne. Jake was more available to care for Sam day-to-day, and his mother came to live with them after I left. I thought she would be better off than being raised by a single, mostly absent mother. I realize that was a mistake, one I can never make up for. With school and hockey, we haven't connected as much as I wanted this past year, but now that I know about her involvement with the Mercer person, I have to do something. Steve has told me about the conversation you had with Ruby today. I haven't spoken to her in years, but I'm aware that she's stepped in to help Sam whenever she could. I'll definitely call her and try to get directly in touch with Samantha and Jake.

"I know she's afraid to talk to her father, and I believe that if I could just get her away from the farm and down here with me, she would eventually tell me the truth about what's been going on. Then, if you guys can somehow come up with the money, I'd be willing to sign any papers necessary to put a detective on this Mercer fella's trail."

"That would probably be the fastest and most efficient way to get to the bottom of what is happening to Samantha at the hands of Jerome K. Mercer," Steve agrees. He clenches his teeth to control his rage as he imagines what the truth will reveal.

"So, how is this going to get started?" Alice asks him. "Like I said, I have no money I can put up to hire a detective or anyone else, like a lawyer."

"I'm working with several nonprofits that help young women in these circumstances and might be willing to set up a GoFundMe account for you, using an alias, of course. If I can pull this off, then we are literally in business."

• • •

Abby is at the airport the following morning as David walks through the doors and into the terminal, a small carry-on suitcase in hand. As Abby embraces her brother, she is surprised that he appears older than his age; his hair is thinning, and she notices strands of gray around the temples. His usually animated brown eyes seem lusterless, and worry lines stretch across his forehead. Abby feels a momentary rush of affection for her little brother. At the same time, she isn't sure how to be with him now that she knows about the episode with Margot. A surge of fury and jealousy simmer just under the surface of her sisterly love. Still, she is somewhat appeased, knowing that even their mother's special devotion is no longer able to protect him from the vicissitudes of his daily life.

They drive straight to the hospital. When they enter their mother's room, her bed is still in the same position as yesterday, and the TV is on. Immediately, David rushes over to her, takes her hand, and bends down and kisses her cheek. She stares directly at him, but her expression doesn't change. He settles on the edge of the bed and starts talking to her in a soft voice, too low for Abby to hear.

Abby is disappointed that their mother shows no sign of recognizing David, nor does she seem to notice that Abby is even in the room. She approaches the other side of the bed but does not sit down. Bella glances at her briefly, then fixes her gaze on the TV as if she were alone.

Fifteen minutes later, the nurse enters the room and tells them that they must leave for now. David and Abby each kiss their mother goodbye then exit the room into the hallway. Abby notices that David is dabbing at his eyes that are now glassy with unshed tears.

As soon as they arrive back at the house, David makes his way into the den. He spends the next hour at the desk sorting through bank and investment statements. He also pays all the bills and then sets up auto-payments online for as many of these vendors as he can.

Abby still hasn't approached David yet about Margot nor what he meant when he said, "It's complicated, and not just about work." She suspects he has issues with his wife, Beth, and goes so far as to speculate that he could be having an affair, possibly with a much younger woman. The more she thinks about it, the more she convinces herself that this conclusion is true.

David finally joins her on the lanai. As he drops into the lounge chair opposite her, he is confronted with the stoked emotions that Abby's contorted face directs at him.

"What's going on, Abbs? You look like you've just seen a ghost." He utters a nervous chuckle to defuse whatever she might be ruminating about.

Unable to spill the ire building up inside her just yet, she backs off and asks in as neutral a voice as she can manage, "What did you mean when you said your life is complicated?"

David uncrosses his legs, hangs his head, and says in a wobbly voice, "Beth wants a divorce, well, a separation, but I think if that happens, it will lead to divorce." He glances at Abby to scrutinize her reaction. "She has a *boyfriend*, Abby, someone she met at a bar! Apparently, she and a friend from the gym have been barhopping like college kids for the past few months. I knew they were going out together now and then, but I thought it was more of a group thing. Anyway, that's what she hit me with three weeks ago, in the middle of the third-quarter tax run-up. It's a mess! And no, the kids don't know—yet."

Abby stares back at him, weighing whether he's telling the truth or exaggerating a situation to gain sympathy. "Are you sure she isn't trying to pay you back for something you did first?"

"What?" He jerks his head up and gawks at her in disbelief that she would insinuate such a thing about him—David the Perfect, David the loving husband, father, son, and brother, David the honest, trustworthy, and dependable accountant to several hundred clients.

But Abby witnesses that he is seething with anger rather than projecting hurt or even shock that his sister could think he ever cheated on anyone. "David, I know about what you did to Margot when she was thirteen. It traumatized her to the point that she couldn't talk about it—even to me! I found the journals she's been keeping all these years, struggling with self-loathing and shame, because she believed it was somehow *her* fault—emotions you should have been dealing with, not her."

"You can't be serious! How can you think I would ever do something to a child, much less to my niece?"

"Because I've read her journals. Either she's crazy, or I have to believe something happened. Looking back, I realize that Margot was never interested in going to parties or dances, even as a young teen. She's never mentioned a boyfriend, and Sarah was always teasing her for not wanting to date."

"I never did anything to her! Did it ever occur to you that

she could be a lesbian?"

Abby notices that David is no longer looking at her as he continues to deny any wrongdoing. He has an edge to his voice; his eyes are screwed up into slits, and his body is hunched over like someone about to spring from the chair and either attack or flee from the room.

"Look. David, she never accused you of rape, but you need to recognize that you did touch her inappropriately. Maybe that's not the only time something like this has happened, and Beth found out about it. I would try to forgive you, and Margot might too if you would stop being in denial and tell the truth. Otherwise, except for this crisis with Mom, I don't think I want to have a relationship with you anymore." Tears glisten in Abby's eyes as she waits for David's response.

• • •

Margot spends another fitful night. Even before the glow from the rising sun lights up the eastern sky over the Bay, she gives up any hope of going back to sleep. After they met with Alice yesterday and drove from Annapolis to Venton and back, Margot is concerned about what might have transpired between Ruby and Sam. Although it is still fairly early, she taps in Ruby's number.

"Hullo," a raspy voice croaks into the phone. "I thought it might be you, or I wouldn't of answered."

"Sorry if I woke you, but I've been so worried about you and Sam that I haven't slept very well."

"Me neither. Sam was a mess yesterday. She did let me in, but then all she did was cry. I think he forced himself on her. I couldn't get her to say it outright, but I ain't never seen her like that before."

"What about Jake? Does he have any idea what's happening?"

"I think so, but he didn't say nothin' to me, and I ain't said nothin' to him neither."

"Steve and I met Alice yesterday in Venton. Did she call you? She said she would."

"Yeah, but I was with Sam, and I ain't called her back. What am I supposed to say to her?"

"She'd like to take Sam to her place so Mercer can't find her. She also agreed to sign papers so we could hire a private investigator. Steve and I are hoping you could help Alice by talking to her and then to Jake about all this."

"Sam used to go to her mom's a lot on weekends, but that was a few years ago. I ain't sure Sam will agree to go anywhere with her anymore. As for Jake, I'm damned certain he don't want to hear it. But if it'll help Sam, then I'll try."

"I know your name is Ruby, but you're a real pearl when it comes to your niece. Good luck."

"Ain't nobody never called me a pearl before. Thanks."

After Margot clicks off the call with Ruby, she focuses on her mom and what she must be going through with her grandmother in Florida. She forces herself to put Ruby and the Wheelers, and even Steve, out of her mind as she re-reads the email she received from her mother yesterday that she has yet to answer.

Dear Margot, Gran is doing well enough to be moved into a rehab facility in a couple of days. She did have a stroke, but the doctor is hopeful she can recover. I plan to fly home with David on Monday to take care of some important matters at work. I think you'd be interested in the Ayer Homes case. It involves the Monocacy River, so it's pertinent to your work. It would be great if you could come the following Friday and stay through Labor Day. We could do something over the weekend to pre-celebrate my birthday. Bisous, Mom

Margot gets that Abby is hooked into other, more pressing worries, but apparently, her mother has forgotten that she has left the CBLAC and is now assisting Steve on issues related more specifically to chicken farming. She's especially upset that there was no mention of her having a confrontation with David. Margot assumes that the subject was never broached. She is frustrated and hurt that her mother tries to show up when it suites her but is evidently unwilling or unable to support her when Margot needs her the most.

After eating breakfast, she texts Steve, telling him that she'll meet him at his office around 9:00. Later, she plans to get caught up with the two online classes she has set aside. In the meantime, she calls her dad to see how he's getting along while her mother is in Florida. She assumes that he is happy on his own without his life revolving around three women vying for his attention and putting demands on what little spare time he has.

Michel picks up after the first ring. "*Pitchoune*! I didn't expect to hear from you so early. Everything okay? Have you spoken to your mother yet today?"

"Yeah, I'm fine. Mom emailed me yesterday. She told me that Gran's doctor plans to move her into a rehab place on Sunday. I also heard from Sarah a couple of days ago. She wants to stay in France."

"Yes, I know. I've been corresponding with Marie-Laure. She wants Sarah to get her papers to apply to the university, but I'm not sure they'll accept her with only one year of college here. Still, I would like her to try and see what happens. If she gets in, then it's fine with me. If not, then she should come home. But you know, you are both old enough to make some of your own choices about what you want to do in life—as long as you keep moving forward."

"Well," Margot utters, as she stifles a sigh, "I guess I'm moving forward. Steve and I are working on a story that could expose some criminal activity if the allegations are true. It's slow going, but right now, we seem to be making progress."

"When do you start your online class?"

"I already have, and I'm taking two classes, thanks for asking." She tries to keep any sarcasm out of her voice. In the end, he's just like Mom. He doesn't seem to care that much about what's actually going on in my life.

"Sure, *Pitchoune*. I'm very proud of you, you know. When are you coming home?"

"Mom asked me to come next Friday to pre-celebrate her birthday. Have you planned anything around that?"

"Not yet. Do you have any ideas?"

"Well, maybe we could get tickets to something at the Kennedy Center."

"Yeah, why not? I'll look into it over the weekend. Let's talk tomorrow or Sunday. *Bisous*!"

"*A toi, aussi.* To you, too."

Hi, Mom. I'll do my best to come next Friday. I hope everything goes well with Gran.

Dry, dispassionate, detached—my way to stand my ground, Margot determines as she hits *Send*.

26

SEARCHING FOR ANSWERS

Early September– Mervilla, Montauban, Caussade, France

After returning from Dr. Cohen's, Sarah is anxious to initiate a heart-to-heart with Marie-Laure. Although she longs to dig deeper into her cousin's motives for helping her remain in France, she also has trepidations about how Marie-Laure might react, especially if Sarah decides to terminate the pregnancy.

"*Alors*?" asks Marie-Laure.

"Thanks for making the appointment," Sarah replies as she sits on the couch next to her. "Dr. Cohen asked me a lot of questions that I have to answer for myself soon if I decide not to go to term. It would be tremendously helpful for me to know if you've ever experienced anything like what I'm going through. I don't know any other way to say it except to ask you outright if you've ever been pregnant."

Marie-Laure drops her head and clasps her face with trembling hands as if she were going to weep. Sarah wishes she could take the question back, as it strikes her that she has trespassed into some tragic place in Marie-Laure's life that she has kept locked away—until now.

"Oh, God, Marie-Laure, I'm so sorry. Please forgive me. It's not my business ..."

"It's okay, Sarah," she interrupts, then casts her moist eyes and a weak smile at Sarah. "I'm glad you asked. It's not something I've ever discussed with anyone except Jean. But I understand why you would like to know. I don't want my answer, however, to influence your decision about your own choices."

"But that's why I'm asking! I'm so confused. I suspected you might have gone through a similar experience; it would be helpful for me to know what happened."

"I lost a baby to a miscarriage that was fathered by the love of my life at the time. Soon after, he left me to take a job abroad. I was alone to cope with the loss and the abandonment. I had to take a leave of absence from teaching for a semester because I almost fell apart. As a result, I've never been able to completely trust any man again—until I met Jean.

"I never told anyone in my family. My mother was religious enough that I was afraid she couldn't forgive me for becoming pregnant out of wedlock." Marie-Laure reaches over and takes hold of Sarah's hand. "So, you see, my dear, I do have an ulterior motive for wanting to help you. I would be overjoyed to have a child in my life, even knowing that you could ultimately decide to return to the States. But more importantly, I genuinely want you to do what's best for yourself."

Now tears do start to flow down Marie-Laure's cheeks. Sarah hands her the box of tissues from the side table and then gives her a long, tight hug.

Sarah blinks hard, trying not to start crying as well, then whispers as if to herself, "Having someone totally dependent on you is an awesome responsibility, maybe at times a joy, but to me, it's also terrifying. I don't know if I can deal with it."

"Becoming a mother is fraught with risk," Marie-Laure agrees, "but it's also an irreplaceable gift of pure love, as one person gives life to another, hopefully forging a bond between them that cannot be broken."

Perhaps this was the moment that Sarah decided to keep her baby. Marie-Laure genuinely wants her to do what she believes is best for herself. And because she has faith in Sarah's ability to make that decision, with her help and support, Sarah knows deep down this is the only option she can live with.

• • •

The next day, as promised, Jean arrives mid-morning to drive Marie-Laure and Sarah to Montauban. Hopefully, they will confirm what Sophie has told them about Jacques Aubert adopting Suzanne's daughter and possibly find out if she's still alive.

For Sarah, this trip has taken on the proportions of a mission. She knows that becoming a single mother happens to many women, but it turned into a tragedy for Suzanne. And because her grandmother, Bella, could never overcome her own abandonment, Sarah longs to pick up the broken pieces for all three women and make them whole again.

Jean has already found records online indicating that Suzanne Aubert was born in Montauban on April 12, 1921. There was a note in the margin indicating the date of her death, March 25, 1946, in Caussade, about fifteen miles away. These records, however, do not mention the birth of a child. He also tried to find where Marie-Laure's great-uncle, Jacques Aubert, lived and when and where he died. There are quite a few men with that name who also lived and died within the region. Thus, many years later, it is difficult to find the one who may or may not have adopted Suzanne's nameless child.

They have lunch in a bistro near the records office in Montauban. While they are talking things over, Jean searches online for convents and orphanages in the Tarn et Garonne department, of which Montauban is the administrative center. The art dealer in Toulouse told Sarah that Suzanne was taken in by Carmelite nuns. Jean finds some information about several such convents converted to modern B & B's. As for psychiatric hospitals, he finds only one near Montauban that existed during the War and is still functioning today. It's located in Caussade, where Suzanne died. At least by going there, Sarah hopes they might be able to reassemble a few more of the shards of Suzanne's shattered life.

They set out along a two-lane road with plane trees bordering both sides. Carpets of field daisies grow between tended fields ripe with sunflowers bobbing their heavy yellow and brown heads in the stiff breeze. In season, the town of Caussade attracts tourists who come to explore its medieval past and picturesque surroundings. In early September, *les grandes vacances*, the long summer break, is over, and the town is relatively quiet.

The psychiatric facility is a few blocks southeast of the main square. From the outside, it appears as austere as it must have been during the War, with its faded brick façade and rusting metal shutters. Inside, however, there are now paintings on the light gray walls and sheer, white curtains covering the windows. The waiting room has the look of a small hotel lobby, with colorful upholstery on the couch and several club chairs.

Marie-Laure has requested a short meeting with one of the psychiatrists who hopefully can tell them whether Suzanne

Aubert was ever a patient here and what became of her baby.

After a short wait, a middle-aged, roundish man with a long nose, dark eyes, and a receding hairline invites them into his tiny office. Marie-Laure explains her family ties to Suzanne, who was probably admitted here as a patient during the War and possibly died within these walls soon after that. It naturally follows that they would hope to uncover any information about the baby girl she was said to have given birth to and consequently gave up for adoption. The doctor listens attentively, then shakes his head.

"I'm terribly sorry, Madame, but most of those records were destroyed during or soon after the War ended. If you have researched your cousin's records at the *Préfecture* in Montauban and there is no indication of the birth of a child, then I cannot help you. What makes you so sure that the infant even survived the War? The only other thing I can suggest is that your cousin may have given birth in another town and became a patient here later after her baby was put up for adoption. You might want to visit some of the other villages nearby and inquire. Now, if I can't help you any further, I hope you will excuse me."

On the street, Sarah appears to shrink into herself from disappointment. Marie-Laure bemoans the fact that they seem to be going around in circles. Jean and Sarah sense that she's had enough, but the two of them are not quite ready to give up entirely.

"Is it possible that someone in your more immediate family could fill in any of the gaps?" Sarah asks Marie-Laure as they drive back toward Mervilla.

"Unfortunately, I haven't made much effort over the years to stay in contact with most of my relatives. As an only child and living farther away from the cluster who settled around Montauban, we weren't that close. After my father died, my mother sought out her clan, who had settled farther south. The only cousin I made an effort to stay in touch with is Michel—maybe because he's also an only child. But I'm glad I did because here you are!" Her mood shifts from somber to light as she smiles back at Sarah through the rear-view mirror.

"I'll see what I can find out by posting something about Julien, Suzanne, and her daughter on the genealogy site I use," Jean promises. "Let's not give up entirely just yet."

• • •

As they approach Toulouse, the traffic thickens as people head home toward the outlying towns and villages, which haven't changed much in over a century. They still have their monuments from the past—a traditional Catholic Church, a town hall probably in need of renovation, a covered marketplace, and a plaque or statue engraved with the names of hometown soldiers who died in one of the World Wars. The charm of the visible past is still present in the buildings' stone facades and rose-tiled roofs, with faded wooden shutters and geraniums flowing from iron-railed balconies. However, not far from town, the woods and fields are slowly being replaced by look-alike subdivisions, boxy shopping malls, supermarkets, and areas zoned for industrial activities. Fortunately, Mervilla is too far off the main roads and as yet is still undisturbed by the encroachment of numbingly impersonal suburbia.

"Would anyone like some tea?" Sarah inquires as they arrive home. Marie-Laure and Jean settle into the deep leather couch in the living room, now crinkled and faded from use and exposure to the glaring sunlight pushing its way through frayed, voile curtains. It is a portrait of the cycle of life itself, slowly erasing the freshness of youth and replacing it with an unraveling that eventually happens over time as one repeatedly uses a fragile, hand-tatted doily. Sarah can observe the weight of time, even though she had barely been affected by it. As she surveys the scene of Marie-Laure, still beautiful but no longer in her first youth as the French expression goes, and Jean, more marked than she by the accumulation of passing years, Sarah can't help but wonder how she will be when she reaches their age.

She pours the tea, then sits in the empty armchair facing away from the windows, her own shadow obscuring the teak wood table between them. She mulls over the day in Montauban as her heart throbs with sadness, acknowledging the probability that Suzanne's daughter is most likely lost to them for good. Suzanne's life was torn apart due to a deep passion for a man who may have shared its intensity but didn't believe in its longevity. Slowly, however, her sorrow lifts as she experiences a swelling of gratitude flowing through her, knowing that her fate will never be that of Suzanne Aubert. She might mourn the narrative of Suzanne's life and death, but Sarah is finally able to cease identifying with it any longer.

Sarah is deeply affected by the image before her of Marie-Laure and Jean, their faces partially lit from the fading sun, full of love and contentment. She can't resist the urge to give them each un *gros bisous*, a real kiss—one that is different from *les bises*, the pecks on the cheeks, that French people often exchange with each other whenever they meet.

"Where did that come from?" Marie-Laure smiles, her face glowing with affection.

"I am so glad not to be facing what Suzanne had to go through."

"What made you think you ever would?"

"I don't know. Suzanne's story is so pathetic. I guess I identified with her because misery needs company. I accept that we'll probably never know what became of her daughter. But I do know what will become of my child. I want to stay here and raise her in this place that has become my world too."

"*Her*?" asked Jean. "What makes you so sure it's a she? You haven't even had a sonogram yet."

"Just a gut feeling," Sarah replies. "Poetic justice, maybe. More tea?"

27

COMING INTO HER OWN

Early September—Gaithersburg, Annapolis, Maryland, Washington, DC, Sarasota, Florida

Abby arrives at BWI airport late in the afternoon, exhausted from the emotional turmoil of seeing her mother in decline and witnessing her brother's inability to wrap his mind around his vile behavior toward Margot from years ago or the shambles of his marriage now. David decided at the last minute to prolong his stay in Sarasota for several more days as their mother settled into the rehab facility.

Michel is at the airport to greet her. What a comfort he is as Abby falls into his bear hug, knowing at this moment how treasured she is! As soon as she gets into the car, Abby calls Jim to tell him she is back, at least for a while. He has set up a meeting with Ayer for Thursday, perhaps their last chance to convince Ayer and his cadre of advisors to scale back the number of units they appear intent on building. Jim promises to email her the pertinent documents to be discussed on a conference call with his entire team tomorrow afternoon.

Abby senses that her karma is shifting in her favor, even though she is struck by how the vicissitudes of a lifetime flow and change. They are like whitecaps on a calm day that bump around but barely turn over, while others will become stormy waves that swell and gain force until crashing into the shoreline like a runaway train. The only thing that marches in a straight line in life is time. Abby knows her mother's time is draining through the hourglass. Just how fast is what she is struggling to face.

Later, she sits on the back porch under the ceiling fan, reading the documents that Jim emailed. After studying the material that rehashes all the building regulations and restrictions now in place or about to be activated, she is dismayed that the attorneys on Jim's team continue to use these dry and uninspiring facts as a strategy. As she contemplates putting forward a more convincing argument, she suddenly remembers Ingrid's suggestion from the last meeting—build less, plant more. I think I've figured out a way to persuade them that they've already committed to Ingrid's outcome, and I can prove it to them by using their own words.

Her ringing cell phone jars her out of her bubble and back into the pesky present moment. It's Margot.

"Hi, Mom, how's Gran? How was the trip?"

"Both as well as can be expected. David is staying a bit longer to make sure Gran will be okay as she settles in the rehab facility. What about you? Will you be able to come home on Friday?"

"I plan to. However, we are at a crucial junction with this situation in Princess Anne. We're arranging for a private detective to get involved, and we're hopeful that he can document facts about an agricultural inspector who is harassing a girl half his age and her father."

"Whoa!" Abby interrupts her, "Can we talk about it when

you come? I'm in the middle of something right now."

Momentary silence. "Uh, sure. I understand. I'll call you later in the week."

"I have this all-important meeting on Thursday and a prep conference tomorrow. Better if you text me when you leave Annapolis on Friday. Love you. *Bisous*."

Click!

Margot still has her mouth open to say goodbye as the words fade into the space between her lips and the phone. What was that about? She realizes now that she should have called her father instead. Why do I get the impression of bumping into an invisible wall of resistance when dealing with Mom? She remembers the conversation she and her mother had about her uncle's abuse when Abby declared that she believed something despicable had occurred. Now Margot is concerned that Abby and David discussed it during their trip and that he emphatically denied it all. Maybe her refusal to engage with me indicates that she's flipped back to not believing my story.

Margot also wonders if Sarah ever also felt that their mother blocks out the unpleasantries of their relationships and will only engage with either of them on her terms. Margot checks the time. It's not even 9:00 pm in France. Even though it's expensive to call there, she punches in Sarah's number anyway.

Sarah picks up after the first ring and asks with some urgency, "Margot, is everything okay? God, did Gran die?"

"No, nothing that drastic. I'm just missing you so much right now. I had to hear your voice." Her voice has a tremble that Sarah detects immediately.

"What's going on, Sweet Pea?"

"Please don't call me that! Mom only calls me that anymore

when she wants something from me; at least that's how it feels."

"I detect some grievances. What's going on with you two?"

"Don't you sense it as well? Do you think Mom is really interested in what you have to say when you talk to her?"

"I haven't spoken directly to her since leaving home back in May. Any communication between us has been through text and email. And since she sort of ordered me to go to Florida to replace her when Gran comes back from rehab, I haven't responded at all. She's sent me emails about you being so focused on your education and a possible career path, as she likes to word it, implying that I'm out there somewhere in left field just twiddling my thumbs. What has she said to you that's gotten you so upset?"

"That's just it; she acts totally disconnected as if she's having a one-way conversation with herself."

"Look, let's face it, she's going through some trauma with Gran. Maybe we both have to give her a break for now."

"No, I get that. But for some reason, all this stuff is coming up for me about how we've interacted for years. I realize that I lost that feeling of closeness and trust at some point. And even back when—Mom didn't want to be home taking care of us. She was dying to finish law school and then get a job."

"I'm sure Papa pushed her along in that direction. All her friends were launching careers and trying to juggle work and family. At least Mom recognized she wasn't capable of handling that much stress."

"But why take it out on me? She is different with you."

"To some extent, I guess so. But I think it's more because I'm different with her. I kind of let it all slide off my back. Ever since I started playing basketball in middle school, I've had a way of letting off steam. You should try focusing on something that doesn't require our mother's approval. It's quite liberating!"

"Right now, I'm laser-focused on this family who are victims of extortion and the sexual abuse of their seventeen-year-old daughter. When I was doing my internship, I used to think that in some very small way, I was helping to save the Bay. But now, it's obvious that I won't be able to go very far in any field unless I finish my education. The other issue is that I earn very little, so I must rely on the parents to get by. I admit it's driving me crazy!"

"I feel that way, too. But we aren't even twenty—yet. I believe it's their duty to help us until we're able to acquire the experience we need to be successful on our own. Some of us take longer than others. I'm still trying to figure out what continent I want to live on. Try to lighten up on yourself. You don't want to become Mom until you're somewhere in your forties, do you?" Sarah chuckles, then Margot joins in. "How I wish we could be together," Margot laments. But she leaves unsaid how much she would love to tell Sarah what's really troubling her and why it's so difficult when she senses their mother pulling away.

• • •

During the conference call on Wednesday with Jim and his team, Abby argues that there is a more forceful way of approaching their problems concerning Ayer Homes. "This lack of willingness to compromise, in my view, has as much to do with Charles Ayer's ego as it does with making money. I think we can prove to him that he can be a hero and still make money." When she finishes outlining her proposed presentation, the group is initially skeptical, but after some discussion, they accept her plan.

"If you can get an entire group of lawyers to agree on anything," Jim quips,"then, Ms. Aubert, I think you are very well-positioned to make your case tomorrow."

• • •

The following morning, Abby spends extra time getting dressed, fixing her hair, and applying makeup. Although she has gained some weight over the summer, she's satisfied with how she looks in her fawn linen suit and white silk blouse. As Abby walks from the car to the Metro platform, the heat and humidity cause her mass of curly hair to frizz around the back of her neck. As the train approaches, she removes her jacket and notices a half-moon of dampness forming on her blouse under her arms.

No seats are available in the car she has boarded, and her swelling toes begin to pinch inside her heels. But then, miraculously, someone near her gets up to leave at the next stop, allowing Abby to sit down and partially kick off her shoes. The AC vent above her projects a flow of cool air that eases the sweat oozing from every pore. Abby is surprised that even something as uninspiring as a ride on Metro begins to lift her spirits and confirms that sometimes things can work out as one truly hopes.

• • •

The conference gets underway, and Abby is soon called on to speak. "I would like to talk about your target buyers, a diverse group of people between the ages of twenty-nine and fifty-five years old, who earn somewhere in the neighborhood of $80K to $130K per year. They are mostly working couples with children who prefer a larger living space and would rather commute to urban centers than to live in them." Then she activates a slide show using images from the Ayer Homes website and their marketing materials.

"You have featured these same people in all of your advertising. They are brimming with enthusiasm evident in their brilliant smiles, some with kids, happily hiking in the nearby hills, biking along the banks of the Monocacy River, shopping and dining in the charming city of Frederick. In almost all these photos, trees, grass, flowers, and blue skies with puffy white clouds are present in the background. Your choice of words, both spoken and written, extoll the beauty of the natural setting and Ayer Homes' respect for the environment. Now look at the architectural renderings of the entire plan," she says as she projects them onto the screen, depicting row upon crowded row of various townhome models interspaced with a few newly planted trees and low bushes.

"It's obvious from watching this presentation that the advertising doesn't accurately represent the true scope of the project, which is visually so out of sync with the surrounding natural backdrop."

For a few moments, nobody says anything. Finally, Ingrid speaks. "That was a very persuasive slide show, Abigail. I think you've made your point, and we see the business advantages to reworking our plans. Tony has already begun looking at creative ways to refigure the overall number of units in favor of additional common space."

Charles doesn't say anything to correct her, but his jowly face scrunches into a resentful scowl.

"We'll be with you every step of the way," Jim reassures them. "We can assist you with the revised building permits and not keep track of all those billable hours. I hope that helps."

Charles rises as if to leave, so everyone else follows suit. "I didn't think it would come to this," he laments, "but as long as we can move quickly and break ground close to our target date, I bend to the advice of *most* of my team." Then, he exits the conference room.

Ingrid hangs back a moment and says to Jim and Abby, as the others are filing out, "The good news is that we won't have to redo any of our marketing materials. Thanks." Then she leaves right behind Tony Pierson and Leonard Costa, the silent accountant.

• • •

After Margot ends her call with Sarah, she returns her concerns and attention to the Wheelers and especially how they can make sure that Jerry Mercer's remaining time as a free man will come to an end quickly. Margot searches online to see what a PI is legally able to dig into as the investigator gathers evidence from a person's online history. She rightly assumes they are blocked from hacking into someone's social media accounts, but they can follow all the trails left from surfing, sharing, commenting, and creating personal profiles.

Margot decides to make doubly sure that the PI Alice and Steve hire will be well-versed in the technology and have the patience to follow through with these searches, no matter how deeply they might be hidden within the dark and obstructive tangles of the web. She speculates that Mercer has left a digital trail of correspondence with Sam to include photos of other underage girls on porn sites.

Margot is sure Steve has thought of all this, but she sends him an email anyway. When she hears back, he admits that he was initially more interested in someone who could work in the field, following Mercer to find out where he went, how often he engaged with Samantha, and who else he saw in his free time. But given what they all suspect has happened, Steve agrees to prioritize the technical part.

Meanwhile, Jillian has followed up with several nonprofits on whose boards she or her husband have served. Several are willing to set up a GoFundMe account for Alice Wheeler, but one working with sexually abused young women offers even more support. The site invites comments from the public to weigh in anonymously concerning sexual harassment of any age group and gender. Before the week is over, the GoFundMe site is activated. Within forty-eight hours, enough people have reported threats of violence against themselves or someone they know, so that Steve urges Margot to drop everything else to monitor and report on the influx of contributions and complaints.

• • •

Bella Herschel lies in a hospital bed, her eyes closed, unable to understand what she is doing here. She wants to ask someone, but she can't make the words come together. Bella tries to sit up, but her body isn't responding. She detects some light filtering into her room from just beyond the door, yet she wonders if she's asleep after all and caught in the middle of a slow-motion dream. She seems to recall that someone spent hours trying to get her to say her name, but she could never get it right. Now, she is drained of her limited energy. Her head is pounding, and her heart is racing, but she is powerless to call out.

She lies back and closes her eyes again. Suddenly, she hears a familiar voice—someone she knows well, but she can't quite remember who. Then, she senses a man approaching her bed, but he is completely in shadow. For some reason, she is not afraid. "Who are you?" she asks. Surprisingly, she can suddenly lift herself onto her elbows and have a better look at the man as he draws nearer.

"It's Bill, your husband. Don't you recognize me?" He is very close now and extends his hand toward her. She slips hers into the warmth of his large, gentle grasp. "Yes, Bill."

"I've been waiting for you. I am going to take you to the river. Remember the river behind our house? You were always afraid one of the children might fall in. Now, it's our turn."

"But, all I have on is my nightgown. Won't I be cold?"

"No," he says softly. "You will never be cold again."

She rises from the bed and allows him to put his arms around her.

"I've missed you so much," she whispers.

As he bends down slightly to pick her up against his chest, she catches a reflection of herself in the mirror. The reverse image of a much younger woman smiles back at her.

"I'm not sick anymore, am I, Bill?"

"No," he answers. "Now, let's leave here and never come back."

"Yes," she mummers. Then, she closes her eyes, his arms strong around her, as he carries her out of the building and toward the river.

28

LOST AND FOUND

Early September—
Gaithersburg, Maryland; Sarasota, Florida

Margot arrives in Gaithersburg early on Friday, avoiding the Beltway traffic as people leave town for the long weekend, marking the unofficial end of summer.

Miraculously, before leaving, she was able to reach Ruby on the first try. Ruby had managed to convince Jake that he had to seriously consider what she had witnessed between Jerry Mercer and Samantha throughout the summer. Ruby also told him how Margot and Steve have been targeting Mercer, first by finding Alice and then persuading an organization to create a GoFundMe account, enabling them to hire a private investigator.

At first, Jake was apoplectic that all this activity had been occurring without his permission. Sam echoed his anger by refusing to be isolated at her mother's, moving away from her friends and giving up hockey. Eventually, however, Ruby and then Alice convinced Jake that the best way he could protect his daughter was for her to leave the farm and live with her mother as long as Jerry Mercer was still a free man. Once Jake accepted this plan, he persuaded Samantha to go along for her own safety. "It's just until Jerry Mercer is indicted and taken away in handcuffs by the local police—if I don't shoot the bastard first," he told her.

• • •

Michel purchased tickets to the Kennedy Center for a Saturday matinee performance of the musical revue *Ain't Nothin" But the Blues*. He also made reservations at Chez Martin, Abby's favorite French restaurant downtown. Abby was ebullient since most of the attention over the weekend was focused on her, starting with a champagne toast for her upcoming birthday, luscious food served on delicate Limoges plates, and a bottle of smooth, fruity wine from a renowned Burgundy vineyard. When they got home, they watched a classic movie on Hulu, *The Philadelphia Story*, but both Abby and Margot fell asleep before it was over.

What seems to Abby like a short time later, she hears her phone ringing. Am I dreaming? What time is it? 3:23 am? Why would someone call … Oh shit, it's got to be about Mom.

"Abby," her brother utters in a hushed voice, "the night nurse checked on Mother about a half-hour ago when her monitor flatlined. She passed away in her sleep."

Michel is now also awake. From the tears flooding his wife's face, he knows that her mother has died. Michel gently takes the phone from her and asks David what they can do. "I'll get in touch with the girls," Michel reassures him. "I assume you'll want to leave for Sarasota as soon as possible."

"Mother belonged to a temple, although I don't think she and Dad attended services very often."

"We'll take care of all that when we get there. I'll handle the airline tickets."

"Thanks, Michel. See if you can get us a direct flight sometime later today. And could you also get in touch with Maria?"

"Of course. I'm so sorry. I've been through all this too. I had convinced myself I could handle my mother dying, but it was still a wrenching shock when it happened."

Michel calls Sarah first. "Your grandmother passed away in her sleep early this morning. I will get you a ticket to Paris and then to Miami or Atlanta—whatever works best for the connection to Sarasota. Can you leave tomorrow?"

"Oh, my God, yes, of course. Mom must be devastated. Can I talk to her?"

Silence, then the sound of sobbing.

"Mom? Oh, Mom, I'm so sorry—for Gran, for not being in touch, for not coming home when you needed me to." Sarah is crying as well.

"Just come as soon as you can."

"Papa is taking care of it now. I'll arrive tomorrow. I love you, Mom."

"I love you, too."

Margot was still sound asleep when her father knocked on her door. She sits up in bed, then recognizes the shadow in the doorway. She knows immediately why her father is there.

"Gran has died, hasn't she," Margot says it as a statement rather than as a question.

"Yes. She passed away in her sleep sometime during the night. I'm about to make arrangements for the whole family to fly to Sarasota later today." Michel sits down on the edge of the bed and gives her a long hug. "I know you're all tied up with the investigation and all, but you have no choice. Sarah is coming back as well."

"Of course. Oh my God! Mom—where's Mom?" She lets go of her father, rushes down the hall into her parent's bedroom, then into her mother's arms.

• • •

Despite it being the day before Labor Day, Michel managed to purchase tickets for all seven of them, with David and his family, on evening flights with two different airlines, arriving forty-five minutes apart. He booked Sarah on a flight from Atlanta for late the following afternoon. Before leaving, Michel contacted the rabbi at Temple Beth-El, where the Herschels were members. The rabbi agreed to officiate at the service and provided information about the funeral home Mrs. Herschel had chosen when her husband passed away. They scheduled the service for Tuesday, giving the family enough time to make all the arrangements and to contact their mother's friends and neighbors.

• • •

Late the next afternoon, just as the sun begins its daily descent into the Gulf of Mexico, Michel, Abby, and Margot arrive at the airport in Sarasota to greet Sarah. Their reunion at the baggage claim area is emotional. Sarah is especially weepy from jet lag, fatigue, and the fear that her expanding waistline will give away her secret. She purposely wore baggier clothes than she normally would, but no one seemed to notice. Once in the car, however, their mother brings up the subject of attire to both girls.

"I hope you each have something appropriate to wear to the funeral. Did either of you bring a dress?"

"No, Mom, I don't own a dress," Margot replies. "What about you, Sis?" Sarah just shakes her head. "Maybe we can hustle over to one of the department stores at the mall early tomorrow," Margot suggests.

Sarah feels like a rabbit caught in a trap. If she had to try on clothes in front of her sister, her condition wouldn't be a secret anymore. She knows that she'll soon have to tell them all anyway, but hopefully not before the funeral and her mother's actual birthday the following day that are about to collide.

Abby vaguely thinks about her birthday on Wednesday, as she recalls birthdays of long ago when her parents would come to Maryland and treat the whole family to dinner at a nice restaurant. Her mother would take her and the girls shopping for that special something that she wouldn't buy for them or herself. Bella was like a different person at these times—nonjudgmental, spontaneous, even loving.

Abby begins to grapple with the notion that she has just become the matriarch of the family and a surrogate for her mother. Grandmothers bestow another level of love for their grandchildren by focusing all their attention on them whenever they're together. The matriarch is the communicator of family lore and traditions. She wants to say "yes" when the parents say "no." She sets goals that are sometimes higher than those of the parents but are presented as a gentle wish rather than an expectation. Abby lovingly remembers this about her own Grandma Sarah.

As she ponders her new persona, she recalls her twins' special experiences with their Grandma Bella and speculates why they so adored her. They likely wanted to feel treasured by a maternal figure in the family as their mother began to slip away from them into a new realm of her own. The girls had started elementary school, and Abby was suddenly alone a good part of the day. She remembers thinking that she was just marking time, waiting to let go and focus more on her future.

This painful truth squarely confronts Abby as it overwhelms her with such remorse that her mind and body recoil and falter. She grabs onto the kitchen counter where she was putting groceries away. Michel, who had just come into the kitchen to help, sees her trembling and notices her face as white as the porcelain sink. Abby bursts into racking sobs that everyone believes is grief. Michel leads her out onto the lanai and tells Margot to bring her a glass of water. Sarah falls into the chair next to her mother and tries to comfort her.

Abby is barely able to compose herself enough to choke out, "Oh, Sarah, I've been so harsh with you. I'm so terribly sorry!"

"Mom, what are you talking about? I'm the one who left you, not the other way around. I know you're devastated because of Gran. We all are." And with that, she, too, is overcome with tears. When Margot returns with the water and witnesses the two of them, she crouches down between them as all three cling to each other and weep.

• • •

The following morning, the family gathers at the funeral home. The casket is open. When Abby stares down at her mother, she's shocked. She hardly recognizes the woman lying stiff in the coffin. Bella has been made up in a way that makes her look grotesque—pastie skin plastered with heavy foundation and rouge, her curly hair pulled straight and then teased, like a throwback to the sixties. Abby starts to say something, but David orders the funeral director to close the casket. Sarah bends over and places a final kiss on Bella's sunken cheek. Then the lid is shut and locked.

Closing the casket has brought death and its unbearable

finality more into focus. The service on Tuesday will be a formality for the family and Bella's friends, coming together to honor a woman who was part of their life and whom they will remember in their thoughts. But a funeral also reminds everyone attending what is in store for each of them, a glimpse of the inevitable, waiting in the wings, as this drama in which they are all actors draws down its final curtain.

• • •

The day after the funeral, the family gathers at Bella's home, where she lived for more than twenty-five years. It's still too raw for either Abby or David to make any definitive decisions about what to do with the house.

Beth, her children, and Michel have tickets to leave the following morning. Margot would prefer to go with them, but she wants, even more, to spend time with Sarah, to finally bare her soul to the person to whom she feels closest.

The family begins taking a hurried inventory of Bella's possessions, rifling through drawers and closets, the garage, and the small attic above the garage for anything that someone might want to keep or take as a memento. They also agree to set aside something special for Maria in thanks for her dedication to Mrs. Herschel.

Ari and Rachel, David's children, are assigned the task of checking out the attic. They navigate the rickety, pull-down steps into a hot, confined space, just large enough for the children to stand up and not bump their heads. They find a dozen boxes that are then brought down. Three have been labeled: *Old Photos and Souvenirs, Personal, and Children.* The twins open the one marked "*Children*" and quickly discover that the children in question are not them or their cousins but their mother and uncle.

"Mom, come see," Sarah calls to her. "I believe some things in here belonged to you."

Abby joins her daughters as Sarah unpacks a plastic bag of handmade baby-girl clothes that smell musty but are otherwise well-preserved. Sarah can't help thinking, I'll be needing these soon. Two shoeboxes under the clothes are filled with metal matchbox cars and trucks that David must have collected over the years. There are also a few Dr. Seuss, *Babar the Elephant*, and *Curious George* books tucked on the sides.

At the very bottom is a linen pouch containing a stuffed elephant in a pink, puffed-sleeve dress and undies to match. The darker plaid material on the elephant has faded and is worn through in places, showing some inside stuffing. Abby immediately recognizes Cutie Pie that her grandmother gave her for her fourth birthday. She is flabbergasted that her mother saved this one keepsake all these years! Her eyes brighten with tears as she cuddles her favorite childhood toy in her arms as if it were a real baby.

Meanwhile, going through some drawers in the living room, David discovers a key in an envelope along with a combination that had to belong to a safe. But where? No one remembers Bella ever mentioning a safe.

"Maybe it's a bank safe," Margot suggests

"Let's see if we can find a safe here first," David replies. A search begins akin to when children hunt for the hidden matzoh at a Passover Seder. They look behind paintings, then in all the closets, and search throughout the laundry room and the garage.

Finally, David decides to call the bank. The manager informs him that the key was probably from years ago before the bank updated its security system. David makes an appointment for the following day to bring the necessary proof to reclaim the contents of Bella Herschel's safety deposit box.

The two families spend their last evening together at Le Café Belge in town to honor their mother and grandmother and 'commemorate' rather than 'celebrate' Abby's forty-second birthday. They order a bottle of Veuve Clicquot from Champagne, France, and offer a toast to her as well as to Bella's life.

• • •

In her dreams that night, Abby recalls tender memories of her family together in a place of vibrant beauty. She believes she is at a bed and breakfast with Michel and the girls on Chincoteague Island in the early spring. The weather is still cool, but the flowering trees are budding pink and frothy white as April unfolds. Abby is thrilled to witness her young daughters' curiosity and delight being on this small island, watching the wild ponies graze, smelling the briny air, and walking barefoot across the chilly sand on narrow beaches along the waterways. She remembers the rhythmic surges of elation and gratitude throbbing through her. That time of feeling so close to their girls, so needed, is now gone forever, as is her mother, who loved her but didn't know how to show it.

Once she is fully awake, these warm sensations quickly fade. Michel used to warn Abby, "We rarely appreciate how happy we are in the moment, and later, when we try to recall the feeling, we can only catch a glimpse of it as a memory."

Abby is overcome, knowing that she closed her eyes and her heart in so many ways to the wonder of what was unfolding as her twins were growing up. Now, with the death of her mother and so many of their issues left unresolved, Abby also mourns what she has allowed to slip from her grasp.

Abby opens her eyes and sits up. Michel is standing by the night table, gathering his keys, wallet, and phone. He comes around the bed, kisses her on the forehead, then takes her hand. "I'll call you later when I arrive, Abbs. Take whatever time you need here. Don't think about work or home. Just be with the girls and with David."

A stab of deep regret and throbs of grief swirl within her as she watches Michel leave the room. Then, she turns her face to the wall and muffles her dry, choking sobs into the pillow.

• • •

After David drops Michel and his family off at the airport, he drives to the bank. He returns with a briefcase full of papers and some jewelry—Victorian and Art Nouveau pieces that dated back to the early 1900s. Abby and the girls are on the lanai, still in nightgowns and slippers, having coffee. David opens the briefcase and lays everything out on the glass table. Sunlight flows with the breeze through the screens and flickers off the gold and platinum jewelry. Among the papers are expired passports, their parents' marriage license, and their mother's original birth certificate and adoption papers, with a new name and a new set of parents.

Abby can hardly believe her eyes. Her mother was born in Chicago in 1943 to an underaged girl named Ida Kohen, barely past her childhood. No known father. Ida named her baby Hilda and cared for her for three months before giving her up for adoption. She had undoubtedly nursed her and bonded with her; then, one day, that special intimacy was abruptly torn apart.

"Oh my God, David," Abby bemoans. "Can you imagine?

Mom knew all this time the identity of her birth mother. What if, at some point, she tried to find her and failed?"

"I don't think she had access to this information until after Grandma died. A cover letter from Grandma's attorney dated May of 1997 was sent to Mom after the estate was settled."

"I wonder why she never said anything to us about this heartbreaking part of her story. Once she found out, it must have been so difficult for her to grapple with knowing her birth name and even her birth-mother's name. Then this poor woman was erased when she was adopted and given a whole new identity."

The four of them spend the rest of the day and well into the evening going through all the boxes. The one marked *Old Photos and Souvenirs* is the most intriguing. Inside are albums and scrapbooks going back to Bella's adoptive parents' wedding and after her adoption with congratulatory cards. Several albums hold photos arranged chronologically of her on special occasions—birthdays, summers at her grandmother's house in Wisconsin, high school and college graduations, and finally, as a bride. The scrapbooks contain pressed flowers and cards from her wedding, souvenirs from her honeymoon, and programs from concerts and plays dating back to the 1960s.

The *Personal* box is also filled with photos—piles of envelopes containing the negatives and printed images of Abby, David, and their parents. They are all labeled with the occasion and date, abundantly commemorating the days of their childhood, adolescence, and adulthood. Abby finds it strange, however, that none of these hundreds of photos were ever mounted into photo books. She remembers seeing many of them as they were taken and developed. But she instinctively believes that this lackadaisical way of storing their family's visual history is a result of negligence at best or indicates some deep dysfunction at worst.

Abby decides to ship this box back to Gaithersburg and scan all the photos into the computer or put them into albums herself. Still, she recognizes that she probably won't devote that much time to this massive project, especially since she hopes to take on a wider role at work. They will likely end up in her attic just like they did here.

• • •

Margot has kept a low profile over the past few days, especially around David. He hasn't interacted directly with her except when it couldn't be avoided. No one else seems to be aware of any awkwardness. David has always been somewhat of a loner, whom everyone always assumed was due to shyness. But Margot suspects that the real reason is guilt. She is surprised and then relieved, noticing how he has begun to age, how he moves among them with a sour expression and averted eyes, as she becomes increasingly confident that she isn't afraid of him anymore.

However, she is anxious to return to Annapolis. She and Steve have been exchanging texts and emails, keeping her informed of any progress in Somerset County. The PI has brought in an assistant to take on the technical end of their investigation. At the same time, he continues to shadow Jerry Mercer, who has been photographed several times alone in his car parked near the Wheeler farm.

Jake allowed Sam to move in with her mother, but he is resistant to hiring a lawyer. Recently, Alice also told Steve and the PI that Sam is still very shut down and will seek some counseling for her daughter as soon as possible.

• • •

That evening, after sorting the items from all the closets, Abby and David retire earlier than usual. Both twins are uneasy, bottled up within themselves. Margot senses her own and Sarah's reticence to start a conversation, speculating about what might be troubling the other.

Margot finally breaks the silence. "Sis, what's up? I've been trying to figure out what you're hiding from me. I know it, and you know it, so out with it!"

Sarah drops her head and stares at the floor. Then she looks into her twin sister's face and sees the mirror image of herself. Not the physical attributes that are so different, but the intuitive knowing, the shared perceptions of the other as a pathway into themselves.

"I'm going on four months pregnant. Maybe no one noticed that I've put on weight—at least no one has said anything. I wouldn't have let you leave without telling you, Margot, but I haven't even told our parents yet.

"Mom has too much trauma to deal with it right now. I'm going back to Gaithersburg with her and stick around for a week or so. I probably won't stay until our birthday, though. I want to enroll in the university in Toulouse, and I need to have all my paperwork ready by the end of this month. But maybe we could get together in Annapolis before I leave the country."

"Wow, Sarah, I'm blown away. I noticed that your body has changed, but I also know, we aren't the body type to hold onto a lot of extra weight. I just figured you were enjoying the food in France. Who wouldn't? But knowing about your relationship with Daren, I wonder why I didn't think about this possibility myself. Does he know?"

"No, he doesn't, but at some point, I'll probably be in touch." Sarah turns away again as if it pains her to talk about her circumstances or Daren. Then she fixes on Margot with a tender smile. "So, what about you? What's going on with you and Steve? We haven't been able to talk like this without Mom or David being around. Tell me everything."

Margot hesitates because she doesn't know how to broach the whole David thing. Instead, she begins with Steve. "Right now, there's nothing to tell about Steve and me as an item. Our relationship is strictly professional and platonic. I know we have feelings and an attraction for each other. But he's not going to act on that—at least not as long as I'm working with him. Once I go back to Georgetown, the distance will become another obstacle. Who knows? We're both trying to get over some trauma," she lets drop into the conversation. "He's been a great mentor and a source of support whom I value as much as anyone I know outside the family. He's also helped me realize that not all men are only out for sex. It's been a breakthrough for me to become comfortable with trusting a man again."

"Why on earth would you say that? Did something happen at school that you haven't told me about?" Sarah is as stricken as much by Margot not confiding in her as by whatever might have provoked her reticence.

"It's a long story that I've never told anyone, except Mom, although not voluntarily. But I want to tell you now before we part again for who knows how long." Tears well up in Margot's eyes as they glisten with grief.

"When we were thirteen, David cornered me in the hall when he came to our Seder that year. He ran his hands all over me, then pushed me against the wall and worked one of his hands into my undies as he pressed against me. I could feel his erection, Sarah. I was terrified, but at the same time, I felt what I guess amounts to some sort of sexual arousal as well. I was too young to know what it was exactly, but I've been ashamed and feeling like it was all my fault ever since I figured it out. You teased me about not having dates or being interested in boys when we were in high school. I know you all thought I was probably a lesbian, but the real reason was fear—of boys and myself—that I would end up wanting them to do to me what David did.

"I started keeping a diary that year that turned into a journal about my feelings. It was a way to vent, and eventually, I also read a lot about the sexual abuse of young girls, which has helped me heal. It was a one-off, and I was traumatized but not seriously abused. I've just hated the hypocrisy I've seen in David and his dismissal of the whole thing—like it didn't matter.

"Mom went through my drawers after I left for Annapolis. Undoubtedly, she did that in your room, too. She found one of my diaries and then searched the house until she found the others. Mom and I met in Annapolis, and she admitted all this. At first, she didn't believe me, but then she did. We haven't talked about it since, and I have no idea if she has confronted David. Right now, I prefer not to get snared into some come-to-Moses moment between them."

That gets a chuckle from Sarah, but then she puts her arms around Margot and holds her close.

"Oh my God, Margot! That's so sad—what you've been through! I'm flabbergasted, and I'm really angry at David. What a shit-face! It's going to be hard to ever smile at him again. I wish you had told me years ago, so you weren't alone having to deal with such betrayal, but I get that you were afraid I might blab it to the parents. And speaking of telling the parents our secrets, I haven't said a thing about the pregnancy. I thought for sure one of them would notice that I was getting bigger by the day.

"Meanwhile, I want to go back to Mervilla and stay—not forever, but I'd like to see how it goes. I plan to enroll at the Uni in Toulouse, although I have no idea what I want to study right now. I don't even know for sure they'll accept my one year of college as the equivalent of the baccalaureate. That would be a deal-breaker, but if I can get past that hurdle, then I'll stay."

Now both girls are exhausted, especially Sarah. They amble into their grandmother's bedroom and get ready for bed. They've been switching off who sleeps on her side, but then Margot claims it for the second night in a row.

"It's okay, Sarah. It's sort of comforting. There's an indentation in the mattress from her sleeping here for so many years. I feel held by her this way."

29

SEPARATION AND REVELATION

Mid-September–
Sarasota, Florida; Gaithersburg, Maryland

"David just told me that you and he will leave on Friday. Is that true?" Sarah asks Margot.

"I'm not happy about traveling with him, but yes, I need to go back. Mom told me she called him out for what he did to me, but apparently, he denied it or claimed that whatever he did was just to tease me. That's not what happened, and I can't forgive him, but at least I don't fear being around him anymore. Mom also told me that Beth wants a separation, and she confessed to some sort of affair. Maybe she's retaliating for things he's done in the past. What goes around comes around, and maybe he finally has to deal with the consequences. What about you? When do you plan to leave?"

"Mom and I have to stay here until we've finished dealing with the rest of Gran's stuff. But once we're here alone, I'll tell her everything, although I'm pretty sure she suspects that I'm pregnant. The fact that she hasn't mentioned it yet makes me believe that she's too disappointed in me to bring it up first."

Margot forces a strained smile, then grabs Sarah's hand.

They both tear up as they hold each other's gaze.

"No matter where in the world we are and how far apart," Sarah looks deep into Margot's moist eyes, "you're my best friend and always will be. I feel like I'm about to open a door behind which lies a heap of pain that will overwhelm Mom and me both. But I have to go there with her, and I can't leave until I do."

• • •

Abby and David are leaning toward selling the house. They are both too young to retire, and neither has expressed much attachment to it.

Sarah is wistful about this news. Instead of going to sleep-away camp, she and Margot would fly down on their own for a few weeks every summer when they were old enough. They each have wonderful memories of their time here with their grandparents. Grandpa Bill tried to teach them to play golf when they grew tall enough to handle the clubs, but neither she nor Margot took to the game. It was too slow a sport for them both.

However, the girls loved that they got to try new things that they couldn't do at home. Gran found an equestrian center nearby and signed them up for riding lessons a couple of times a week. Their grandparents took them to the Ringling Museum of Art, and they even went to an opera once. Sarah remembers that the theater was small and elaborately decorated with red velvet seats, marbled walls, and gilding on everything else. She and Margot got bored and fell asleep, yet Sarah still fondly recalls the setting.

What the girls loved most, though, was spending days at the beach. They would usually go to Siesta Key, romping on the crystal sand and swimming in the warm, calm waters of the Gulf. Occasionally they would take a boat ride to several mangrove islands to watch pelicans, blue herons, and even the occasional dolphin and manatee. It was exotic, like a trip to Disney World, but without the artificial surroundings and the hordes of other tourists.

• • •

Abby and Sarah continue to sort through the remnants of Bella's household. In addition to all the clothes, there are many heirlooms passed down from one generation to another—an elaborate set of sterling flatware and serving pieces, hand-monogrammed tablecloths and napkins, and a complete set for 12 of gold-trimmed, white Limoges china, including four different sizes of plates, soup bowls, teacups, and demi-tasses.

Abby has labeled a few boxes to be shipped to her or David, but most of Bella's things will be consigned, or donated. Bella's clothes will go to various charities, except for a couple of upscale handbags, including a small Yves St. Laurent evening purse and a Coach handbag that Abby intends to give Maria with a generous check tucked inside.

Sarah decides to go through the drawers and closets one last time to check that nothing has been overlooked, such as folders of old papers that need a final flip-through before consigning them to the recycling bin. David had already separated the most important papers—tax returns, bank and credit card statements, and recurring bills concerning the house. Much of the rest has been boxed and marked "keep" or "toss."

Sarah begins in Bella's bedroom. The bureau and night-table drawers are empty, but Sarah notices several shoeboxes and plastic bins in the large walk-in closet that appear to have been overlooked. She fetches a stool then brings the containers down from the top shelf. Sarah lifts the lids of several shoeboxes that hold dressy heels and sandals that Bella probably hadn't worn in years. She is about to conclude that everything here will get donated when she retrieves the last box that is longer and wider than the others. Sarah speculates that this box must hold boots and is curious why Bella would have high enough boots to warrant such a big box. She certainly wouldn't need them in Florida, and even before Grandpa Bill died, she avoided coming up north during winter.

When Sarah removes the lid, there are no boots in the box; instead, there are several large manilla envelopes containing letters and other papers. Sarah plops down on her grandmother's bed and spreads out the contents of one of the packets that contain a passel of envelopes stamped from France when Abby lived there over twenty years ago.

She's stunned to discover that her mother had kept up such an active correspondence with her parents after abruptly leaving them, in no small part out of anger at her mother. The contents of the second packet are even more surprising. They are journals that Bella wrote in which she recorded her deep feelings toward her daughter. Presumably, she never intended to share them with Abby. Sarah gathers them up and returns them to the boot box that she places under the bed. She plans to retrieve them to read once her mother retires for the night.

Abby has made an appointment with the owner of a high-end consignment shop to look over the tableware, the furniture and accessories, such as lamps, vases, knickknacks, and artwork. It's painful for Sarah to participate, as she realizes that so much of what her grandmother cherished in her later life will be dispersed. Many of these objects had intimate, personal meaning to Bella Herschel that helped define her. It seems that neither Abby nor David wants many of these things for themselves, even to eventually give to their children, regardless of any sentimental attachment or intrinsic value they held for their mother.

• • •

In the evening after supper, Abby brings a large glass of white wine into the den, turns on the TV, and settles into her father's old recliner. Sarah follows her in but hangs back. "Is it okay if I get a small glass of that, too?" she asks, even though she knows she shouldn't drink alcohol while pregnant. She keeps telling herself the wine would help her relax, and then maybe she could work up the courage to tell her mother about, well, everything.

"No, my dear," her mother replies calmly without taking her eyes off the TV. "You mustn't be drinking alcohol in your condition." She turns to her daughter, who's now standing in front of her, then glares at her with so much hostility that Sarah takes a step backward. Abby's aggrieved eyes bore into Sarah as she spits out at her, "Do you think I'm not aware that you're pregnant? I knew when you first arrived from France the minute I saw you. Just when were you going to say something?"

"Uh, right now? That's why I wanted the wine. I thought it could help lead us both to an intimate moment."

"Oh, bullshit! And don't tell me you haven't said anything before now because of Grandma." Abby knows this aggressive reaction isn't entirely fair, but now she has crossed a line that has broken through any constraints.

"C'mon, Mom. I didn't want to upset you even more than you already are. Did you expect me to just blurt it out in front of David and his kids? 'Guess what, everyone, I got knocked up in Ghana! La-dee-da!'"

"This is why you stopped emailing me, isn't it? Because you were ashamed!"

"Are you ashamed of me, Mom? Because it sure sounds like it. So, I guess I did the right thing, then, by not coming home over the summer and not being in touch." By now, Sarah is crying, torn between leaving the room altogether or just going to fetch a tissue.

Abby pauses for a moment to drain her wine glass and then says with less vitriol, "No, Sarah, I'm not ashamed. I'm hurt because you didn't feel you could tell me. I always thought we were closer than this. Does the father know?"

"It's complicated, this situation with Daren," she replies. "I thought he was in love with me. I knew we were both way too young to get this involved, that it would be just a time or two. But then we couldn't control it—until it all blew up. But no, I haven't told him yet. It turns out he's gay, Mom. I was there as a prop so his parents wouldn't guess about his sexuality. His family is very religious, and he really can't tell them. For a while, he thought maybe his orientation was just a passing curiosity. But then he hooked up again with his high school partner. That's when I left."

"Why couldn't you have come home to us? Did you think we would force you to do something you didn't want to do?"

"When I left Ghana, I had no idea I was pregnant. I didn't want to come back home to an internship and basketball, partly because I couldn't handle your disappointment. Plus, Marie-Laure did need my help."

For a few moments, silence hangs between them like a room-darkening curtain. Abby's body appears to fold and shrink down further into the couch as her head and shoulders droop. "I felt abandoned. That's probably too strong a word, but Margot had decided to stay in Annapolis by then, too. Your father was also away a lot over the summer."

When Abby looks up again at Sarah, some of her anger appears to have been released. "I guess you're planning to go back to Toulouse," she says matter-of-factly.

"Yes. I don't know that I want to spend my whole life in France, but I'm happy there for now. I'm needed, and I think it's a good experience to live abroad. You did it, so why not me, too?"

When Sarah has finished talking, her mother is smiling at her. "Come here, You," she says, holding her arms out as a comforting smile spreads across her lips. Sarah is so relieved that she collapses against her mother, like an overwrought child.

• • •

When Sarah can access the boot box in private, she sets aside her mother's letters from France and decides to read her grandmother's papers first. She hopes to glean something from them about what went wrong between Bella and Abby. Sarah wonders if their issues with the mother-daughter entanglements had all been predestined, given Bella's birth and upbringing. Bella's writings are in the form of a loose journal dating back to late 1993 after Abby had left for France. It was mostly a commentary about her difficult first pregnancy that exacerbated her anxiety about becoming a mother. She described a traumatic delivery that ended in an emergency C-section. Bella even hinted at her disappointment that she had given birth to a girl. Throughout, there was no expression of joy or any positive feelings of anticipation—only dread.

Sarah is saddened that Bella never expressed any joy about having a child—fearing instead that she wouldn't measure up—tormented with feelings of insecurity and confusion about caring for a tiny, fragile infant. She stated over and over that she felt like she was going to fall apart. Sarah speculates that her grandmother was going through some postpartum depression. Bella wrote about it, but she never indicated that she told anyone.

The experience of pregnancy and birth that her grandmother survived rather than relished has deeply affected Sarah. She intuitively believes that Bella's hellish pregnancy and lack of confidence as a new mother directly affected Abby's tendencies toward negativity and anger stemming from childhood. Dr. Cohen told Sarah that the growing fetus senses its mother's stress and other negative emotions even in the womb. Because of her circumstances, Sarah worries that her child could also come into the world anxious and fearful.

Sarah longs to discuss all this with her mother, who gave birth to twins under trying conditions. It's possible she was so overwhelmed that she withdrew from them initially. Sarah knows that Abby didn't breastfeed them. Was her mother able to be in touch with her own emotions at the time? Sarah doesn't want to bring any of this up now; her grandmother's death is still too raw. She packs up all the envelopes to bring back to Gaithersburg so she can finish reading them there.

• • •

When Abby closes and locks the front door to Bella Herschel's house for the last time, she and Sarah share a sense of loss, as a significant phase in their life has ended. Maria came by the day before they left, and she was surprised and very pleased by the gifts of the Coach bag and especially the ample check that she so richly deserved. The three of them hugged, promising to stay in touch, knowing that they probably wouldn't, over time.

30

BUTTERFLIES

Mid-September—Gaithersburg, Annapolis, Maryland; Somewhere over the Atlantic Ocean

When Sarah and Abby arrive at the Gaithersburg house, before Sarah even lugs her suitcase into her room, she phones Margot. She's anxious to know how the investigation in Somerset County is progressing, and she also wants to finalize plans to meet up before she leaves the country.

"Hello, Stranger. Why didn't you answer my texts or emails these past few days? And don't pretend it's only because you've been too busy."

Margot releases an audible sign. "Well, Sis, that is part of it, but you're right; I've been avoiding the whole situation down there. You guys went into overdrive going through boxes and closets. I thought we were supposed to choose a memento from all of Gran's things. Instead, it turned into a frenzy of how to get rid of almost everything she owned. I guess I withdrew, and nobody seemed to care."

"Oh, God, Margot. I'm so sorry! I just wanted everyone to leave to have 'the talk' with Mom. We did, and I guess it went okay. I haven't told Papa yet, but I'm pretty sure Mom has, and

I still feel it's my responsibility to tell him anyway. So, what *is* going on with you?"

"First, let me tell you that, on the plane, David apologized to me for his behavior. He blah blabbed with excuses about just wanting to tease me or whatever, but finally, he admitted that it was inappropriate, and he took responsibility. I don't think he has ever thought much about how his actions have affected me since then, but it does help to finally hear that he regrets what he did.

"As for the situation in Somerset, the private investigator and his team have uncovered some pretty damning stuff about Jerry Mercer. For one thing, Sam finally did tell her mom that when Jerry took her to his house, he convinced her to pose in the nude, and then he forced himself on her. Later, he posted those photos on a deeply hidden site on the internet. It would appear that he's been trafficking in online porn for quite a while. I get emotional each time I think about what Samantha must be going through. She's younger than we are! Look at how long it's taken me even to be able to talk about my own experience. How does she ever begin to heal from such trauma?

"On a good note, however, the GoFundMe account has raised enough money for the Wheelers to hire a lawyer, who plans to file a lawsuit on Samantha's behalf in criminal court. Given that Sam is almost eighteen, many judges are skeptical about sexual abuse accusations, and the burden of proof is legally on the victim. I find it appalling on its face, but the lawyer has been granted a search warrant that will hopefully include Mercer's computer. We've also received some similar complaints through the GoFundMe site about harassment of teenage girls, and we're hopeful that even more people will come forward. Jerry Mercer might not be the only perpetrator, and all these additional claims should put more pressure on the authorities to act quickly.

"Meanwhile, I'm following up on more than a dozen incidents alleging attempted extortion. The lawyer has also asked the judge to order Mercer and some of his fellow ag inspectors to turn over their bank statements and other financial documents." Margot breathes in deeply, as if she had managed to say all that without coming up for air.

"Wow, Sis! It's amazing what you and Steve have accomplished. I'm so proud of you! What's going on with him, by the way?"

"Steve is very stoic, but I think if I were to stay here, our relationship could evolve into something more intimate. I'm committed, though, to going back to school in the spring. The timing for us is just off right now, and little by little, I feel less sad to let go and more open to other possibilities down the road. So, I guess you could say I'm trying to get over him."

"I also called because I want to nail down when we can get together," Sarah says. "I'm hoping to leave by the end of next week."

"If you guys can come to Annapolis, then it can be whenever you want—this coming weekend is good for me."

"I'll check with Mom and Papa and let you know. I love you, Margot. Just thinking about how long it might be before we see each other again makes me weepy."

"I'm pretty sure it wouldn't take much to convince the parents to fly over for the birth, and hopefully, I would be able to come as well. When are you due?"

"Mid-March, but you know these things don't always

happen exactly on schedule."

"What are you going to do about school if you enroll this fall?"

"I can take all my classes online, but I'd prefer to attend in person through February and then finish the year remotely. Let's talk about all this when we get together. Meanwhile, *Bisous*, Sis, and I love you too."

They hang up just as Sarah suddenly remembers that she forgot to tell Margot about their grandmother's journals.

• • •

Michel has planned a celebratory meal for their return and intends to prepare it himself. Sarah asks her mother's opinion about when a good time would be to talk to him. "After dinner tonight," Abigail responds, an expression of scorn frozen across her face. Sarah would like to be angry. What is this game of flipping from forgiveness to suddenly treating me like a piece of shit? But then she releases some of her hostility. I don't know—maybe if I were in her shoes, I'd act the same way.

Instead of moping, she goes into the kitchen to see if her father needs some help.

"You can set the table if you have nothing better to do," he says to her in French, turning on his sing-songy accent and his cheerful smile.

"*Avec quoi*?" With what, she asks.

"*Une nappe et les belles assiettes*." A tablecloth and nice plates. Sarah retrieves the table settings that her mom uses for guests.

When they sit down to eat, the conversation is focused mainly on the meal itself—how copious, how delicious, how grateful she and her mother are that Papa has spent so much time planning and prepping. After the food is gone and the wine bottle empty, Sarah clears the table and cleans up the kitchen.

When she seeks out her parents in the den, her father is watching a football game on TV, and Abby is reading the paper. Sarah is determined, however, to have it out with them both. She picks up the remote and clicks off the TV. Her father shoots her a what-the-hell look, but he doesn't act all that surprised.

She approaches his side of the couch and kneels at his feet. Then, she takes his hands in hers, looks him straight into his dark, velvety eyes and declares, "I'm almost four months pregnant, Papa. I want to go back to France and have the baby there. I want to go to university in Toulouse in the fall, and I want you two and Margot to come for the birth in mid-March."

"*Rien que ça*? Is that all?" he asks with exaggerated astonishment, but Sarah notices his eyes twinkling as a loving smile breaks out across his lips.

"*Oui, rien que ça*. No, just one other thing. I want us to go to Annapolis and have an amazing meal with Margot somewhere really nice for our pre-birthday treat. Would that be okay?"

"Sure," he affirms but then looks over at Abby, who is also smiling.

"It would be wonderful to have just the four of us together—maybe for the last time for quite a while," Abby says. "Because when we see you next, you'll probably be a mother. And from then on, for the next twenty or so years of your life, your child will always come first."

• • •

Over the next few days, Sarah looked for an opportunity to get her mother alone so that she could bring up the subject of Bella's journals. She has so many questions about how Abby adjusted to motherhood, especially having twins. Sarah knows her mother is introspective enough that she's surely thought a lot about all this over the years.

She wonders if Abby ever compared herself to her mother, to come out of that rivalry feeling like the winner, that whatever mistakes she's made as a mother would pale in comparison. Sarah speculates if this could be driving Abby's off-and-on again coldness toward her. She would like to reassure her mother that whatever the reason, it's okay, but she doubts that Abby would admit as much.

Since Abby has been putting in extra hours at work, it's been hard for Sarah to find her alone. Finally, the day before they meet Margot for dinner in Annapolis, Abby doesn't go to work. After her father leaves that Friday morning, Sarah joins her mother in the kitchen, where she is emptying the dishwasher.

"Mom, I found a box in Gran's closet that contained some packets of papers, including all the letters that you sent to your parents from France. The others add up to a kind of journal that she started writing after you left. She wrote about being pregnant with you and the delivery and how she tried to adapt."

"Let me stop you right there. I know all about what a terrible pregnancy my mother had and the C-section, so I don't see the need to go over that again—like it was somehow all my fault."

"She never mentioned anything in her letters about any of it being your fault," Sarah says reassuringly. "Quite to the contrary—she was very anxious about what kind of mother she'd be. She worried if she could even bond with you. Did you know she had postpartum depression?"

"What?" Abby's eyes bulge with shock. "She certainly never mentioned that to me— not ever! Who are you now, Dr. Freud? Was she diagnosed with postpartum depression? And I'll tell you another thing: she was over the moon when David was born. She never showed any sign then of being depressed. It wasn't until many years later that she started taking medication for anxiety."

"Just because she had PPD the first time doesn't mean she would experience it again. And no, I don't think she mentioned how she felt to anyone. I believe she was ashamed. She was supposed to be happy, and she wasn't because she was so worried about being an inadequate mother."

"Well, take my word for it, in many ways, she was. And just what are you insinuating, anyway—that I've been an inadequate mother, too?" Abby backs away from Sarah as tears quickly wash into her eyes and are released in a gush.

"I'm sorry, Mom, but I thought it would help you to know that Gran was so traumatized and depressed that she was incapable of caring for you the way you needed her to."

"Please, let's not talk about this! You can't understand what I went through as a child just by reading a few pages of Gran's journal. It feels to me like you are comparing me to her. I stopped working to take care of you two, and I've always tried to be there for you."

Sarah starts to regret that she has stirred up this much bitterness as her mother's swollen eyes stare sadly back into hers. "Mom, Mom! No, I'm not saying that at all. You are not your mother! I just thought it would help you—and me as well—to know what Gran experienced."

Abby sits down at the kitchen counter and uses a napkin to mop away her tears. When she looks up at her daughter again, her expression has softened.

"Look, Sarah, I know you are in a difficult situation, and I want to support you, but stirring up all these memories is hard for me. And anyway, Gran is gone now, and no one can change the past. I have always been afraid of becoming like her, and in many ways that I prefer not to name, I have succumbed. I recognize, though, that it was not all her fault. I just don't want my mother's past to define me anymore.

"I was excited to become a mother, but I admit it was hard with the two of you. I was very grateful that Grandma Marguerite was there. She helped me through the first couple of months until you both finally started sleeping through the night. I don't think I had a problem bonding with either of you. But it sometimes takes a while. I went through all that pain, and then I, too, had a C-section. When I woke up in even more pain, a nurse handed me two little lumps of flesh with tiny, squished-in faces. I remember thinking that after all I went through, the result was a pair of wrinkly, wet, and wailing preemies!"

New tears drip from her eyes, but this time it's from laughter. "I've never seen a newborn baby," Sarah remarks as she wipes her eyes as well. "We weren't that premature, were we? Are all newborns that ugly?"

"I hope not," Abby cracks up. "And anyway, within a few weeks, like most babies, you and Margot started to fill out and look all cute and cuddly. Nothing ever stays the same throughout life. We go from one phase to another, hardly noticing how we change. Only when we look back and see ourselves as we were in photos and our private memories do we realize how different we've become over time—and I don't mean just physically." Her face clouds over again.

"My mother rarely showed much understanding or even any interest as to why, when I got to be a little older, I kept pushing her away. She treated me like my anger was coming from a place that had nothing to do with her. Then, I left for France that put even more distance between us."

"I wish you could have had a conversation like this with Gran," Sarah says as she covers her mother's hand with her own. "I plan to read her journals and your letters, but I'm going to leave them all here when I leave. What you do with them after that is up to you." Abby manages a weak smile as Sarah slowly walks out of the kitchen, leaving her mother to her thoughts.

When she returns to her room, Sarah regrets bringing up anything about Bella suffering from postpartum depression. She certainly is not qualified to offer an opinion about the mental state of her grandmother after giving birth. The more she anticipates it, the more she's frightened about going through childbirth herself and how she might react to that wrenching experience.

She also tries to imagine what birth is like for the baby, being violently expelled from the security of the womb into a cold, insecure, and turbulent place. She is perplexed why people say that babies come into the world like blank slates—innocent, sure, as opposed to being guilty of anything, but instead of comparing them to something hard and dark that should be worked on until they end up like mini-versions of their parents—or what the parents wanted themselves to become—why aren't they each treated more like a fragile butterfly that has developed inside its chrysalis and has now broken free to evolve as the beautiful creature it was meant to be?

Sarah keeps circling back to the real reason why she left so abruptly for Ghana and then fled to France. She blamed her first decision on parental pressures and the second on the collapse of her relationship with Daren. Sarah is beginning to grasp at a deeper level what motivated her to make those choices in the first place. Tears sting behind her eyes as the answer hits her in the gut: maybe all along, I was just trying to get Mom's attention and, at the same time, to punish her for the lack of it. Her mother had admitted as much herself when she told Sarah why she had left with her father for France.

Now Sarah must consider that a human being is growing inside her, someone totally dependent on her. Her heart starts to pound, and her breath comes in raspy gasps as she is overwhelmed, knowing that her child's entire future will evolve according to the decisions she will make for many years to come.

For Sarah, this is much more than a moment of self-discovery. It's about finally accepting responsibility for a life-altering outcome she certainly didn't wish for but allowed to happen. As a result, if she becomes immersed in guilt and assigning blame, she might not be capable later of giving her baby the unconditional love and care it deserves.

Suddenly—like a firecracker going off over her head—once the smoke clears, Sarah experiences a jolt of excitement rippling through her as she visualizes herself emerging from a confusing fog and into the light. She will go to university, study psychology, and train to help those who want to explore and accept their uniqueness.

First, however, she will begin by recognizing and then breaking free from the weighty '*shoulds*' that are indubitably passed down from one generation to another as part of an initiation into a tribe. Can I find a way to do that and still be accepted by those I love? If they truly love me, then the answer has to be "Yes"!

• • •

The night before Sarah leaves for France, they drive to Annapolis to meet Margot at O'Henry's Grille, where Margot and the parents had been over the July 4th weekend. When they are seated, and before conversation begins, Margot proudly announces that she's just talked to Steve and that a district court judge in Somerset County has ordered Jerome K. Mercer to turn over his computer, bank statements, and cell phone to the DA. They expect an indictment to be handed down soon.

"Jake and some of his neighbors have agreed to testify that Mercer threatened to report them for over-dumping chicken waste into the Bay if they didn't pay him to look the other way. Can you imagine? Those courageous farmers are willing to risk being fined and sanctioned to get Mercer before a jury. But the best part is that Alice Wheeler's attorney has filed criminal charges against Mercer for possession and distribution of child pornography, attempting to corrupt a minor, and statutory rape." Margot chokes up as she utters this last word.

"Meanwhile," she continues after regaining her composure, "I plan to keep working with Steve, at least until the end of the year. However, I've made arrangements to return to Georgetown for the spring semester."

Abby and Michel are beaming at Margot with love and pride. Sarah recognizes that if she intends to live up to her sister's standards, she will have to dig deeper and work harder than she ever has before.

Sarah sits back in her chair and observes the family dynamics playing out before her. She's happy for Margot that the parents' attention has been focused on her for most of the meal. Margot has a beautiful smile, and when she shows it off and then directs her dark, probing eyes into yours, she makes you feel like the most important person in the world.

When the time comes to say goodbye, the twins fall into each other's arms and can't let go.

• • •

The Air France Airbus 350 turns onto the runway at Dulles Airport, revs up its turbo engines, and roars down the tarmac to lift off, then cross the Atlantic Ocean toward Paris. Sarah is sad to leave her family but not so much the United States. She wants to get back to Mervilla and to the coziness of the house, to see Charlotte and the chickens whose names still confuse her. Sarah has missed eating vegetables from the garden and pears off the trees. She thinks a lot about Sophie, who's become a much-needed friend, and Bernard, who was so devoted to helping her throughout the summer. But most of all, she can't wait to be with Marie-Laure again, who has become a second mother to her.

Michel—and Abby, more reluctantly—have agreed that Sarah can stay in France as long as she's accepted into the *Université Toulouse, Jean-Jaurès*, that offers a major in psychology, her chosen field of study. Sophie will be at the same campus, so Sarah knows she won't have to cope all alone with what already presents itself as a daunting learning curve.

Sarah feels confident she can handle the work, the pregnancy and becoming a mother, with all the physical and emotional challenges along the way. One day at a time, she tells herself. After all, isn't that what adds up to life? Living and accepting who I am on any given day?

The meal has been served, and Sarah searches for a movie to hopefully put her to sleep. As she goes through the list, she sees that the film she watched on the flight from Accra to Paris, *Bienvenue à Marly-Gomont*, is still being shown. Sarah remembers how Dr. Seyolo Zantoko worked hard to be accepted by the people of this rural town in the north of France. Now, it was her turn to show her world that she, too, will be able to overcome any obstacle.

As she settles back in her narrow seat, a pillow behind her head, a blanket spread over her growing belly, Sarah exhales the anxiety and stress from this trip and then savors a long, deep breath. How wonderful to finally experience a sense of calm, contentment, even confidence. I'm about to turn twenty. Hopefully, I will have more days ahead of me than I can count. Time is on my side, and all that matters is how I use that time going forward. Her eyes close as her head nestles further into the pillow. In a few hours, I'll be back in France. In a few more hours after that, I will finally be home.

ABOUT THE AUTHOR

Carol Bouville has published one other work, a children's book, *Yellow Bird*, that she wrote and illustrated. Carol has a master's degree in American Literature from La Sorbonne in Paris, France, where she lived for 18 years with her husband and two children. Upon returning to the United States, Carol worked in marketing and project management while attending evening classes and multiple workshops in the visual arts. She eventually left the business world to paint and teach. She and her husband continued to spend time in France, where her son and his family lived for many years, and went to visit them in the Ivory Coast, Ghana, and Gabon as they relocated to these countries. Very recently, the family has reunited in Los Angeles, where her daughter also lives. Carol, her husband, and their two cats now split their time between Bethesda, MD, and LA.

The Chrysalis Phase and *Yellow Bird* are available for purchase from Carol's website: www.carolbouville.com